FOOTLOOSE & FAERIE FREE

This is a work of fiction. The characters, incidents and dialogues are products of the author's imagination only.

Footloose & Faerie Free/Rowena May O'Sullivan
ISBN **978-0-473-30027-2**

Cover by Novakillustration

Publisher Rowena O'Sullivan

FOOTLOOSE & FAERIE FREE

An Oaktree Falls Romantic Tale

Love, Laughter & Magic

Rowena May O'Sullivan

Dedication

Thank you to my wonderful family.
You bring joy to my life each and every day.

Acknowledgement

I need to thank those who have helped me get this book ready for publication. First of all there is the wonderful *Beth McLaren* who agreed to proof this book for me and for her friendship since we were but young and innocent and barely out of school! We giggle like schoolgirls whenever we are together! Thanks also for a final proof for print by the wonderful *Vanessa Gulik*. My gratitude to *Andrea R Cooper, Deborah O'Neill Cordes, Carole Brighouse* and *Julie Davis* for beta reading this manuscript for me.

Lastly, thank you to my wonderful family. You bring joy to my life each and every day. Love you heaps.

≈ CHAPTER 1 ≈

Bud Chandler, consulting psychologist for Oaktree Falls Precinct, nearly choked on his can of cola. Sergeant Delaney, a bad-tempered old coot who should have retired from the force years ago, sneered at him down his large bulbous nose and said, "She's a faerie. With an a-e and i-e."

Great! Just what Bud needed to round off an altogether day from hell. "A faerie?"

Delaney was clearly tickled by Bud's ill humor because his response was irreverent and altogether unsavory. "Very."

Bud crushed the empty can in one hand and tossed it into the trash and wondered whether this was a wind-up. "And I suppose there's an elf in lockup as well. Or maybe the Easter bunny has arrived early with a basket of goodies?"

"Oh she has goodies," Delaney leered. "I nabbed her skulking behind a dumpster naked as the day she was born. She was flashing her bits front, back and all, and headed for the loony bin for sure. She put up one hell of a fight too."

Bud ignored the derision in the sergeant's voice. Logically, it was likely she'd taken drugs and had divested herself of her own clothes at some stage during the night. "What exactly did she do besides appear naked in public?"

"She tried to bite me when I arrested her." Delaney nursed his left forearm where Ms Faerie had sunk her teeth and failed to break his skin. "I caught her down on Wisteria Boulevard rummaging through a dumpster."

"She was hungry." Bud shrugged his shoulders. "So what? It's a minor charge. Tell her to put her clothes back on and fly home?"

Delaney hefted his considerable frame out of his chair, reached for the charge sheet and shoved it across Bud's desk. "Maybe she ate her clothes. There were none to be found when I came upon her."

The officer waved a womanly shape with his pudgy hands just in case Bud had not understood. "She says clothes are not always worn in the Faerie Realm."

Bud checked his watch. Why now? Being called out in the middle of the night wasn't his idea of a good time. He attempted to shift the conversation out of the gutter. "So, she thinks she's done nothing wrong?"

"Nuh-uh."

"Did she actually say she's a faerie?"

"Sure did. She also says she's a princess and claims she can't return home until I say the magic words."

This story was getting crazier by the minute. All Bud wanted was to go home, curl back up on the couch and finish the book he'd been reading while polishing off a glass of whisky. It had been one hell of a tough day filled with some very disturbed people. Now he had to deal with someone who apparently lived in an alternate reality. Surely this could have waited until tomorrow?

"Did she tell you what the magic words are?"

Delaney's eyes lit, two dull coals of meanness in a rotund face. "I wrote it down on the charge sheet." Tapping the paperwork with his pencil he added, "See for yourself."

Bud picked up the report and scanned the page. He grinned, his mood lightening considerably. He fixed his gaze on Delaney. "I hope you gave this a try?"

Delaney flushed. "What do you think I am? Stupid or something?"

Bud's grin grew. Yep. That's exactly what he thought. "What do you think I think?"

"Ah-hah!" Delaney pointed at him. "I'm too smart for that psychobabble stuff Doc. Save it for Ms Faerie with an a-e and an i-e. She's the one who's delusional."

Bud wasn't so sure about that.

***

Glory didn't appreciate being shoved into the gloomy, depressingly cold concrete room. There was very little sunlight except through the small barred window set high in the wall above her. At least her physical attachment was now transferred to the officer standing guard on the other side of her cell. Lacey, she thought she'd heard someone call him.

"Come on. Please?" she pleaded one more time. "Three times is all it takes."

Lacey stood, feet planted apart, his arms folded over his broad chest. His eyes narrowed and he leered at her in such a way she swiftly reconsidered her opinion that he was a better choice than the human who had arrested her.

Great slimy toads! Glory decided the officer might be handsome, but only on the outside. Her closer inspection of his aura told her he was not a kind man. She swallowed and her heart sunk to her toes. 'Twas a predicament she found herself in for sure.

She turned her attention to the silver buttons lined down the front of the officer's jacket. Mayhap, she could distract him while she muddled a new plan together in her head. The buttons gleamed under the artificial light with an odd brightness. "I'll grant you a wish if you say the magic words." Spotting the spark of interest in his mean eyes, she added an offer to further tempt him. "As an extra special treat, I'll polish all your buttons to a wondrous sparkle."

For some reason, the officer thought her generous offer funny. He laughed and laughed. Right in her face! She inhaled an awful stale odor of garlic and almost keeled over on the spot.

He might be handsome, but his manner was offensive and the voice emerging from those perfectly shaped lips was odious. "Don't need no three wishes to get what I want from a buxom bitch like you."

The lecherous undertone in his voice was unmistakable. A kernel of fear caused her heart to skip a beat. Glory shuffled on her feet and felt a strange heat rush to her cheeks. "I am not that kind of faerie!"

"Yeah! And I'm the tooth faerie," Lacey sneered. He took a step closer to the cell.

"You most certainly are not!" Glory put him straight. "You're nothing like the tooth faerie!"

The officer laughed even harder and her skin crawled with alarm.

He sneered once more. "I think I may have a button that requires polishing." His hand rubbed the material near his groin. "It hasn't been shined in a while."

Glory understood why. There was no mistaking his intent, and she felt her fear turn icy. What was going on inside his head did not match the outside in any shape or form.

A hand moved to his belt and Glory's heart fluttered weakly behind her ribcage. The only buttons she wanted to see were on his jacket. Her stomach almost heaved its contents then and there. She quelled her queasy stomach but then decided that mayhap heaving would not be so bad. If he got too close, she would consider it Faerie Duty to empty the contents of her stomach down his front. The idea held considerable appeal.

Her fear diminished and she allowed a small smile to turn her lips upwards. She narrowed her eyes and shot him an assessing glance. She was in trouble and now trouble owned her as well. Alone in this awful, dark room with the slick sleaze from hell, Glory did something King Aloysius, Supreme Ruler of All Faerie, told her she was never to do.

Waving both hands in an expressive and dramatic arc before Officer Sleaze Ball, she muttered several rhythmic sentences without feeling any remorse whatsoever. "Mayhap now you'll believe in faeries!"

≈ CHAPTER 2 ≈

When Bud entered the detaining cell a sight that defied any psychology lesson he'd ever learned confronted him. Opening and closing his eyes several times he then removed his glasses and cleaned them thinking that might help. It didn't. Perhaps that whisky he'd been drinking before being called out was more potent than he thought.

He pinched his arm just to make sure he wasn't dreaming. Ouch! Yep. Wide-awake at Oaktree Falls Precinct. And no. He couldn't make any sense whatsoever of the message his eyes were sending to his brain.

Lacey, who Bud considered lower on the evolutionary scale than the slimiest slug or even Delaney upstairs, sat inside the same cell as his prisoner, wedged between the concrete wall and the toilet, stark naked except for boxers that advertised red pouty lips. He was trussed more tightly than a turkey at Thanksgiving with what looked to be… cobwebs.

There was a wild look in Lacey's eyes. Bud couldn't blame him. He was feeling that way somewhat himself. Ms Faerie, Bud assumed it was she, sat on the floor on the opposite side of the cell with Lacey's official jacket over her knees. She was pulling the official precinct buttons off and threading them through her hair. They dangled from the same mysterious stuff encasing Lacey.

The sergeant's highly prized badge, only six months old and gleaming as brightly as the day it was first pinned to his chest, now held his white shirt together over Ms Faerie's shapely curves.

Speechless, Bud gaped. His glasses fogged over. He spun round, walked out the door, closed it and stood in the hallway for several long bewildering moments. His brain refused to assimilate what his eyes had witnessed. Ensuring his lungs were filled with oxygen, he turned around, opened the door and walked back in, expecting…? What exactly, he didn't know.

Nothing had changed. The scene remained the same and all that fresh air in his lungs rushed out, leaving him shocked and lightheaded.

Ms Faerie was singing what sounded like an old
Celtic folk song his father used to sing while she spun a web-like substance from her fingertips. Apparently she was finished with the buttons. Upon his re-entering the room, she looked up at him, stopped spinning and smiled and his heart did an involuntary flip-flop in his chest.

"Hello," she said, her voice lilting and sexy as hell.

Clearing his throat, Bud managed a respectable, "Hello. Ms Faerie, I assume."

Ms Faerie laughed and a tinkling sound filled the room. "Yes. I am she."

Bud stared hard. He could have sworn he had seen a spangle of lights gathered about her like an aura. He also thought he'd seen the faint outline of wings poking out the neck of Lacey's shirt she wore so well.

Nah! Couldn't be! None of this was real! He shook his head and peered over the top of his glasses. Thank God! No wings! He sagged with relief.

"So what did you do to Lacey?" And how, he thought? The man was taller and wider than his prisoner. How had she got the better of him?

"I sealed his mouth shut," she informed him as if it was nothing unusual at all.

But what with? That was the question. "Why?"

"'Twas a necessity."

Bud felt his eyebrows lift. He blinked as the cogs in his brain stopped altogether. He tried to crank them back into action. "Can I ask why you would think so?"

"I sealed his evil lips with Faerie webbing for he was making such a palaver. And the language! Never before have I heard words such as the ones he spoke. They were bad. My poor ears are ringing with offensity. Plus, I have no desire to be deflowered by him. I had to do something to teach him a lesson."

Offensity! Deflowered? Did she mean what he thought she meant? He looked to Lacey and then to Ms Faerie. "He attacked you?"

"Oh no," she replied. "But I could see his intention in his aura. He's a bad man."

Bud couldn't argue with her there. He'd wondered on more than one occasion how Lacey had made it into the force. Bud scratched the side of his head. Something he was prone to do when faced with a problem he couldn't solve. "But he took his clothes off?"

"Nay," she replied. "I took them from him."

Bud closed his eyes and shook his head from side to side. "None of this makes sense," he mumbled, more to himself than to her. How the heck had she removed most of Lacey's clothing?

The conclusion Bud came to, was that Ms Faerie must have bamboozled Lacey with her ravishingly beautiful self. There could be no other explanation. Even then, he knew he was reaching for straws. The woman was stunning. Although she remained seated on the concrete floor, he ascertained she was statuesque and rounded in all the places that counted.

There was much to admire about Ms Faerie, even when dressed in Lacey's voluminous shirt. If wearing it was an attempt to hide her curves from the lecherous Lacey, she had failed. Instead, they were accentuated. The neckline gaped and he glimpsed the swell of her white breasts straining against Lacey's badge pinned strategically at her mid-riff. His gaze moved downwards. Down to where the hem of the crisp, white material ended and her legs began. Magnificent, long shapely ones and they went on and on all the way up to her....

Testosterone rushed to his groin as his imagination took flight. Yes, it said. It's time you had some action. Jeez! He was fantasizing about a woman who had run naked through the streets of Oaktree Falls.

Shoving the fantasy away, he scrutinized the reality in front of him. Neither was believable. Still, he found himself captivated and uncharacteristically wanted to believe her ludicrous story.

Very thick, long blonde hair framed her face like a halo. She looked back at him, her heart shaped face open and honest, her eyes the deepest, clearest pools that seemed blue and yet green as well. Those eyes were staring back at him with open curiosity and interest.

It was a pity she thought herself a faerie princess.

"Are you planning to eat Lacey at Thanksgiving?" He nodded towards her prisoner. "Because I can tell you, he'll be tough as old tree bark."

Glory's eyes darkened to a deep azure. "'Twould be wrong to eat a human. All faerie are vegetarian. He's a horrible weed of a human. Mayhap I should turn him into a lizard." Her eyes lit with what he could only describe as glee. "What do you think?"

A lizard was an apt description of the man. Bud found himself thinking it would be good if she could
turn him into a dark green one.

***

Glory had taken one look at the human coming through the door and had made a snap judgment. She knew to whom she would much rather belong. There was something different about this human. He was tall and possessed shoulders so broad she immediately wanted to rest her head against them to see how it felt. Truly, she hoped his character was as solid as his physical image suggested.

There was also a gentleness in him that wasn't present in the other humans she'd encountered. One glance told her many things. This human possessed the dreamiest eyes encircled by the most ever so shiny silver frames. That and the fact he clearly spent a lot of time outdoors. Skin tanned to a dark bronze, hazelnut hair bleached to a lighter shade from many hours in the sun, and crease lines marking the corners of his eyes. He laughed often. She was sure of it, and a man who laughed had to be inherently good. Right? His jaw was square, nose straight and his gaze… well it was a little confused right now, but she figured he was an honest man who lived an honest life. Someone she could connect with.

Glory didn't doubt this knowledge, for she could see it plainly in his aura and an aura never lied.

Mayhap he would be the one to release her from this predicament she found herself in. Rising from the floor, she tamped down her fear of touching a human and moved into his personal space. Close enough to inhale his musky scent. An aroma so hypnotic her knees grew weak with an unfamiliar fancy.

"I can tell you're not like Lacey at all. I don't think you're rude or horrible like he is." She paused as she made her assessment. "Dependable is what I believe you to be."

He huffed. "I was hoping for something a little more interesting than the word dependable."

Glory noted this human's pupils dilate behind the shiny frames and heard his breath quicken. Standing almost eye-to-eye she spoke, attempting to use the Art of Charming as taught by her Master Tutor, although she did not think 'twas necessary. She could discern his spark of interest reaching out and encircling her.

She tried dazzling him with her best smile. "Forgive me. I have not formerly introduced myself."

"There's no need." Bud took a step backwards. "I know who you are."

"Oh, but there is." She sank into a deep curtsy with all the grace expected of one from the royal court of Faerie. One knee almost to the floor, she bowed her head for several seconds before lifting her hand and head in unison and looked directly into his eyes.

"I am The Most Royal Princess, Gloriane, youngest daughter to King Aloysius and Queen Celandine of the Faerie Realm. By the colors in your aura, I note you are not a foe. You may call me Glory. All my friends do."

***

Bud was extremely disappointed as he reached out and took her hand and tugged her back up onto two feet. For some bizarre reason he'd wanted her to have a genuine reason for her strange behavior. Regrettably, she was as nutty as his Aunt Esme's walnut loaf and destined for the psychiatric ward at Oaktree Hospital for sure!

Clearing his throat he said, "Bud Chandler. Attending police psychologist." He glanced at Lacey, still bound and wriggling like a worm in a cocoon as he tried to break free. Shrugging off his unease, Bud released his hold of Glory's hand and forced his feet to move towards Lacey while asking, "Where did this stuff come from? How did you do it?"

"Oh 'tis but a simple glamour taught to me when I was a youngling. Faerie webbing is one of the first things we learn to create."

"I see." If he played along, maybe he would understand. Eventually. He leaned down and tried to free the prisoner. Sticky stuff clung to his fingertips like taffy, and as he removed the silken substance it instantaneously replenished itself both on Lacey and himself.

He waved cobwebbed fingers in her direction. "Perhaps you

could get rid of this stuff, what did you call it?"

"Faerie webbing? It's glamour. What you humans call a spell." Glory pouted. "Do I have to remove all of it?"

"What do you think?"

"I think he hasn't been punished enough."

Privately Bud agreed with her. "Take it all off." He was beginning to wonder if this was just a bad dream. That he'd fallen asleep on the couch at home and he would wake up in the morning and it would be business as usual.

"Fiddledeedee!" Glory's long locks seemed to lift with static electricity. "I like him better the way he is."

Nevertheless, she raised her arms out to the side and for one moment, Bud thought she was going to flap them and fly. Instead, she recited words Bud couldn't comprehend and just when he was thinking she should be in show business, the cobwebs miraculously disappeared.

Bud jumped backwards. He knew his eyes were darting in their sockets. First to Glory and then to Lacey and back again. He felt like a loony stuck in a toon!

"Mmmm," Lacey mumbled as he crawled free and scooped up his jacket, which Glory had dropped, to the floor. "Mmmm," he said again, pointing to his mouth.

Planting fists on her hips, Glory's voice took on a cautionary tone. "Do you promise never to foul the air with unseemly language ever again?"

Lacey made a vigorous single nod. "Mmmm."

"A promise once made can never be broken." Glory wagged an index finger at him as if her prisoner was a naughty schoolboy. "Otherwise I'll have to take more drastic action."

Alarm flared in Lacey's eyes. "Mmmm."

Loosely translated, Bud decided the mumbling sounded like *I promise.*

Glory, it seemed, thought so too, for once more her hands danced in the air and she muttered a bevy of indecipherable words while Bud marveled at how it took only one woman, the wave of a hand, a threat and a promise to bring Lacey to his knees.

Lacey's mouth flew open and was accompanied by a loud popping sound. Glory's hands shot to her mouth and her eyes grew wide and round. "Great Snapping Crocodiles! I may have overdone the glamour a trifle."

"Ahhhh." Lacey's jaw was hanging open wide enough to net a school of fish. "Ahhhh."

Bud found himself enjoying his workmate's discomfort far more than he should. Lacey could not close his mouth. Bud was speechless and stared unable to find anything to say that would make sense right now.

Glory's lips pursed into a delightful grin. "I'll make a few adjustments here and there this time." Her hands danced through the air once more and then fell to her sides. "There. All done."

Bud found himself grinning back.

Lacey didn't seem to see the funny side. His mouth snapped shut milliseconds after a fat lazy blowfly flew into his mouth. He coughed and the fly wafted out and wavered about before coming to rest on a wall.

Bud shouldn't laugh. He really shouldn't. But he did and Lacey shot him a hateful leer that only made Bud laugh louder and longer.

"Thank the heavens!" Glory was clearly relieved. "I wasn't certain 'twould work."

"You're a witch!" Lacey spat the words out, his expression a mix of fear and disgust.

"Consider yourself lucky I'm not. A witch would have done far worse than I."

"Faerie. Witch. Whatever."

Glory assumed what Bud could only call a Peter Pan stance.

Elbows bent, knuckles on hips, chin jutting forward. Her eyes narrowed. "Do you want me to show you the difference?"

"No!" Backed up against the cell wall, Lacey made his bid for escape faster than a magician.

Completely bamboozled, Bud asked the princess, "How did you do that?"

"Magic." Glory winked. "Want to see some more?"

"No!" Bud dropped his face into his hands. He couldn't believe he was even having this conversation. He raised his head. "I've seen enough."

Musical laughter filled the cell. And, because Bud could not think of any particular reason not to, and also because he was beginning to consider the outrageous claim Glory was making was true, he laughed right along with her.

Then she twirled. Spreading her arms out in a wide arc, all the precinct buttons and silver tabs woven into her hair glinted under the single cell light. Suddenly, he found it difficult to breathe. A strange sensation shot like liquid fire through him, sending confused messages radiating to his heart. He drank in the sheer pleasure of looking upon someone so beautiful, so appealing, so… so certifiably crazy.

Damn it!

He intoned darkly to himself, *I don't believe. I don't believe. I don't believe.*

***

Glory stopped spinning and studied her new master. There was confusion in those wonderful grey eyes. Confusion and… what? Was it fear?

She didn't want Bud Chandler to be afraid. Not of her. A deep-seated sigh started somewhere in the region of her toes and twirled its way up through her heart and out past her lips. What she wanted from this man she would never have. She was faerie and he human.

The two didn't go together and if she stayed in his world, there'd be trouble and she was in enough of that already.

She must leave as soon as possible. But before that could happen, her new master would have to set her free.

"Please," she implored, her heart full of regret. "'Tis time for me to go home. Will you release me?"

"It's not in my power."

He seemed genuinely sorry but she didn't want his pity. She wanted her freedom.

"It's up to the courts."

"Each time a human touches me I then belong to that person until released by their reciting the magic glamour. You're the last person to touch me. I am now yours. You hold all the power. You must release me to let me return to the Faerie Realm. My true home."

His regret was genuine. "I can't."

"You can. Just repeat the magic glamour three times. 'Tis easy."

Bud's eyebrows lifted a fraction. "Not a good idea."

"Please?" she pleaded. "'Tis not a great hardship to be kind to another in need."

Jeez! Now he'd feel hardhearted if he didn't give Glory her wish. She was the patient and yet here he was considering her request to recite what she called glamour.

"Please. I would not ask if it were not important."

"What are the exact words?" Bud's tongue had gone from neutral to top gear in one second flat without going through second or third. His intelligence had left his head and now resided due south.

Light leapt back into Glory's eyes and Bud felt insanely delighted to see it there. Her eyes were so clear and so… so inviting. He felt he could drown in their liquid depths. "Now let me get this clear," he said, because he wasn't about to do this twice. "All I have to do is say this glamour aloud three times?"

Glory nodded, her face a picture of what he could only describe as delight. How could he disappoint her, and besides, it would put paid to any further fanciful thoughts on his part because he knew it wouldn't work. He didn't have to ask what the words in her glamour were either. He'd read the charge sheet. He remembered them clearly.

He sighed. "Only if you promise not to tell anyone about this."

Glory was ecstatic. "Thank you, Bud. I will never forget your kindness."

Bud was about to perform an act of lunacy and he wanted no witnesses to the fact. He poked his head out the door and scoured the hallway for any loitering personnel, before locking the door behind him, and wondered who the sane one was here. Locking himself in with a prisoner to recite a spell was the craziest thing he'd ever done.

"Wait." Glory interrupted when his lips began to form the first word.

"What?" What now?

"I have a rare gift for you to thank you for your kindness. Three wishes shall be yours. However, before I go, there is one other favor I would have from you."

Bud was suddenly cautious. "You would?"

A seductive smile played on her lips and she twirled a curl of her hair in her fingers. "Aye. I would."

Before Bud realized her intention, she leaned in and pressed her lips against his in a searing kiss that made his toes curl and his testosterone hit an all time high. Man. His mind went numb and a certain part of his anatomy swelled to alarming proportions. Just as he decided he might as well join the madness and wrap his arms around her, she stepped away out of reach.

"I'm ready now," she smiled happily, seemingly unaffected by their momentary tryst.

Me too thought Bud, and before he could pull her back into his arms for another taste of heaven, he recited the magic words.

"Faretheewell

Faretheewell

Fly Faerie Free"

***

Glory sensed the physical hold that kept her in the human world lift, leaving her feeling light, but not totally free. How odd. 'Twas as if part of her now resided with Bud. Somehow, they were still connected. 'Twas inexplicable, although mayhap it was because their lips had touched. She would ask Triumphant upon her return home. Triumphant knew everything.

Bud finished his recitation for the third time. "You're still here then?"

"Of course," she replied.

"Aren't you supposed to vanish?" He flicked his hand in the air. "Disappear."

"Oh, I will. In a moment or two. But first there is something else I must do."

"Another kiss, perhaps?"

Glory grinned and her heart tapped a mini happy dance. He liked her well enough to want another kiss from her. "Alas no." She waved her hands through the air, crafting another glamour. "Lacey has to forget about me."

Glory looked longingly into Bud's wonderful eyes. "Everyone has to. Including you. I've removed the record of my arrest from the charge sheet and soon no one will recall anything about me."

"Oh, I won't ever forget this," Bud assured her. "No one in his right mind would ever forget you."

Glory felt herself blush the color of the brightest fuchsia. "I thank you for your kind words. I will not forget you either." She would never forget the touch of Bud's human lips on hers or his great kindness.

Then she waved her hands before Bud's eyes, released her glamour and disappeared from the cell.

***

Shrouded by an invisibility glamour Glory, now her usual size when in the forest, approximately six inches tall, flew through to where Lacey huddled by Sergeant Delaney's desk. However, before Glory released her final glamour, she did something else her Father told her not to do and felt not one ounce of remorse or guilt.

"Oh, what a wicked faerie I am," she uttered as she completed the maneuver.

Delaney, the odious officer who had arrested her, sat bolt upright in his chair, and then, with an agility Glory would never have thought him capable of, he clambered, no, sprang onto his desk as if he had springs in his short, fat legs.

Crouched, legs apart, knees bent frog-like at right angles, his hands and tummy rested on the table, supporting his immense weight. His jowls jiggled and his eyes bulged as he surveyed the room with a watchful, intense regard. A fat, lazy, extremely disoriented fly, smelling suspiciously of garlic flew way too close and to everyone's amusement, Delaney's tongue darted out and then in, and the fly was gone. He croaked a series of deep, guttural, extremely satisfied grrrrribbits.

As for Lacey, another spell had him quacking like a duck, going backwards and forwards resembling a target at a fun fair.

***

Bud walked into the room just in time to witness the entire event. An elusive image of a very naked and extremely voluptuous blonde with silver buttons in her hair wavered in and out of his vision. He blinked rapidly. A six-inch, naked nymph winked at him, but, before he could digest what must only be a hallucination, she was gone.

Man! Did he need a holiday or what!

≈ CHAPTER 3 ≈

Glory assumed the King had not yet heard through the Faerie Chain what she had done or she would have been summoned to the Royal Throne by now. Still, she swore Triumphant to secrecy before revealing a single detail of her escapade into the Human Realm and her subsequent capture.

"You realize," her sister advised, "Father will find out. He always does."

Glory's shoulders sagged, her expression woeful. "He will? He does?"

"Unquestionably."

Triumphant was the wisest person Glory knew. "But you're not one hundred percent certain." Glory perked up a little at the doubt she saw in her sister's aura. "If Father knew, he would be hovering around like a persistent bumblebee just like all the other times I've done something wrong. Truly, he would have summoned me long before now if he'd heard an inkling."

Triumphant sat down on the bed beside Glory, picked up one of her hands and squeezed it gently in a comforting gesture. Glory felt her sister's love pour through her hands as she continued, "You do indulge yourself in them, do you not?"

Glory's eyes coalesced to a murky green. "In what?"

"Fantasies."

"It's true my imagination is a trifle overactive. I do not intend it to be so. Why am I fooling myself? You are never wrong. Why should now be any different?"

Any last trace of rosy color bled from her cheeks and Glory bit down on her bottom lip to prevent it from wobbling. "I'm truly worried." She paused, gulped back her tears, and exclaimed, "I wish I was more like you."

Her parents still spoke of the day Triumphant was born and how the heavens opened and God's angels played trumpets and sang with joy.

"What did the heavens do when I was born?" Glory once asked a long time ago, hoping for an equally notable entrance to the world. A disconcerted look had passed between her parents and she had not understood why until much later. "What did the heavens do?" she had asked again. The heavens had opened and deluged the earth with a million Morning Glory and rose petals was the reply.

Overcome with joy at being so special, Glory had from that day invested time and energy into befriending all the different varieties of Morning Glory and rose to be found in Newberry Forest. She was Princess Gloriane, Faerie of Morning Glory. Her favorite was always Morning Glory because it was also her name when shortened. Especially those colored with just a hint of cornflower blue tipping its delicate edges. It was as if someone had dipped each petal into a pot of diluted ink. If you held them up to the light you could just about see right through them, and they felt so soft, so fragile.

Several weeks after her parents' revelation, while playing amongst the old gnarled roots of their home—an enormous sprawling ancient oak, which had stood in the forest since almost forever—she had heard her parents' familiar voices drifting down from a leafy arbor nearby. Good faerie princesses never eavesdropped, but she was hardly ever good even when trying her hardest, so she'd listened and discovered the terrible truth.

It was not petals to fall from the heavens upon her birth, but rain. A deluge of big, fat droplets had cascaded from the sky, enough to create a new river on the outskirts of the forest. The rain had lasted for nearly as long as the great flood the Ancient Ones always talked about with such awe.

She loved her parents but was unable to conceive how they could have told her such an untruth. The pain of their deception sliced deeply into her soul and on that sad, sad day when she learned the facts of her birth, she cried enough tears to flood her own bedroom within the Tree Most Royal.

Even then, she couldn't find it in her heart to be jealous or resentful of her older sister. Almost certainly, she would have drowned in her own sadness if not for Triumphant who courageously swam against the swell of Glory's tears to hold her against her gentle and benevolent heart until every last teardrop had fallen.

Triumphant had then held her close and explained all about little white lies, and slowly, Glory began to forgive and understand why Mother and Father had done such a dreadful thing. Truly, who would want to admit to their child that the skies had wept upon her birth?

Not in her nature to be jealous or envious, the auspicious arrival of Triumphant into the world was truly more awe-inspiring than her own, without question.

Anyone would have forgiven Glory if she had shown even the teensiest trace of envy, but she never had. Instead, she loved her sister all the more for her gentle, caring sensitivity. Triumphant was the kindest, most perfect, most wonderful sister any faerie could ever hope to have.

"What am I to do?" she cried. Triumphant was also the wisest faerie she knew. Apart from the Ancient Ones of course. They were the wisest of all. Faeries who, once accepted into the Ancient Circle, could live for hundreds of years. Sometimes thousands.

Triumphant looked at her and firmly declared, "You will do nothing."

Deep worried eyes, a strange swirl of blue and green, widened in confusion. "Nothing?"

Squeezing her hands encouragingly, Triumphant nodded. "Mayhap Father is waiting to see what you do next. I expect he's not as displeased as you think."

Glory had a horrible gnawing feeling in the pit of her stomach he would be extremely displeased if he knew all the facts, and that Triumphant was employing one of those little white lies she'd told her about all those years ago.

"Does he know everything?" And when her sister nodded an affirmative, she declared dramatically, "I'm never leaving home again. Never!"

***

Somewhere over Oaktree Falls Plains

Wind whipped through Bud's hair. Icy freeze-your-ass-off invigorating wind. So cold, he could barely suck in a decent breath. Bud didn't care. It was all part of the adrenaline surge coursing through him.

It happened every time he flung himself from a plane.

Ten thousand feet in the air and freefalling.

He likened it to the all-consuming rush that flooded his veins during sex and yet, not even sex came close to describing how he felt right now. He was still to meet a woman who could engender the feelings he was experiencing right this second. Doing what he loved most.

Parachuting was the closest he ever came to what he imagined flying was like. Except when cushioned in dreams and in the naiveté of childhood, he had dreamed nightly of flying. That was why he jumped from planes with a parachute on his back. He was attempting to recapture the magic of weightless dreams.

With the ground charging up to meet him, the thrill of waiting as long as he could before pulling the ripcord to open his chute was pure exhilaration. He felt alive and vital. All the negative experiences of the past week had been placed into perspective, and, by the time he touched down on terra firma, he knew he would have regained his perspective on life.

At peace with himself and the world.

With one strong tug of the ripcord, his parachute deployed, slowing his descent. Jack "Daredevil" Diamond, his best friend and jumping buddy, shot past in a blur of speed, and Bud acknowledged his passing with a thumbs up and a gregarious grin. By the third jump of the day, all his stress had evaporated. Energized, he concluded all he'd needed was a few days away from the precinct to regain some balance in his life.

There was absolutely nothing wrong with him.

Life was good.

The only thing missing to make his life perfect was a woman who understood just how spine tingling flying unfettered through the air could be. Someone to keep him warm at night and share his hopes and dreams.

Bud laughed aloud at his fanciful thoughts and spoke out safe in the knowledge no one could hear him. "Where is she, God? Where's the woman for me?" Of course, there was no reply. "I wish I could meet someone who loves to fly as much as I do."

"Hello."

Bud chuckled inanely. God had become a woman and was speaking to him. He continued his descent, gliding ever closer to his target.

"Hello."

There it was again. He swiveled his head to the left and then to the right. Nothing.

"Hello."

"Damn!" Bud swore. Suddenly, his newfound peace and happiness dissipated, unraveling his short-lived and oh so craved for, peace.

***

When Glory experienced the call of Bud's wish she fought leaving Tree with all her might, but a wish once given was a power too strong to be denied.

Away from the safety of her home, she landed with a plop and a bounce right on top of a bright royal blue parachute canopy. Shinning along to the edge, she lay on her stomach and peeked over, allowing herself to dangle from the edge, her hair cascading down like tassels on a pillow.

Naturally, it was Bud. She had given no other human three wishes. Ever! Moreover, because of the glamour she had cast, he probably didn't remember she had given them to him. A slight flaw in her plan.

Glory's eyes twinkled with mischief. A naughty giggle escaped her lips, her tears forgotten. If she was to incur the wrath of Father for her misdemeanors then she may as well add another to the list. What would one more matter?

Waving her hand, she made herself human sized, but remained as light as a feather and somersaulted from the edge of the chute like a trapeze artist to flutter down to face Bud. "Hello."

***

A strange tension gripped Bud, contorting his features into stunned horror. His knuckles whitened as his fingers clenched around the ropes and he veered off course as a result.

The vision flew on over to join him.

The hazy images of a nymph-like creature, which had been flitting in and out of his memory and dreams all week, had flit back and this time she possessed a set of wings and was using them. They were whipping up a frenzy, almost creating an updraft as she kept pace with his descent.

His eyes behind his prescription goggles glazed over and his libido kicked in. How could it not? She wore no parachute. In fact, she wore nothing at all except a set of sheer wings. Not a single stitch of clothing adorned her incredible curves.

Once more, his hands jerked on the ropes and he swerved even further to the left, well away from his target on the ground.

The apparition followed and winked wickedly at him. "'Tis good to see you again," it said.

Bud sucked in a huge breath. "Where? What?"

"You called," she explained. "And I came."

"I did?"

"Uh huh," she said. "You probably don't remember, but you have three wishes. Apparently, you just used one."

This time Bud deliberately veered to the right in an attempt to get away from this hallucination and back to his target.

The creature followed, a frown on her brow. "What was your wish?"

"Shouldn't you know what it is?" He was having a conversation with his hallucination. Bud was extremely concerned for his safety, let alone his mental health.

The creature quirked her head to the left and studied him as one might a perplexing jigsaw puzzle. "When one makes a wish, one usually knows what it is. 'Tis usually obvious."

"'Tis? I mean, it is?"

"Yes." She frowned at him. "But, I haven't a clue what your wish is."

Bud returned her gaze warily because he knew what his wish had been. To meet someone who enjoyed flying as much as he did. Blinking, he damped down a hysterical laugh. Well, he was flying and so was the creature before him? And she was definitely female.

He raised his face to the heavens and shouted. "Is this your idea of a joke?"

His hallucination looked upwards as well, searching the great expanse of blue sky above. "To whom are you talking?"

A bubble of laughter erupted from Bud's mouth. "Who do you think?"

His hallucination shrugged and she smiled. "Is this a game? I love games."

The shock value in the situation was waning. His heart thudded less dangerously in his chest, his breathing less shallow. Bud inspected the naked woman closely, while trying to appear as if he spoke to naked women all the time. She seemed real enough and perfectly formed as well. Except for those blasted wings. What was that about?

It was odd, but she reminded him of someone. Who the hell was it? It was right on the tip of his tongue. "Where did you come from?"

"The Glory Tree."

The Glory Tree. Of course. Why not? Nymphs lived in trees. Didn't they? "Are you a…?" Bud couldn't believe he was asking this. "…nymph?"

Glory beamed. "Some would call us that. Nymphs are naughty creatures who like to stir up trouble on purpose. I'm a faerie."

Bud nodded as he floated ever closer to the ground. He had lost his hold on reality. He was way off his target and when a rescue party finally picked him up and listened to his raving about naked faeries they would cart him away to the funny farm. And he would go willingly.

"Naturally you're a faerie," he muttered more to himself than to her. "How could I have got it so wrong?"

"I fear you're having trouble believing," his faerie spoke softly. "Do not be overly concerned. Most humans don't believe we exist." She giggled and he was reminded of a bubbling brook he'd sat beside once. "Just tell me your wish and then I will be away. What was it?"

Some things were best kept secret. Even if she wasn't real. "None of your business."

"Of course 'tis my business."

"And why is that?"

"I gave you the wish. It stands to reason that if I gave you the wish, I should know what it is."

"It would also be reasonable to assume that if you gave me the wish, you would know what it is as well." And that I should know you. "Why did you give me a wish?"

Puffing her cheeks out with air, she planted her fists on her hips. Bud followed the movement and felt nothing reasonable about the way his body responded.

He attempted to will the unwelcome reaction away. Don't stare he told himself. Don't look. Nevertheless, he had to admit he had seen enough to know she was an outstanding vision. So was his groin. It appeared his imagination was far more creative than he'd ever thought.

"You helped me recently and as a reward I gave you three wishes."

"Who are you?" He shifted his gaze to somewhere just above the top of her head. In the blink of an eye, he had seen all he needed to see and that was everything. It was wonderful. Every inch of this faerie was a red-blooded man's dream. "I would have remembered if you'd given me three wishes."

"My name is Glory. You helped me return to my world."

"Glory." Bud rolled her name over on his tongue. It felt right, familiar. "Are you sure?" He supposed he must have dreamed her up along with the three wishes in the past. It's a pity he couldn't remember that particular dream.

Tossing her head, her wild mane glistened in the sunlight and something shiny captured his attention. Round, silver objects were threaded in her golden locks. They looked like the tabs you pull from the lids of cans and was that an official Oaktree Falls precinct button as well?

"Of course I'm sure. 'Tis my name," she said with indignation.

Again, Bud experienced a ripple of recognition. Goosebumps popped up all over his body. He had definitely heard that musical laughter before. "So we've met before?"

His hallucination nodded her very attractive head.

Bud wondered why he was so relieved. He was talking to a faerie for heaven's sake! He gauged the length of time left before landing. A couple more minutes of freedom, then the little men in white coats would whip him away for the rest of his days.

"Maybe I'm having an out-of-body experience," Bud conjectured. "And when I touch ground I'll be jolted back into my body."

"What is this nonsense you are spouting?" A puzzled frown creased Glory's brow.

"If you don't know," Bud responded, "I'm sure I don't."

"Are you well? Your eyes are overly large behind those big round things on your face."

Bud snorted rudely. "They're prescription goggles and I'm as well as can be expected. As for my health, well, perception is everything. It depends on where you're coming from I suppose."

"Oh, I see. I come from the Faerie Realm," Glory responded innocently.

"I was being sarcastic. I'm talking to a naked faerie. I've lost my target and who knows where I'm going to land. I'm not well."

"Is that all? I thought it to be something serious," his faerie declared.

"It is serious." Bud almost shouted. "I'm a lost soul."

"Don't you worry about a single thing," said Glory. "'Tis nothing a simple glamour won't fix. Just leave it to me."

It occurred to Bud it was a definite sign of insanity when you put your trust in a hallucination. "Leave it to you?"

"Aye," she nodded. "But first, just a trifling matter. What is a target and where can I get one?"

Why fight the madness? He was a lost cause anyway. "It's a marker painted on the ground. Large enough for me to see where to land. I was on target before you materialized."

"Do not be concerned." Glory spoke confidently. "I shall locate your marker and be back in the twinkling of a starburst."

And POP! She was gone. Just like a cartoon. Scanning the horizon, he could see nothing except the sky above and the ever-approaching ground below. It was only a matter of seconds before his feet touched earth. How could she help him now?

POP! She was back. Bud shot off to the left.

"I've found it," she cried, zapping after him.

"Too late," he muttered. "I'm about to become a tree ornament." He indicated with a nod of his head to the stand of pines below. He determined he was located on the southern perimeter of Newberry Forest.

"Oh, no you're not," Glory declared and instantly recited something unintelligible. Bud heard a loud buzzing and then another POP, followed by what he could only describe as a WHOOSH! Wind rushed against his skin, dragging it tight against his cheekbones and flattening his hair against his skull. The world whirled about him and moments later he found himself several thousand feet higher than he was two seconds ago.

Glory hovered so close to him he could feel the fan of her wings against his cheeks. "I'm supposed to go down. Not up," Bud yelled. He never yelled. But he'd never gone up and not down when parachuting, either. He wondered inanely why the material of his chute hadn't collapsed and tangled around his limbs.

"Do not be concerned. I've everything covered."

Except for that delicious body. "I'm glad one of us does."

"'Tis my pleasure to be of service."

"This is not the kind of service I had in mind." He gulped and tried to control his raging hormones. "What is the point in putting me back up in the sky?"

"To get you back on course."

"Of course."

"Nay. On course."

Bud stared blankly at Glory. She shook her head and batted her eyelashes at him. Naked and flirting, he thought. This hallucination was a doozy.

"I've brought you back to the exact position you were in when you called upon your wish. Your target is a little to your right. I'll stay with you until you land."

"Are you my faerie godmother?"

Glory managed to look nonplussed for a moment or two. "Do I look old enough to be a godmother?"

Bud didn't hesitate. "No. But you do look good enough to eat."

Another fit of giggles escaped her cherry red lips and suddenly Bud wanted to more than taste this amazing creature. He was filled with a need to bury himself into this fantasy and press his mouth against hers and kiss her senseless. "Come closer and let me see," he muttered, wondering if she was tangible enough to actually touch.

As senseless as he already was, he needed a whole lot of loving, especially after being put through such terrible torture. This might be his last chance to kiss a woman before they carted him away to hospital. Ever!

"I don't think I'd taste that wonderful."

"Let me be the judge of that." He beckoned with a nod of his head. "Come over here."

Although she appeared reluctant, Glory hovered a little closer.

"That's it," Bud encouraged, when she was only a flutter away. He breathed in and the scent of flowers triggered a sense he should remember something.

"What perfume is that?"

Glory fanned her wings a little more and her scent surrounded him. "Do you like it?" When Bud nodded, she added, "'Tis my own special blend. I call it eau du Morning Glory."

"Eau du Morning Glory," Bud whispered and leaned forward. "Wonderful." In the same breath, he found himself uttering the words, "Kiss me."

***

Glory forgot to flutter her wings and she dropped several feet before remembering to fly. "Kiss you?"

She had thought of little else since first setting eyes on Bud Chandler and wanted nothing more than to repeat their first and only kiss. She wanted to kiss him silly. Wanted him to kiss her silly.

Disappointment pooled in her eyes, her face a picture of heartfelt longing. "I cannot."

"Yes, you can," Bud urged. "Fly on over here and pucker up. I want to see if you taste as delectable as you smell. I've wanted to since…" He frowned. "… I don't know when and I don't care. Just kiss me."

At a loss as to why the glamour she had cast had not completely eliminated all traces of his memory of her, Glory debated the pros and cons of his request. There was nothing more she wanted than to do as he asked. There were other parts of her body begging just as equally to get up-close-and-personal with him as well.

Another small glamour was all it would take to get rid of those cumbersome ropes and coarse human clothes he was wearing and then she could kiss him all over with the rest of her body.

There would be a price to pay for touching a human. Did she have the courage to pay-up? "Will you promise to release me once you've had your way?"

Bud was clearly eager because there was no hesitation in his reply. "I will."

"Do you know the magic words?" She wondered if he remembered anything else about her.

There was no hesitation on Bud's part. "The magic words are kiss me quick."

"Nay. Not those words." No recognition of having met her before registered in his eyes despite her appearance in full-sized human form. She rather liked being this size and so did Bud, it seemed, from the open appreciation in his eyes.

"All this talk and no action is wasting precious time. I've so little of it left. Will you kiss me if I promise?"

Glory wavered, but only for a moment. "Yes." She loved how he looked at her. As if she was a gift that he wanted to unwrap.

There was no hesitation in his response. "I promise then."

The promise was all it took because she'd seen his answer in his aura before he uttered the words. She allowed herself the luxury of inhaling his seductive, musky aroma. Tentatively, she leaned in and touched her lips to his. Rockets went off in her head and shot off elsewhere. She kissed him once more to see if it would happen again. It did. His lips were soft and inviting, their pressure insistent, and she opened her mouth just enough to allow his tongue to run along her top inner lip. She sighed into his mouth. He was just as she remembered. Except now his lips were not enough.

"Put your arms around me," she ordered, eager to feel the hands of this human on her skin. Bud's wonderful, gentle, yet masterful hands.

"I can't," he answered, and indicated his hold on the parachute ropes.

"Oh tish-tosh! Another trifling matter." Glory waved her hand. "You can let go now. You're on automatic pilot." It was a term she'd heard before when listening in at the edge of the forest to conversations between other humans.

***

Automatic pilot! The mind a wonderful instrument. He might as well trust her. After all, she had wings and was flying without the aid of a parachute. He let go of the ropes and yes, he remained headed towards his target. If this was insanity, he rather liked it.

"Now you can put your arms around me." Glory plastered herself right up against him. Every glorious naked inch of her. "Kiss me again. I liked it."

"I liked it too," he spoke gruffly, completely undone by an emotion so foreign he had no words to describe it. Bud didn't need further encouragement. Before she changed her mind and flew away, he buried his head into the crook of her neck and inhaled the essence of her perfume. His body responded like a hormonal teenager.

This hallucination…? Delusion…? Whatever it was, was turning out to be one hell of a doozy. No wonder some of his patients preferred living a life of fantasy instead of living in the real world.

As his lips touched once more with Glory's, he gave himself up to the madness and savored the experience instead. What a wonderful, heady madness it was. There was nothing about her that wasn't glorious. Skin so smooth, so pale and unflawed. His coarser hands trailed down her back beneath her wings, feeling every indentation as they made their way to cup her bottom. She melded so neatly into him, moving with and against him. A perfect fit. Hot need set him afire, threatening to erupt into something far more volatile. Unfortunately, there was something very sad about a hallucination engendering a passion he had never felt for anyone other than this unworldly woman. Ah… faerie.

***

Nobody had ever explained to Glory exactly why a faerie should never touch or kiss a human other than stating the fact she would then belong to whoever touched her. Nobody had ever told her how brilliantly blissful it could be either. Bud's tongue probed her mouth and her breath mingled with his. Her speech was barely coherent. "This is…. oh. This is…. oh my. This is heavenly."

She clung to him more tightly than the vines of Morning Glory clinging to her home and reveled in the play of his hands tracing pathways across the sensitive skin of her back and buttocks.

Opening her mouth under the insistent pressure of his, she nipped at his bottom lip with her teeth, imprinting, moistening, and leaving her mark. Tracing her tongue around the outline of his lips she matched his equally adventurous probing when he slanted his mouth to cover hers and they joined in a deep, electrifying exploration.

"Perhaps I'm in heaven." Bud muttered between kisses. "If this is what heaven is, then I never want to leave." It was a statement spoken heatedly against her skin as he discovered the rosy peaks of her breasts with his thumbs.

He cupped full, rounded bundles of flesh and Glory's wings went into overdrive. Their descent slowed, stilled and then changed direction. Together they shot up through the air, purely from the force of her feelings.

"I want to stay with you forever," she cried as he nipped the lobe of an ear.

"You can," Bud growled against her throat. "You're a part of me. You're in my head. We can be together in hospital."

"Hospital!" Glory leaned back to stare at him. "Why would you want us to go there?"

"I don't want to go, but it's where I'm going when we land." He resumed nibbling at her neck.

His thumbs massaged her perfect, pale pink nipples. He flicked them, enjoying the rapid increase in Glory's pulse. Pleased at her response, he cupped both breasts and pushed them together and upwards, then bent his head to taste and suckle their sweet scented roundness.

A strange explosive desire coiled through Glory, sending surges of hot need rushing into her womb. "Why?" The heat spurred her wings into overdrive once again and they surged upwards.

"Because I'm certifiably mad."

She reluctantly tugged at his head, lifting him away from her breasts. "'Tis not anger I see in your eyes or in the feel of your lips." She bent down and kissed his eyelids one by one. "'Tis desire."

"No. Not angry. Mad. Nuts. Insane."

"You're not insane."

"I am," Bud insisted.

"Why would you think such a thing?"

"I'm suffering from a severe case of delusional psychosis. Only crazy people see and speak to naked faeries. Only insane people believe they are flying with or making out with one in broad daylight."

Glory raked her long fingers through Bud's wind-whipped hazelnut hair and nuzzled back into his neck. "You're not crazy. I'm real. You can feel me, can you not?"

Now there was an understatement. He could feel everything and loved it. Unable to speak, he nodded.

"Faeries exist. One day I'll take you to my home and you will see."

"I'd like that." He also very much liked what she was doing with her tongue in his ear. "If they ever let me out of hospital, I'll be happy to visit."

They were dropping again, and Bud judged it would only be another minute or so before they reached the ground. When Glory pushed herself out of his arms, he protested, "No. Don't go."

"Do not concern yourself. I will soon be back in your arms." Glory looked down at the people milling about, waiting for Bud to land, no doubt with a million questions for which there were no answers.

Silently she wove a glamour and cast it upon the crowd gathering below. No one except Bud would remember a thing.

She hoped.

With the glamour released, she snuggled into him, her breasts pressing against the rough material of his jumpsuit. She fit perfectly and knew Bud thought so too, because he whispered as much against her ear before he resumed nibbling on her lobe. Even better, he also whispered about how much he would like to remove his clothing and fly naked with her across the sky.

"One day we will," she promised. "One day soon." Then she took his mind off everything by kissing him with a promise of things to come.

***

Bud touched down, making a perfect landing. His hallucination had vanished and Jack was jogging towards him. Pulling in the ropes of his parachute, he geared himself for the inevitable? But all Jack did was slap him on the back and congratulate him on another successful jump. Surrounded by other jumpers who were milling about, none hinted his descent had taken longer than usual or that he had mysteriously gone up and not down, several times. And finally, of course, no one hinted at seeing the voluptuous woman in his arms. Alas, she had definitely existed only in his head.

He wouldn't be carted away after all. Maybe he would have to do it himself.

Or just maybe he could go home and continue his hallucination in private.

Then a woman flew into his arms. "Oh Bud. That was wonderful."

"Ah, thanks," he managed, before she covered his lips in an energetic and overly familiar kiss. "I think?"

The scent of eau du Morning Glory pervaded his nostrils and he stiffened, his arms falling to his sides. She was back! Only this time she was clothed, thank God, in a flowing, flimsy lemon paisley thing, some would call a dress. There were no wings in sight.

A ribald remark from Jack broke through his confusion. "You

old devil. Where did she come from? You never told me you were seeing someone."

Glory turned round in Bud's arms to face Jack. "'Tis so new. You might say I flew into his arms."

The apple bobbed in Bud's throat as he gulped back his stunned surprise. He spoke to Jack, his throat constricting with bewilderment. "Can you see her?"

Jack frowned. "See who?"

Bud winced. "Glory. Can you see her?"

"Of course I can see her." Concern marred Jack's handsome forehead. "Are you okay? You seem a little confused."

Glory nodded. "I said the very same thing." Craning her neck to look over her shoulder at Jack, she allowed the inflection in her voice to rise as she spoke to him. "He should never have got out of bed this morning. I think he's fighting off a virus."

"I think he's lost the battle," Jack laughed, and held out his hand. "It's a pleasure to meet you, Glory."

Her stomach sank. She could not let him touch her, but if she ignored Jack's offer of friendship he would think her rude.

She turned on her best charming smile. "Forgive me if I don't shake your hand. I wouldn't want to pass whatever Bud has on to you."

She sighed inwardly with relief when his hand dropped away.

"I do not have a virus." Bud was feeling hot, but not from some physical ailment.

"Oh, you do," Glory stressed and milked the role of concerned lover for all its worth by placing a gentle palm on his forehead. Her gaze locked with his. "You're burning up."

"Well, I do feel a little feverish," he found himself saying weakly. For a brief moment he felt a whole lot better, but then he remembered it still didn't explain Glory's existence or the events of the past half-hour. Nor did it explain how everyone on the ground appeared to accept Glory's sudden appearance without question.

"I think I should go home to bed." He began to undo the straps of his harness.

Jack grinned like the sly fox he preferred people to think he was. "I would too if I had a girlfriend like Glory to tend to me."

"She's not my girlfriend," Bud stressed through clenched teeth.

"'Tis true. I'm not." Glory's eyes flickered her annoyance, and she added, a glint of defiance shining in her azure eyes, "But I *am* his Faerie Princess."

≈ CHAPTER 4 ≈

"Did you have to say that?"

"Say what?" Glory bit into a huge rosy apple that had appeared out of nowhere and continued to stare out the passenger vehicle window.

"That you're my Faerie Princess."

The conniving little minx grinned. She waved the apple in her hand. "'Tis true enough."

"'Tis… it is not." Bud's fingers clenched around the steering wheel and he made an effort to keep the edge of annoyance from his voice. Unable to convince her there was no way on this earth he was taking her home with him, she had simply ignored his protests and now shared a seat in his jeep, chatting inanely about nothing in particular, as if she did so every day.

He wanted to evict her from the jeep.

He wanted to be sane.

He wanted her in his arms again.

He glared once more at his Faerie Princess. If there was one thing he knew from his brief encounter with her in the sky, she was not in the least shy and she was leading him on a merry chase and enjoying every second.

Locking himself in his jeep at Oaktree Falls Parachute Club in an effort to discourage her from following him hadn't worked. Somehow-he guessed it was magic-she had managed to unlock the passenger door and clamber right on in. So now he was stuck with her and he didn't know whether to be pleased or pissed. To kiss her or tell her to get lost.

Glory munched noisily on the apple. A rivulet of juice dribbled temptingly down her chin. Unconsciously he licked the corners of his mouth. He had an urge to trace the same path the juice took with his tongue. She would be delicious and sweet.

Concentrate. Keep your hands on the wheel. Eyes straight ahead. Keep driving. It was a tall order. Bud steered the vehicle through the late afternoon traffic in an effort to keep his hands where they should be and not threaded through Her Royal Highness's hair.

Tension gave him a stiff neck and a throbbing ache in his shoulders. Desire gave him something else altogether. "Can I drop you off somewhere?"

"Nay." Glory shook her head. "I'll be staying with you tonight."

His foot slipped on the clutch and the jeep lurched, nearly rear ending the car in front. "I don't think so." Taking his eyes off the road for a second, he gave her what he hoped was a convincing show of authority. "Not a good idea."

"I belong to you now," she said. "I will stay by your side." She took another bite of apple.

Moistening his lips with his tongue, his gaze locked onto her mouth. He tamped down the growl threatening to rumble from his chest and out his mouth.

"I like you," she said in that lilting come-hither voice. It turned him boneless and helpless but to agree with everything she said.

What should he say? I like you too. I especially like your kisses, tantalizing body and your lack of inhibition. "You can't fly into my life and then say you're going home with me," he protested.

"Why not?"

"No respectable woman goes home with someone they've just met! I might be dangerous. I might be a serial killer."

Laughter filled the air and a heat that had nothing to do with fear shot straight to his groin. "Are you?" she asked without a hint of fear.

"No. But I could be."

She waved her hand dismissively. "'Tis not possible. Your eyes are too gentle."

"You shouldn't take people at face value."

"'Tis the color of your aura I trust most. You're not dangerous. You're kind and you like me."

The corners of her mouth tilted upwards in a disarming smile, and he thought, but I'm afraid of you.

"Besides, my lips know much about you already."

"First you make me promise to release you and now you don't want to go."

Bud slammed on the brakes realizing he'd just driven past his apartment. The car stalled and Glory was propelled forward in her seat. The apple from her hand bounced against the windscreen and landed somewhere around Glory's feet.

Glory arched an eyebrow at him. "'Twas an abrupt halt. Do these mechanical vehicles always stop so suddenly?"

"Not usually," Bud harrumphed and forced his gaze away from where the seat belt sliced a defining pathway between her breasts. He was reminded of how they had felt in his hands. He clenched those hands into fists on his thighs and peered skywards. Glad no one had tail-ended them he put his hands back on the wheel, started the car again, and pulled into a spot just down the road from his apartment. *Why me?*

"You're different from the others."

Had he spoken aloud? "Different how?" Not liking the direction his thoughts were heading, he unclipped his seat belt and turned to face Glory. He had no right to feel possessive over anyone. Ever.

Beautiful, clear eyes stared earnestly into his and he found it difficult not to believe her when she said, "I want to learn more about humans. Even if it does break Faerie Law."

During the forty-minute drive from Oaktree Falls Parachute Club, other images had begun knocking at his memory and all of them included the beauty sitting beside him. He was remembering way more than he cared to. "Does that make you a bad faerie?"

Glory inhaled apple and coughed. "I'm not bad." She hesitated, her look of guilt unmistakable. "Just a trifle naughty."

This was something Bud had already surmised. "It was more than a trifle naughty to remove most of Lacey's clothes. And what was that webby stuff all over him?"

"Fiddledeedee! Can I never do anything right?" She continued to cough. "'Tis a dilemma. If you recall who I am, others might too." Her cheeks flushed a delicious shade of pink, almost as rosy as the blush on the half-eaten apple now rolling around somewhere on the floor of the vehicle. "I'm all hot with embarrassment," she said, waving a hand in front of her face.

Bud moved a little closer ready to clear her airways if the need arose. Or that was what he told himself. The rest of him wasn't so gullible. Bud's breathing quickened, his chest rose and fell as he sucked fresh oxygen into his lungs. He felt his own version of a hot flush rise up his neck as he failed to hide his reaction to her.

"Are you hot too?" She shuffled closer into the crook of his arm resting along the back of her seat.

"No." Bud croaked out an outright lie. He cleared his throat, but another frog took up residence when she pressed her lips against his neck and began nibbling. No. She was definitely not shy. "I refuse to believe you are a faerie," he choked out.

"Mmmm," was all she said.

Her lips appeared to be speaking a language he could understand. Two quick nibbles and he was a-gone-burger. He made a weak attempt to strengthen his resolve, but her mouth wove a moist trail of delight along his jaw and what was left of it dissolved into a big Forestball of sweet nothing.

Glory nibbled her way to the corners of his mouth. "'Tis a want I sense in you."

Bud shifted uncomfortably on the leather seat. He stretched his neck upward to avoid her sensuous lips that begged to be plundered. "Are you sure faeries are allowed to do this?"

The kisses stopped and she dropped her forehead against his chin for the briefest of seconds. Putting a hand to his chest she pushed back and scuttled away to her side of the jeep. Damn it! He wished he hadn't reminded her of her responsibility. "You mentioned something about breaking Faerie Law."

"Why did you have to remind me?" Leaning down she foraged for her apple. Finding it, she surged back in her seat and pouted at him. "The Master Tutor says the lips of a human must never touch those of a faerie."

"So it's too late for that." He hoped there was a very good reason for such a rule. "Surely it can't be that bad."

"I don't know," she wailed noisily. "If only I had asked why."

Bud nearly laughed. She looked so put out. He mourned the loss of her lips that had never quite made it to his this time. It was one thing to ask for kisses when in the middle of a delusion, but his memory was returning and it was filled with all strange images of Lacey being naked and wrapped in some kind of cobweb. All the same, he hoped he never had to publicly admit Glory was one of those little people with wings that lived in the bottom of someone's garden.

Other people's gardens. Not his.

He switched the ignition off, climbed from the jeep, and moved around to open Glory's door. She certainly didn't resemble one of the little people. She was a tall, curvy, sassy blonde who oozed oodles of sex appeal. Another plus was she was nearly as tall as him.

Bud took the apple core from her hand and tossed it into a trash can on the sidewalk. "What will happen to you if we take this attraction between us further?"

Glory replied as if challenging him to find out. "'Tis a mystery to be sure."

He didn't want to give her the wrong impression, but he sure did want to take her inside and put Faerie Law to the test. Instead, he turned and began to walk down the sidewalk to his apartment.

Glory bounced along beside him, curiosity shining back at him from her fathomless eyes. When he walked up several concrete steps and unlocked a huge, wooden door she hesitated.

"Is this where you reside?" She looked upwards at the large brownstone building, a hint of uncertainty in her eyes.

Bud pushed the door open and stood aside to let her in. "You don't have to come in. You can return home to wherever that is."

Glory bit down on her lips for all of two seconds. "I want to come in."

Bud nodded and waved her in with a gallant flurry of his hand. "Faeries first."

She rewarded him with a blinding smile. "You believe me?"

"I'm reserving judgment till later."

Glory stepped into the hallway and shivered. "Why do humans choose to live surrounded by cold, hard stone? There's no life, no lightness to these walls. They're dead."

Bud surveyed their surroundings. Glory was right. There was no life in this dark, dismal building. The entranceway was, as always, cold and forbidding. Paint was peeling off the walls in great ragged chunks, the floor was littered with fast food wrappers, old newspapers and other unmentionable objects requiring thick rubber gloves before picking up. Dust and cobwebs screamed for a broom and mop and then there was the ever-present odor of damp hanging heavy in the air.

He had learned to ignore the negatives. Used to his surroundings, he never noticed them anymore. His apartment on the top floor at the rear of the building afforded him both privacy and solitude, attributes he so sorely craved after dealing with everyone's problems each day of the week.

"My apartment is much nicer," he assured Glory leading the way inside.

"One day I will show you my home," Glory promised with conviction as she closely followed him up a flight of stairs. She kept well away from the walls by hugging her arms about her middle. "'Tis roomy and full of light. My friends Squirrel and Cricket live amongst Tree's branches and keep me company."

"Where do you live?" She lived with squirrels and crickets?

"In the Glory Tree. It is located on the southern perimeter of Newberry Forest. My sister lives nearby in the Tree of Triumphant and my parents, the King and Queen of the entire Faerie Realm, govern from the North Side. Their tree is called Tree Most Royal."

Any hope of a normal, civilized conversation with Glory dissipated as she continued. None of Bud's training and experience in the-big-wide world of psychology had prepared him for Glory. It was profoundly different.

The automatic entry light went on as they reached his floor. His was the only apartment on this level. He pressed a set of buttons next to his door. "My home is protected by a security alarm and I'm very happy here."

***

The apartment definitely belonged to a man. Walking from room to room Glory absorbed the essence of this human that she had taken an unlikely attachment to. It was not what she had expected, but then she hadn't known what to expect having never been in the home of a human before. Her first impression of the ugly entrance and dark stairwells had not prepared her for this. This was a home filled with items she was familiar with, although those that Bud said were technology was something she'd never seen before.

The walls glowed with warm earthy colors and Glory immediately felt more at ease. The creepy crawly sensation that had frightened her as she entered the building did not exist in Bud's home. Bud's home was made for comfort. Certainly not for its aesthetic beauty.

The living area held all the required niceties for a human to be cozy including a dark forest green couch which reminded her of the colors of Tree, her home. However, it was the enormous wall-to-wall bookcase loaded with books on every conceivable subject that divulged the inner workings of Bud's mind and personality.

There were libraries in her world, but nothing that held these kinds of stories. Most of the faerie libraries contained recipe, glamour and boring old history books. Bud's library was far more interesting. Especially the psychology books. Given the opportunity, she could thrill him psychologically and he would never need to read another word. If she so wished, she could keep him in emotional turmoil for years to come.

The kitchen housed all manner of strange devices. Her kitchen consisted of a bowl, a book of glamour and a few implements to eat with. She gave the room a cursory glance and immediately dismissed it. Why waste time cooking when a spell could create something delicious in seconds?

Marching out into the hallway, she walked towards the door at the far end. "Where's your bedroom?"

Bud tore down the hallway after her. "You don't want to go in there." If his memory served him correctly, the last image of his bedroom was that of a bomb site. However, it was too late. Glory was already opening the door he deliberately kept closed in case of unexpected visitors.

"Why ever not?" Glory's glance over her shoulder to him was puzzled, but when she turned to survey the room he could tell she wondered why she had asked.

One glance explained everything.

Glory took a step backwards to avoid the musty odor of socks from hitting her sensitive nostrils. "The stench is almost as bad as the Ponds of Odious Odors."

She waved her hand repeatedly under her nose in the hope it would dispel the worst of it. She peered past the fumes threatening to knock her out to hazard a closer inspection. An explosion of clothes lay scattered where Bud had either stepped out of or flung them. Glory decided they must have been flung, for surely one did not hang shirts over light-shades. Every drawer was open with clothes spilling wildly from each one. His bed appeared to have not been made in weeks. The carpet, she thought that's what it was, was completely cluttered from the fall-out of Bud's careless housekeeping.

Glory turned and stared at Bud in disbelief. "What on earth do you do in here? 'Tis a shambles."

"Sleep?" The word came out more as a question than a statement.

"Where? How? Surely your mother taught you how to make a bed and to pick up your clothes."

Highly embarrassed, Bud admitted the truth. "She tried, but in the end gave up. She said I was a lost cause."

"I would agree with this woman. 'Tis a wise mother you have." Glory rolled her eyes. "You need me far more than I thought." She planted her fists on her hips. "I'm definitely staying, if only to save you from yourself by putting some order back into your life."

Bud looked offended. "Do not touch a single item. I know exactly where everything is."

"Tish-tosh. A lie. I can see it in your aura."

"I like it this way," he protested.

Glory pointed accusingly at the evidence. "You might prefer to live in squalor. I do not. I'm not sleeping in there."

Bud's eyebrows lifted, mirroring the surprise in his eyes. "Who said you're sleeping in here? And it's not that bad. You're exaggerating."

Glory looked hopeful. "Do you have another bedroom?"

"No." Bud shook his head and tried to look sorry.

"Then, this room is where I will be sleeping."

"But this is my room."

"I am willing to share it with you," Glory offered.

"How generous," Bud grumbled.

"'Tis generous indeed. For no other would want to sleep in this… this… odious hellhole the way it is. I shall set about making it habitable, while you go conjure something to eat in that room you call a kitchen."

Bud took exception to the words *odious hellhole*. It wasn't that bad. Was it? "I have no idea what you can do to improve things, but I'm willing to let you try."

"Probably because you hate housework," Glory muttered and he had to accept she spoke the truth there. "There's no way Tree would allow you to make such a mess in my home. He would swat your butt with a branch if you so much as dropped anything on its floor."

***

Glory redecorated Bud's bedroom. With the whisk of one hand all his dirty laundry was washed, pressed and doused with a liberal amount of eau de Morning Glory. The bed linen, an ugly shade of beige, was relegated to the rear of a cupboard in the far corner of the room.

She couldn't comprehend how such a handsome man possessed no imagination when it came to color. She tsked, "'Tis an abomination." She knew she could not remain in Bud's world for long, but for tonight, this room was hers and she would leave something of herself here for him to remember her by.

She crafted a glamour to bring her own favorite set of sheets woven specifically for her by the Royal Silk Wormery. Making them human sized, she set about rectifying a very unsatisfactory situation.

By the time Bud called out that supper was ready, she had rearranged and redecorated the room in hues of butter yellow and dusky pink. A bunch of golden roses edged with a hint of fuchsia sat on the bedside table in an earthen jar she'd also retrieved from Tree and resized.

The horrible striped wallpaper was now covered with vines of Morning Glory and flowers were already blooming on it.

She surveyed the room well pleased with her handiwork. Now she would be able to sleep.

***

Despite the invasion of his privacy, Bud was pleased. Her obvious pleasure when she informed him she had redecorated his bedroom sent a spiral of anticipation catapulting through his veins. What would happen tonight? Would she invite him into what was now her bed? Or would he be banished to the couch in the living room?

His troublesome testosterone was seriously clouding his thoughts. If she allowed him to lie down beside her, would they curl up together, their bodies pressed skin to skin? What then would ensue? He could think of any number of activities to while a night away with Glory.

However, it was early yet. He would have to exercise his patience, and play the wait and see what will happen next game.

After their meal–vegetarian of course–he recalled she'd mentioned that at some stage–Bud introduced Glory to the wonders of music on his iPhone. The fact she'd never used a mobile phone let alone a computer, amused him. She'd spent the better half of the evening changing channels with the TV remote and then switching from song to song on his iPhone in amazement.

Relegating himself to the fireside chair by the bookcase with a glass of merlot he observed Glory without being too obvious. An easy atmosphere permeated the room. He crossed his ankles and propped his legs up on the corner of the coffee table. Sighing, he sipped his wine and let the warmth of her company wash over him.

She lay sprawled across his couch like she owned it and he found he liked her there. Perhaps having a faerie about the house would not be so bad. When she pointed to a silver-framed image on the mantle above the fireplace and asked, "Who are they?" he found himself telling her far more than he intended.

"That was taken last year, just before my father passed away." Unaware of the sudden moisture glistening in Glory's eyes, he continued, recalling the still fresh pain of the death of his father.

"It was a heart attack. Unexpected, and a shock for us all. The woman standing next to him in the photo is my mother." Clearing his throat, he moved on. "Next to me is my younger brother, Alex. My sister, Alice, was overseas on holiday when that photo was taken." Resting his glass on a side table, he pointed to another silver frame positioned next to the lamp. "That's her with her husband, and their two daughters. My nieces. They live in Ireland, so we don't get to see them as often as we'd like."

Glory found herself tongue-tied. What did one say to someone who had lost a parent? Faeries tended to live long lives, healthy until the end. She couldn't begin to imagine what it felt like to lose a loved one. The thought of losing her family was too upsetting to contemplate. "Do you miss him?"

"Who? My father? He was a rock. He came to every single game of basketball I ever played or competed in. Never missed a single event. And there were a lot of practice games between. He was always there for me."

Bud shook his head and it seemed to Glory as if a dark cloud descended over his head. There was a faraway look in his eyes and she saw the internal struggle going on within him as clearly as if his emotions were her own. They were raw, still unhealed. She recalled Father once saying it was healthy to let your feelings out rather than to hold them in. Built-up unreleased emotions tended to make matters worse.

"Tell me about your mother. Where is she now?"

Bud picked up his glass of wine and knocked back the remainder as if it would clear his head and settle his emotions. Instead, the ruby liquid burned his throat and his eyes watered.

"I'm sure she misses Dad. She never says. Mom is not one to look back and wish what might have been. She says she is grateful for the time she had with Dad but is now looking to the future. Always generous. Overly so. I guess the time she spends on committee meetings and church activities are her way of dealing with Dad's absence."

He smiled, but it did not reach its full potential and the effort tugged at Glory's heartstrings.

"Mom is visiting Alice and her grandchildren, my nieces, for a couple of months." Bud continued, losing himself in the tale. "She won't be back until July."

"And you miss her." Glory understood Bud still needed resolution on his father's passing.

"A little. What about you? Won't anyone wonder where you are?"

His question caused Glory a moment of discomfort. "I miss Triumphant. My sister. I was with her when you made your wish. Which, by the way, you still haven't revealed."

"And I'm not about to either," he muttered. "Who is this Triumphant? She sounds important."

"Oh, she is. She's destined to become an Ancient and rule not only Newberry Forest, but also the entire Realm. She is smart, beautiful, and perfect. I love her dearly."

"What is an Ancient?"

"A wise faerie. Ancients live for a very long time. Maybe thousands of years." Glory saluted her glass to him, her words slurring slightly. "This red nectar is scrummy." The ruby liquid sloshed at the rim when she raised her head awkwardly from the arm of the couch and brought the glass up to her lips. She yawned and her eyes drooped. "I have a brother too." She yawned again. "He's a youngling."

"A youngling?"

"Mmmmm," she mumbled. Fighting sleep, her arms and legs seemed to have lost the will to move. "Prince Herald is but a baby." She yawned, deeper and longer and her glass began to tilt dangerously. "He's only…."

Bud surged from his chair and snatched the still half full glass as it slipped from Glory's limp fingers. He set it down gently on the coffee table and gazed down at sleeping beauty. His heart did this unfamiliar flip-flop thing in his chest. She had found her way into his car and apartment, and now, it seemed, she had also found her way into a corner of his heart.

Tucking one arm beneath her knees, he slipped the other around the back of her shoulders. "Thank God I workout regularly," he muttered, easily lifting her tall frame from the couch. Before he could stop himself, he lightly brushed his lips over her forehead. "Sleep well, my beauty," he murmured and carried her down the hall to his bedroom and placed her in the center of his bed.

She sighed softly, rolled over and snuggled up to a pillow. He had lost his mind, not to madness or the red wine, but to the sinking suspicion he was falling for a woman who lived in a tree and called squirrels and crickets her friends.

With reluctance, he dragged his gaze from her sleeping form and squinted in the half-light at what she had done to his bedroom. It was barely recognizable. Where was everything? He crossed to the dresser and then the wardrobe. Every item of clothing he owned had either been washed, pressed, hung or folded. Even his underpants looked as if they had undergone a dramatic transformation. They were pressed flat as if they had just been newly bought.

Even more astonishing was the profusion of blooms dripping from vines meandering across the bedroom walls. He felt as if he had walked straight into a secret garden. Leaning over the nightstand, he inhaled the scent of a rose. Heady, strong scent filled the night air, enveloping him in its magic and he looked down at the silhouette of the sleeping woman who had commandeered his bedroom. He noted, although the light was dim, the pattern on the new sheets covering the bed, and although he could not make out the color, large roses and trumpet shaped flowers were sprinkled like confetti across them. Probably zapped up from somewhere in less than a nanosecond.

Entranced, he sat gently on the side of the bed so as not to disturb the sleeping princess and watched her for a long, long time. Where did Glory really come from? Was she telling him the truth or was he suffering from some kind of delusional psychosis?

Whispering into the dark, he spoke to God, a habit that had recently got him into trouble. "I asked for someone to fly with and look what I got. Now I know what they say about being careful for what you wish for. I should have inserted the word human in there somewhere."

A zephyr of a breeze lifted the sheer curtains from the open window and he shivered. Walking over, he closed out the chill and pulled the heavy, matching drapes closed before returning to the bed to cover Glory with the new duvet.

He lay down on top of the duvet and turning on his side, he rested his head in the crook of an elbow and continued to absorb the wonder of having a faerie in his bed.

In the wee small hours of the morning, Bud eventually drifted off to sleep and dreamed he was flying, naked, with Glory across the skies of Newberry Forest and Oaktree Falls.

≈ CHAPTER 5 ≈

Glory awoke with a start. Shooting upright, the bedding tumbled down low on her hips, leaving her naked. During the night her pretty, paisley dress she had glamoured up yesterday had vanished. But she didn't care. All she knew or cared about was that Bud had left the apartment.

She felt the wrench of his absence all the way through to her elemental core. More alarming was, that with every step Bud took further away from her physical presence, a strange tearing-like sensation ripped its way through her body. She felt as if she was being stretched taut like a rubber band, as if she would snap in two if this continued.

Desperate to ease this horrible, terrifying sensation, she struggled to cast a glamour to take her to Bud's side, but her mind was muddled, confused, disoriented. Dread filled her gut as she fought to string the necessary words together.

"What's wrong with me?" she cried aloud. "Why does it hurt so?" With her questions came the blinding realization that this was perhaps why touching a human was forbidden.

"Come on Glory," she muttered, forcing herself to gather her scattered thoughts into a cohesive whole. "You can do it. Think." Summoning all the skill she possessed she crafted a glamour. It failed. All she experienced was a dull, empty sense of doom and an increase in the tearing sensation. It was excruciating. She was deathly afraid, fearful she did not have any strength left to cast another glamour.

What would happen to her if she didn't? She had to try. She couldn't give up. Life was too precious and she ached to see Bud one more time. Closing her eyes, she concentrated on the glamour and attempted to ignore the increasing fear that this could actually be the moment of her demise.

What did Triumphant always say when things were at their most difficult? *Call upon your knowing.* That was it. *Call upon your knowing. Know you will remember, and you will.*

Her head was full of dandelions floating in empty space. It took all her resolve, all her will to hold herself together long enough to incant the glamour. It was the hardest thing she had ever done and knew it to be the most important spell she would ever cast.

Fear she would fail clawed its way into her brain, but the even stronger fear of dying increased her determination to succeed. The spell would work. It had to. She was not ready to leave this life. To leave Bud. To leave her family.

The few agonizing seconds stretched into what seemed like eternity. She pressed a fist against her mouth to prevent her from crying out in anguish but failed. "Please, please, please. In the name of all the Ancients, let it work."

Even when the familiar vibration of magic swelled within her, she was uncertain how it would go. In her weakened state, she didn't know if it was enough to take her to Bud's side or whether she would be lost between this world and the next.

"You can do it." Her voice was raw with fright. Unable to prevent the wobble of fear in her voice or stop the tears sliding down her cheeks. Summoning all resources, she squeezed her eyes shut and willed Bud's image into her mind and imagined his familiar lanky legs, striding jauntily down the sidewalk.

***

When Glory appeared in front of Bud, disheveled, bleary eyed and undeniably naked, Bud jumped backwards with fright and swore explicitly. He whipped off his jacket and tossed it over her shoulders, instructing her to put her arms in the sleeves.

"What is it? What's so urgent you couldn't wait to put on some clothes before stepping outside?" Spinning her around he gripped one of her elbows and began to march her back towards his apartment.

"You left me behind." She tugged her arm free and looked up at him, accusation moistening her eyes to watery pools.

He frowned as it dawned on him she was more than agitated. He studied her for a second, noticing the damp trail of moisture on her cheeks. He saw distress in her eyes. But of what? What could have happened in the few minutes since he'd left the apartment, leaving her sleeping soundly in his bed?

He cupped her cheeks in his hands. "Why the tears?"

"You left me behind," she hiccupped.

"I was coming back with a surprise from the deli on the corner. They make a mean bagel with cream cheese. I thought you'd like to try a human's breakfast. "What is it?" he repeated, and brushed a fresh tear from her cheek with the base of his thumb. "What's wrong?"

"I must be with you at all times," Glory stressed, as further tears threatened to spill over her lower lashes. "Never leave me behind. I belong to you."

Bud wrapped an arm about her shoulder and hugged her to his chest in an effort to console her, but the sudden appearance of golden wings on her back caused him to let go hastily. The wings from nowhere now poked obtrusively out from the collar of the jacket he'd given her to wear. He tried to shove them back under cover. The attempt was futile. Like proverbial bad pennies, they kept popping back up.

He had an upset semi-naked faerie wearing gossamer-like wings standing beside him and it was broad daylight. Looking surreptitiously over his shoulder and up and down the street, he checked for early risers who might have spotted them.

One or two people were about. Fortunately, they were not looking in their direction. Yet. "Why? I mean, why not?"

"Oh Bud! 'Twas awful! When left alone in your apartment I felt this pain." She clutched a fist to her breastbone. "Right here. 'Twas as if a knife was slicing me to shreds. A hand was reaching in and squeezing the life out of my heart. I was being torn apart. I nearly didn't make it to your side Bud. Much longer and, truly, I would have perished."

Bud heard the sincerity and accusation in her voice. Saw it in the tears on her cheeks. Felt it in the tension of her shoulders. "What? How? I don't understand."

"Neither do I. Just never ever leave me alone again. If you do, I will die."

An insidious feeling of doom settled like lead in the bottom of Bud's stomach. "Perhaps this is why you're not supposed to touch a human?"

"I believe you to be right," Glory admitted. A deep sadness filled her eyes and another tear threatened to spill down one cheek.

He cupped her face with both his hands and looked her squarely in the eyes. "I promise I won't leave you alone again. I wouldn't intentionally hurt you."

There were feelings for this crazy woman he didn't care to examine even though his mind told him he barely knew anything about her and he should send her straight back to where she came from. But he also wasn't ready to be parted from her. Not yet. Not when he'd just found her.

Glory nodded. "Aye. I know it to be so."

Bud brushed a damp tendril from her cheek but nearly jumped when one of her wings popped back up from the neck of his jacket. He tried to stuff the wayward thing back out of sight. "Do me a favor. Get rid of these wings? People are beginning to notice."

Glory tsked. "'Tis but a trifling matter."

"And while you're about it, cast another one of those glamours of yours and zap on some clothes. Appearing naked on the sidewalk in broad daylight is asking for all kinds of trouble."

Interest sparked in Glory's incredible eyes. "What kind of trouble?"

"You don't want to know." Neither did he.

"Will I be arrested again?"

"Most likely." Bud's jacket barely covered the rounded cheeks of Glory's delectable bottom and those wings glinting in the morning sunlight were way, too distracting.

There wasn't a chance in hell they were going to make it back to his apartment unnoticed. She was about to argue with him, he just knew it, so he halted her with a stern look. "Humor me. Zap up some clothes. Now."

So she did. In less than the blink of an eye, Bud's jacket once more rested across his shoulders and Glory was dressed.

Consternation caught Bud gaping. "Not like that."

She looked down at her new clothes. "What's wrong with them?"

He pointed at the skimpy thing she was wearing. "Civilized people do not wear clothes like that on the street."

"Truly? Why not?" Her hands swept down the length of her front. "'Tis beautiful."

It was. Undeniably. It was also a very vibrant in-your-face-red and very, very short. Marveling at the itsy-bitsy straps holding the dress together at her shoulders, the muscles around Bud's mouth spasmed into a tight thin line.

The dress seemed to sparkle while its dangerously high hemline covered no more of her delicious rounded cheeks than his jacket had moments ago. She was now also an inch or so taller than him, for on her feet she wore a pair of disgustingly high platform shoes. Shoes to defy gravity.

"I was hoping you'd choose something a little less… conspicuous shall we say."

"Oh tis too late for that!" she exclaimed.

She was so right.

Any last hopes of making it inside without causing mayhem evaporated when a paperboy rode past on his bike, wobbled and fell into the path of Bud's Jeep parked on the side of the road. In the same moment his neighbor, Mrs Peabody, her hair in curlers and an ancient hand-rolled cigarette wedged in the corner of her mouth, stepped out onto her porch.

The whole transformation from naked faerie with jacket to that of a sparkly spectacle had been witnessed.

The carton of milk Mrs Peabody had just retrieved slid through her fingers. Her mouth gaped and the cigarette plopped onto the concrete and rolled down the steps forgotten.

At the same moment, an old drunk shuffling along the sidewalk, minding nobody's business but his own, became completely unbalanced from what Bud could only surmise was shock and ended up head first in Mrs Peabody's prized azalea bush at the base of her steps.

Bud didn't know whom to help first. He knew what he wanted to do, and that was to rush Glory inside before any further damage was done. With reluctance, he relinquished his hold on Glory and darted over to pick up the young boy and his bike and check for injuries.

Bud made a joking remark about having been to an all-night fancy dress party but was rewarded with a street-wise look of disbelief.

"Yeah right," said the boy. "And I'm the sugar plum faerie."

Bud looked at the boy closely. He was too young to be so cynical. What could he say when it was possible the boy really was the sugar plum faerie. Bud dusted the boy down to ascertain he was unharmed and helped him back on his bike.

Only then did Bud turn back to Glory. The sight of up-to-the-armpits silky skinned legs and a pair of lacy red panties greeted him. He blinked several times. If he was ever put under oath he would swear those panties had winked at him.

Stop, said the panties. Go, said his libido. There was nothing he would have liked better than to continue staring at the rounded bottom wiggling enticingly in his face as Glory struggled to pull the vagrant out of Mrs Peabody's azalea and into an upright position.

However, it was more important to get Glory off the street.

Now. Before Mrs Peabody started screaming.

Before the paperboy started asking awkward questions.

Before anyone else spotted them.

With the drunk resumed to a more reasonable, although not completely upright position, Bud whispered tersely in Glory's ear. "Come on. Let's get the hell out of here." Keeping his eyes on the gaping Mrs Peabody he bolted towards his apartment.

***

It didn't take long for Bud to discover Glory wasn't behind him. A few seconds was all it took for her to disappear completely. Unfortunately it wasn't a case of out of sight, out of mind.

"Shit. Shit. Shit." The words erupted from his mouth, shocking him. He never swore. Well, hardly ever. He slammed the front door closed behind him and charged up the stairs two at a time. He hoped she had used her magic to beat him inside. Only after he called her name and searched every room, did he accept the unsettling conclusion she was gone.

Hell! Where? How? Had she not told him five minutes ago never to leave her side? Had she not just pleaded with him never to leave her alone again? That she could not be separated from him physically? That she would surely die.

His brain must have been overly foggy from the events of the past twenty-four hours because it took far longer than it should have for the penny to drop. When it did, it clanged about in his brain with a hollow sense of doom.

The last person to touch Glory was the drunk who had fallen into that dratted azalea bush. Had she not also explained that whosoever touched her last was her new master?

Concern pumped a surge of adrenaline into his bloodstream, sending him charging out the door and down the stairs onto the pavement so fast he could have sworn he'd grown wings like Glory's. He scanned the street but it was empty except for the paperboy and upon Bud questioning him, he just shrugged his shoulders and continued tossing papers onto doorsteps.

Bud's feelings were mixed. Why should he worry about a woman who said she was a faerie? Did he need this complication in his life? Then came the nagging questions to worry his already over-loaded conscience. What kind of life would she have with a drunk? What if she was separated from her new master and it killed her.

Glory was gadding about the town, sparkling like a fizzy drink and tottering dangerously on platform shoes with an old down-and-out drunk. He tried not to imagine the trouble an alcoholic and a faerie dressed like a hooker could get up to.

He tried very hard, but failed.

Abysmally.

His skin clammy, worry clenched his gut in a vice-like grip. A cold sweat broke out on his brow. Oh he cared all right. He cared far too much. He had to locate her before she hurt herself. Before she created chaos for the entire population of Oaktree Falls.

He could file a missing person's report, but what would he say? That he'd lost a faerie? That she had taken flight and flown away without him. He could envisage the headlines. *Faerie Flits the Coop.* Or worse still. *Psych Flips For Faerie!*

He shuddered and then his mobile rang. He was needed at the

local hospital immediately.

≈ CHAPTER 6 ≈

"Please," Glory pleaded. "Just one more time. 'Tis simple. Truly."

She could almost see wavy alcoholic vapor rising off the old man. She waved her hand before her face to ward off the fumes.

Her new owner stunk of whisky and his words were so slurred he wasn't making much sense of anything.

"Ffffarethewelll. Hic! Ffffarethewelll. Fry ffflaery ffflee. Ffffarethewelll. Ffffarethewelll. Flee, flairy fly." He was clearly pleased with his effort because he grinned at her, revealing brown stained teeth and a gap where there should have been one as well.

Glory, on the other hand, was definitely not pleased. Her shoulders slumped. Was he ever going to get it right? This was the sixth time he'd tried the glamour and every time he'd got it wrong.

She turned full circle, searching for Bud as she had done for what seemed like the millionth time since he'd bolted for his apartment thinking she was behind him. Where was he? Surely he would come for her? Had he not just promised to never leave her alone again?

She gave her new master an irritated leer. "Why did I haul you out of that bush?"

"Because I fell in it." Her new bleary-eyed master replied far too eloquently for one who was heavily intoxicated. He set to blinking with exaggerated concentration. His bottom lip jutted out, revealing an unhealthy lining on the inside of his mouth. "Ah… me darlin'," he drawled, "'tis the drink of course. Murphy can't see straight."

"You can't talk straight either," Glory pouted. She crossed her arms over her breasts, while towering over him. In this human form she felt like a giant next to this tiny human. "How long is it going to be before you're not drunk?"

She hated to think how long she would have to remain attached to him. Definitely until he was sober. The last time she'd tried one of Father's concoctions-Dandelion and Plum Tipple-it had taken hours for her to recover and days to get her balance back.

He tilted his head and looked up at her, the movement causing him to teeter backwards. Unfortunately, he didn't seem to be frightened or wary of her. He hadn't even questioned her story as the others at the police station had that she was of the faerie.

Glory's despair grew. "How long do you think it will be?"

"Can't say me darlin'. Can't say."

"Why not?"

"Haven't been sssober fffor ten years." He shrugged his shoulders again. "Could be ano... ano...." He stopped speaking because his tongue was obviously tangled. He poked it out and wiggled it about before shoveling it back in with a grimy hand.

Glory nearly keeled over from the fumes. Then he opened and closed his mouth several times in what appeared to be a jaw loosening exercise. For reasons she could not fathom, he screwed his mouth and eyes up tighter than a shriveled walnut.

Exasperated, Glory spoke curtly. "What?"

His bloodshot eyes popped open. "Don't know."

"Don't know what?"

"Can't remember."

"Can't remember what?"

"'Tis hard to say."

"Try."

"Try what?"

"Try to remember."

"Remember what?"

"Oh! Oh!" Glory bit down on her bottom lip and balled her hands into tight fists. For the first time in her life, she actually wanted to hit someone and that someone was her current master. She couldn't possibly stay with this creature. She was going to have to find someone else to belong to and hope they were as kind as Bud and as willing to free her as this drunk was.

If she sent a telepathic message to her sister for assistance the King was bound to pick up on it. Triumphant would also have to request permission to leave the boundaries of the forest before coming to her aid.

She weighed up which was worse. Belonging to a smelly drunk or incurring the wrath of Father.

The drunk won. She wasn't ready to admit defeat. Not yet.

Forcing herself to take several steadying breaths she spoke aloud to herself. "Calm down Glory. Mayhap 'tis not as bad as you think."

"To be sure," Murphy agreed but a hint of sadness crept into his cloudy eyes. "A few wee drams of whisky and all your problems will disappear. Murphy can guarantee it."

Murphy resumed walking in a crooked line down the street. Glory lurched alongside him and tried to think of a creative and cunning plan that didn't involve Father hearing all about it.

Great leaping grasshoppers! She was all out of cunning. Instead she exercised the Art of Conversation, something she was better at. The Master Tutor said humans enjoyed discourse, especially when it was about themselves.

"Did I hear you say your name is Murphy?"

"Aye." The man scratched his head and staggered into Glory. "Murphy 'tis," was his muffled reply. He had lost his fight for balance and fallen face first into her cleavage instead of onto the pavement. A softer landing certainly, but not one Glory particularly cared for.

"Why has it gone dark?" he called out, his hands flailing wildly.

Glory grabbed them quickly before they landed on something they shouldn't and shoved him none-too-graciously away lest he got too comfortable and decided to tarry awhile.

"Murphy. What's your full name?" she encouraged, hoping he would forget about her breasts?

His legs wobbled and his eyes almost circled in opposite directions as he made a creditable attempt to regain his equilibrium. She would have asked him to repeat the eye thing again, but she didn't believe he was up to an on-demand demonstration. She couldn't decide as to whether it was a sign of his imminent collapse or if he was overcome from his close encounter with her femininity.

"Jus' Murphy."

He eyed her breasts longingly and she knew it was the latter, even though he also seemed to be somewhat embarrassed. "Tha's a warm place ye have there me darlin'. All soft, like. More comfy than me own place of rest."

"Don't even be thinking it, Murphy," Glory warned.

"Too late I fear. It'll be confession for ol' Murphy in the mornin'."

Fiddledeedee! How did she do it? Was there no mortal male who wasn't overcome when presented with the form of a woman at close proximity? Was this why humans covered themselves in so many layers of clothing?

Only Bud was different. Alas, he had not been overcome. He was the one human she would consider dallying with. She was still, unfortunately, very much in a flowered state. Bud had enjoyed her kisses, but not enough it seemed. Otherwise he would have rescued her by now. Sadly, 'twas likely she would never see him again. She must accept the inevitable and concentrate on getting Murphy to free her as soon as he was sober.

If he ever got sober.

With Murphy as steady as he was ever going to be, they resumed their own versions of walking. She tottered and he weaved his way down the pavement and several short roads for some time. The further from Walnut Lane where Bud resided, the seedier their surroundings grew. Disoriented, a shiver of apprehension ran up her spine. Where were they?

Her new master made a right turn into a darkened alley. Glory followed only to stumble to a complete standstill. Fear curled its evil tendrils insidiously around her heart and gave it a squeeze.

"We can't go down there!" It was dark and a rank odor of evil emanated from its unseen depths.

"Of course we can," Murphy slurred and kept on tottering forward. "This, me darlin', is me home." He waved for her to follow him.

"Your home?" Glory's voice rose to a notch below hysterical. "'Tis down there?" She pointed a shaking finger into the evil depths.

Murphy coughed and Glory heard the unhealthy rattle in his chest and felt a growing concern. She didn't want to feel concern for this man. She didn't want to feel anything. She wanted to leave this despicable place. Now.

"'Tis the only home for the likes of Murphy. But perhaps me luck is a-changin' now God has seen fit to send me one of the wee people." Murphy blinked, swallowed and eyed her generous curves with longing. "If'n you don't mind me saying so, girlie, you're mighty big for one of them wee people."

"'Tis but my human form, Murphy. I wear it only as not to be recognized. Unfortunately, my true form tends to upset humans."

Murphy scratched his chin and nodded his head as if he understood. Perhaps he did. "Well, you should've hidden your wings and worn clothes right from the beginnin'." He patted his chest with a hand in a rat-a-tat-tat motion. "And perhaps a dress with more substance to it. Old Murphy's heart jus' about stopped beatin' back there on Walnut Lane. I thought Gabriel the archangel had come for me 'afore me time."

"When I'm upset I can't control my wings."

Murphy's eyes were as round as an owl's at midnight. "You're not upset now are you?"

"Nay," she fibbed. The alleyway was making her twitchy. Any moment now she was going to forget herself and her wings would make another unwelcome appearance. Her spirits sunk to an all time low. She didn't want a new master. She wanted Bud. Where was he? She didn't want to believe she would never see him again. Somehow, she didn't know why, she felt emotionally connected to him.

Could he feel it too?

Murphy resumed staggering down the alleyway and her train of thought was abruptly broken. "Come on me darlin'," Murphy called out. "Home is but a cardboard box away. There should be a spare one down here for you too."

The hairs on her arms stood on end. Nothing good ever happened down here she thought intuitively. It was depressingly dirty, damp and stunk of rotting food. As far as she could make out, there were no entrances or exits except for the one behind her. It was a dead end. The only sign of life was the scurrying sounds of rats and the hushed tones of two slovenly youths loitering on the lid of a large dumpster.

"Well, if it isn't Murphy," one of them slurred as her master guided Glory in a wide arc past the dumpster. "Whatchagotthere?"

Murphy scooted between Glory and the boys with an astonishing amount of alacrity. He whipped his head round to hers and winked before turning back to the menacing youths. It was suddenly as if he'd developed a backbone. "Don't you be touchin'," he cautioned them and placed a possessive hand on Glory's arm. "She's mine."

"I'm his." Glory stepped in as close to Murphy as her nose would allow. Instinct told her she was far safer with him at her side.

Not caring for the intent in their red and black auras, Glory's skin crawled with alarm. She was reminded of the calculating way Lacey had leered at her in the detaining cell. Instead this time it was a whole lot worse. The odor of danger pervaded her nostrils, and true fear held her immobile. This human world was far more dangerous than she had ever imagined.

"Yeah! Mine!" Murphy's head bobbed up and down. His grip on her arm tightened. Where earlier she would have cringed at his touch, she was now grateful for it.

The lecherous intent in the youths swiftly changed to that of predator. The shift was subtle, but she saw it in their aura before their posture changed. Their gazes met each other in silent communication.

Scared witless, her mind went blank. She couldn't dredge up a single glamour. Instead, she found herself wanting to urge Murphy to flee, but she knew turning their backs on these two youths would be far more dangerous. The smaller one slithered down from the lid of the dumpster, but Glory sensed it was the older of the two who hadn't moved who would prove more dangerous. Evil wore him as a cloak and she truly feared for their lives. She wasn't surprised when his hand eased to his waist. Her watchful eyes followed the movement and she caught a glimpse of the handle of a weapon tucked into his low riding jeans. His hand caressed the handle up and down, his narrowed eyes cold and watchful.

The slimy toad spoke to Murphy. "Hand the hooker over old man, and save yourself a whole heap of trouble. I've a burning sensation in my crotch." He cupped his groin with his free hand and grunted, his intention unmistakable. "That buxom babe is out of your league."

Murphy shoved Glory behind him in a gallant effort to protect her. Considering she towered above her protector, Glory knew it was a total waste of effort on his part, but his valiant actions earned her respect. He may be a drunk, but he was courageous and perhaps not as drunk as she'd first thought.

"She's mine," Murphy defended in his lilting brogue. "God has seen fit to bless ol' Murphy." He spoke confidently, if a little slurred. "An' nobody is goin' to take her from me."

As Glory had feared, their attacker moved swiftly, jumping from the dumpster to land, knees bent, his body primed for attack. His weapon, a razor sharp switchblade, was in his hand, and Glory guessed he knew how to use it given the speed at which he'd whipped it from his jeans.

Murphy reached behind him to grip onto Glory's wrist so tight she feared she would lose the circulation in her fingers.

The youth sneered and flicked the switchblade at them, the blade teasingly elusive in the dim alleyway. "I'm about to persuade you otherwise. Hand the tart over you old coot. Else I'll remove that head of yours from the rest of your body and when we're done with her, her head can join yours to rot in this hell-hole."

Glory gasped. They were going to kill her master. And her. There was no way in all the worlds of mortal or faerie she was going to allow that to happen. Belonging to Murphy wouldn't be so bad as dying or belonging to these two stinking, rotten pieces of humanity.

Determined to survive she said to Murphy. "Let me turn them into slugs. I'll send them to the Gates of Hell for eternity."

"Go to it me little darlin'." Murphy didn't take his eyes off the thugs. "But not slugs. Slugs be too good for pond scum."

A rush of adrenaline kicked her brain into gear. "What then? Tell me. 'Twill be done."

"Before ye zap 'em, frighten the livin' daylights outta them. Show 'em your wings."

Glory's eyebrows rose a notch and her mouth rounded into an O. Usually everyone wanted her to keep them hidden. "With pleasure."

Having spent the last few uneasy minutes striving frantically to hide them, relief flooded through her as her best sparkliest gossamer wings were revealed with the simple wave of a hand. She arched her long neck and glanced over one shoulder. They stretched and flexed, fitting over the low cut back of her red dress nicely.

Both thugs staggered backwards, gaping soundlessly. The knife slipped like butter from the more dangerous of the two youth's fingers and clanged onto the cold, hard concrete.

Who knew a pair of wings would be enough to frighten the daylights out of even the nastiest of humans.

There was stunned silence except for the sound of rapid breathing coming from Murphy. He had twisted around and was staring at her wings, his eyes nearly bulging right out of their sockets.

Registering his stunned expression, Glory concluded he hadn't truly believed she was of the faerie until right this moment. Instinctively, she knew he'd thought it all part of his drunken stupor.

"What shall I do next?" she whispered through clenched teeth.

Silence. Murphy was still staring. She made a snap decision of her own. Her wings eased out and upwards. Slowly at first. The tangible feeling of freedom they engendered as they whooshed through the air helped settle her nervousness. Flexing and stretching backwards and forwards, they gradually increased in speed until they were but a blur. She grabbed Murphy and they rose up to hover like avenging angels over the two youths who both stood goggle-eyed and immobile, watching as her wings whirred so fast they stirred up the dust and litter in the alleyway all about them.

With her wings fully extended the last remnants of her fear evaporated. She could feel her faerie strength, strangely absent all morning, returning, and as her wings gained momentum, she tightened her grip on Murphy and glared down over the top of his disheveled mop of graying hair at the two stricken youths. The quiet one fell to his knees and began to pray, but the evil one made an effort to retrieve his knife.

"Silly boy." Glory amplified her voice. "'Twould be foolish of you to try."

"Whatcha gonna do?" His words were false bravado. "Drop old Murphy on me." He laughed but it came out more of an uncontrolled squeak. His friend squeaked along with him, the terror unmistakable as they both shuffled backwards until pressed up against a moldy brick wall.

"'Tis not a bad idea," she replied with a grin. "What do you think, Murphy?"

Her master's voice was weak with shock. "Don't know," he stammered. "Best if'n you jus' use those wings of yours and flap us outta here."

"But this is your home. We can't allow these pieces of pond scum to keep you from your home. We must do something."

"Magic. Use your magic me darlin'. You can make me a new home later."

"My mind's all a tizz with the number of things I could do to them. Mayhap I'll truss them up like flies caught in a spider's web."

Murphy didn't appear to be reassured. "Well, you'd better be doin' somethin' soon 'cause the baddies are about to make a run for it."

Glory spun round and took Murphy along for the ride. His legs flew out in a wide arc as she rotated almost full circle. When she stopped spinning, his legs fell to dangling again, but not before they banged solidly into her shins.

She managed to find the time to complain. "Ouch! Watch out! I almost dropped you." But she registered Murphy's assessment of the situation was correct. The toady humans were edging towards the street in increments, hoping she wouldn't notice.

"Hey! Where do you think you are going?" She and Murphy flit over to hover above them menacingly. "I'm a faerie. I can make things happen like you wouldn't believe. I can do things to make your hair curl."

'Twas a pity she couldn't think of a single clever glamour right this instant, but something would come to her soon. She was sure of it. 'Twas only a matter of seconds before she would think of something diabolically wonderful.

≈ **CHAPTER 7** ≈

It was past mid-day before Bud got away from the hospital. One of his clients, a habitual kleptomaniac with a record as long as his arm and suffering from depression, had succumbed to the lowest point a human could go by trying to take his own life. The day was turning out to be one hellish nightmare after another.

Pushing through the entrance of Oaktree Falls Precinct he went straight to his small office to file a report before heading out to look for Glory when a commotion caught his attention and his spirits sunk into his shoes. All he wanted to do was turn around and walk back out of the building.

"What now?" he muttered testily and considered backtracking before anyone saw him. *No more mayhem please. I just want to file my report and get on with finding Glory.*

However, luck was as elusive as ever. A door burst open and Lacey raced through it, an inexplicable wildness in his eyes, his complexion an unhealthy shade of gray. "Flies! Cobwebs! Toads!" he ranted.

Bud reached out to halt Lacey's flight. "Say what?"

"Watch out," Lacey blubbered. "Or she'll… she'll bind us up and turn us all into toads." His head bobbed loosely on his shoulders. "I've seen it with my own eyes." He pointed to his glassy eyeballs, one at a time, as if that would explain everything. "She'll turn us into toads as large as houses. Dirty brown slimy ones." A shudder rippled through Lacey. "Why are you smiling? We've got to get out of here before it's too late."

Lacey's ranting was music to Bud's ears. Instead of worrying about his own response to this kind of news, or that of Lacey's outlandish behavior, he was more interested in discovering if his suspicions were accurate.

As a psychologist he should take a moment to reflect on why slimy brown toads, flies and cobwebs should make him so happy, and in the normal course of events he would have. He eyed the closed door with an eagerness belying his earlier thoughts. Nothing was normal any more. Everything had changed since Glory had flown into his life.

Clearly, just as her glamour to forget her previous visit to the precinct had not worked permanently on him, it had not worked for Lacey either.

Ignoring Lacey's wild plea to, "Flee. Flee before it's too late," Bud flung the door open from which Lacey had emerged and scoured the room, searching for any trace of Glory. Of course, she could have conjured something different to wear. Or she could be naked again. But surely he would notice a naked woman in the room.

A huddle of officers near the charge desk commanded his attention but the cacophony of noise coming from that direction was a deafening jumble of voices and raucous laughter. He couldn't make out a single word.

Bud glimpsed a flash of something red and twinkly and relief coursed through him. Sending up a silent prayer of thanks to God, his feet moved forward. A silly grin tugged at the corners of his mouth.

She was back. "Glory," he shouted loud enough to be heard over the rabble.

Her head popped up from the middle of the huddle and Bud's grin grew as she waved her pair of platform shoes above her head. "Bud. Help us. No one believes our story."

Whatever her story was, he knew it would be fanciful and outrageous enough to warrant a good dollop of derision. The circle of officers and various ragtag members of the public turned towards him, creating a gap as he surged forward, allowing him access to its center.

The woman who had kept him awake for most of the night, the creature who he couldn't stop thinking about, stood beside the drunk who had had the close encounter with Mrs Peabody's prize azalea.

He clamped down a childish rush of jealousy. The old guy was plastered way too close to Glory. Bud wanted to push him aside and stake his claim. But he wasn't a six year old so he stifled the urge to behave like one.

The adoring look in the drunk's rummy eyes gave Bud more than a moment's concern. It was clear he would not readily let Glory out of his sight.

Next to them stood two youths wrapped in the same strange opaque cobwebby stuff Lacey had endured only a few days ago. Fear and alarm reflected back at Bud from both sets of eyes.

Glory wagged her shoes at him. "Where have you been? You left me alone. Again!"

Guilt roiled around in his stomach. "Where have *I* been?"

"We've been waiting for you."

Bud presumed she meant the drunk and her two prisoners. At least he hoped they were prisoners. "And I've been looking for you." Or he would have if he'd known where to look. He frowned. "Waiting for me? Here? Why?"

Innocent azure eyes focused earnestly on him. "To explain to everyone we're telling the truth of course."

"Naturally." Bud schooled his features into an *I understand perfectly* expression he often used for his patients. "Which part of the story do you want me to explain?" Wasting time explaining a story no one was ever going to believe wasn't something he particularly wanted to do.

Her reply came out in a rush. "That I belonged to you, but now I belong to Murphy, and that I'm stuck in this city." She pointed an accusing finger at the petrified youths. "These two evil pond scums are our contribution in keeping Oaktree Falls clean and safe."

"Since when did you," he indicated with his head to both Glory and Murphy, "take it upon yourselves to become law enforcers?"

"'Twas a case of necessity." Glory spoke softly but her lips thinned and she shot the prisoners a wicked glare and they both shrunk into each other in fear.

Bud wondered what that necessity was and what she and Murphy had done to their prisoners.

"Truly," piped Murphy for the first time. "With powerful magic and gossamer wings so grand, we tied 'em up and made one of 'em, whatchamacallit, citizen's arrests."

Murphy staggered into Glory. She reached out to steady him. In return he stared adoringly at Glory and Bud wanted to wring the old guy's neck. Was it his imagination or was Murphy staring longingly at Glory's breasts.

Bud forced his attention to the two prisoners and determined with an arch of one eyebrow that whatever their story was it would be a diabolical one. If Lacey's reactions only moments before were anything to go by then these two pieces of flotsam were wise to keep their mouths firmly shut.

"What did they do?" Bud wasn't at all sure he wanted to hear the answer, but the question had to be asked.

Murphy took it upon himself to explain, his cloudy pupils growing bright with what Bud could only describe as adoration. "They were about to decapitate me faerie and me." He combined a slicing motion across his neck with a guttural *schlick* sound.

Bud shuddered. Had Murphy saved Glory's life? Peering intently at the old guy, he searched for the signs of a brave man. How could a drunk, several inches shorter than Glory, have prevented two youths from seriously harming her? If this was true, instead of being jealous he should be thanking Murphy.

"What do you mean, decapitate your faerie?"

"That's me." Glory volunteered. "I'm the faerie and as you can see, I've still got my head."

Those in the huddle snickered. "Got a right one here Doc," sneered an officer. "Next she'll be admitting she's really got wings."

Murphy drew himself up to a full five foot one or so. "Did I not tell you only five minutes ago that she *does* have wings?"

A fresh round of laughter exploded around them and Bud cringed. *Whatever you do Glory don't reveal your wings.*

"Yeah, and I'm the Tooth Faerie," an enormous slob snorted. He was probably being charged with some heinous crime. Tattoos covered most of his face and gold winked in his teeth.

Glory turned on him. "What is it with humans? Why does everyone claim to be the Tooth Faerie?"

The guy wiped his dripping nose on the back of a raggedy sleeve. "Hey lady. Sometimes I'm Tinkerbell as well."

"Yeah," said the weed next to him with a definite nasal twang due to a broken nose plugged with a dirty tissue. "And my name is Sugar Plum."

Slob and Weed rattled with laughter.

"Ignore them Glory," Bud said. He moved into the center of the huddle and stood next to her.

Glory's mouth drooped at the corners. "Humans don't believe in the Tooth Faerie either?"

Bud shook his head. "I'm afraid not." With Murphy on one side of Glory and him on the other, he hoped she would be safe from unsavory hands. Plus, there was no way he wanted her wandering off with Murphy now that he'd found her again.

"'Tis all true, I tell you," Glory insisted. "The Tooth Faerie comes at night to take baby teeth away and leaves a gift in return.

Look at you." Glory pointed at Tattoo face. "You must have been good once. He left you gold."

Tattoo's amusement only increased. "Lady. These teeth didn't come from no faerie."

Glory looked so crushed Bud felt the need to soften the blow. "Children believe." Now wasn't the time to get into a deep discussion on how little his race believed in anything considered magical or otherworldly.

Bud caught the duty sergeant's eye and knew that he assumed Bud was practicing psychobabble on Oaktree Falls latest would-be crime enforcers.

But Delaney belted out, "I don't care if you're all aliens from outer space. I want to know how a hooker and a drunk managed to arrest these two hooligans?"

Delaney made the mistake of fingering the cobwebs and unfortunately, it adhered to his fingertips like taffy. He wiped his hands on his trousers, but the stuff wouldn't budge and the harder he endeavored to rid himself of the gossamer, the worse it got. Soon his hands were tangled completely. He cursed explicitly.

Glory covered her ears as if the foul language offended her. It certainly offended Bud. She whispered to him, "What's a hooker? That's twice I've heard that word now."

"I'll explain later." Considering how she was dressed Bud couldn't blame the sergeant for thinking Glory was a call girl. Having a drunk for a companion only compounded the notion. "We need to get you out of here." He paused, thinking for a moment, wondering how they were going to achieve such an act when surrounded by a bevy of beefy policemen.

Bud spoke softly to Glory so no one else would hear. "What I don't understand is why your glamour that made everyone forget the first time you were here didn't last on Lacey and yet Delaney doesn't seem to recall you at all."

The color rose in Glory's cheeks to a high pink. "I guess my magic didn't reach everyone as it should." She bit down on her bottom lip, her eyes soulful. "'Tis a sad fact that here in your world my power appears to be weaker."

"Do you think your magic will work now? Can you get us out of here? Safely?"

"Sure she can," Murphy leaned in so he could hear their conversation. "Glory's powers were a trifle defunct at first, but who wouldn't be flummoxed by these here scalawags." He waffled his fingers at the cowering duo. "Give her a few minutes and she'll figure out what to do. 'Tis a grand magical power she has." Murphy rabbited on inanely and his voice grew louder. "Her wings are almost see-through." He spread his arms out wide. "They're huge."

Pushing Murphy's nearest outstretched arm back down Bud hissed, "Not now Murphy."

However, the old guy didn't need wings to be in full flight of his mouth. He went on in detail to a captive audience of how Glory's wings had beaten faster than a bumblebee's. How he and Glory had flown through the air faster than a speeding bullet and eventually had spun the webbing around their attackers before bringing them to the precinct.

He didn't seem to care everyone was having a good chuckle at his expense. Not one iota.

Leaning into Glory, Bud spoke more urgently. "Think you can try your forget-everything-glamour again and zap us out of here."

Glory whispered back. "I can but try," she said, her voice uncertain. "What if it doesn't work?"

"I'm prepared to take a chance."

"Me too," said Murphy, his Irish brogue steadily growing broader. "I've distracted them with me story telling. They don't believe a thing. But what of our prisoners?"

So there was method to Murphy's ravings, Bud thought, his

estimation in this small man rising. "Have the charge sheets been filled out?"

Glory nodded. "The odius Delaney wrote the report and Murphy signed it."

The whisper of her lips a mere fraction from Bud's ear lobe sent a rush of attraction flooding through him. However, her next words filled him with concern and all amorous thoughts fled.

"Why doesn't anyone believe us? Murphy and I did something good and instead of being thanked we are jeered and laughed at. Why?"

What could he say? People find it easier to negate all that is good, preferring to dwell on the negative. He shrugged. "I don't know."

Glory released a heavy, defeated sigh, an indefinable sadness clouding her eyes to a murky blue. "I'll try the glamour again. 'Twill cloud everyone's memories certainly. I'm convinced they won't recall a single thing ever again."

"What about me? And the police report?" Bud asked.

Glory's mood lightened marginally. "As long as they don't see me with you they won't remember. I'll remove any mention of myself from the charge sheet before we depart." Worry creased her brow. "We can't let our prisoners back on the street. They're dangerous."

"Don't you be worrying about a 'ting." Murphy patted her arm. "Leave my name there and I'll turn up at court when they're charged. I expect they're going to need counseling when they try to explain what happened to them." He chuckled. "I haven't had a day as good as this in a very long time."

Bud nodded but he wasn't convinced Murphy would actually turn up. He probably didn't know what day it was most of the time. "Come on then. We need to get out of here."

"Clouding minds is a complex process. Especially, if I'm to ensure it really does work properly this time."

"You'll be taking me with you darlin'," Murphy insisted. "You're me faerie now, are you not?"

Glory didn't hesitate. She nodded. "'Tis a strange feeling I have within me, Murphy. With you on one side and Bud on the other, I feel as if we three are bonded."

Bud was alarmed at the thought. "Bonded! This is a temporary condition I hope?" Glaring at Murphy, Bud prayed Glory's comment didn't mean what he thought it meant. "Isn't it?"

Glory shrugged her shoulders. "'Tis not something I have experienced before."

Visions of Murphy with them twenty-four hours a day sent shudders of horror up and down his spine. Not that he didn't like the old guy. Considerably more sober than when he'd first seen him face first in Mrs Peabody's azalea bush he appeared to be a likeable fellow with some moral character still in tact. Plus, he owed him big-time for saving Glory's life.

Once again, Murphy asked, "But you will be takin' me with you will you not?" He looked from Glory to Bud his fear at being left behind acutely obvious.

"Of course you're coming with us." Glory hastily wrapped an arm about his shoulders and gave him a quick reassuring hug. "We'll sort out who I belong to afterwards."

Without waiting, she spread her arms wide and said to everyone standing around them. "Step back. I require physical space. No aura must mingle with mine except those of Murphy and Bud."

Surprisingly, the throng backed away. "I'll do the easy stuff first, as a warm up for the harder glamour," she said and waved her arms through the air.

"Beware!" shouted Tattoo Face in mock horror.

The crowd once again erupted into raucous laughter.

Bud prayed Glory's glamour worked otherwise he was in for a serious amount of flack. It was a small town. People talked. He didn't particularly care to be the butt of their jokes, but if it meant Glory was free then he would just have to deal with it if it happened.

≈ CHAPTER 8 ≈

The removal of Murphy and Bud from Oaktree Falls Precinct was accomplished with an ease Glory never imagined possible. Only moments after casting the glamour, all three were planted in the dimly lit alley next to Murphy's cardboard box.

She had felt the pull of the two humans but instead of their coarser, heavier auras hindering the process by weighing down her magic, it seemed as if instead, they had assisted. Another bemusing facet was that she sensed rather than saw both their auras undergoing a metamorphosis and she wondered if it would be permanent and what did it signify?

Bud's aura, always strangely brighter than any other human she had encountered, glowed with rays of golden light. Faerie Light. It twinkled and sparkled about him lending him a glow she had only seen in those of her own people.

As for Murphy, his dark depressed aura, which had given her cause for concern only a scant few hours ago had lightened and was now far less dense. Although still gray, promising flashes of color broke through the bleak clouds and she could sense within him, a growing hope for his future.

"There," Glory announced, pleased the first and easiest of the glamours had gone without a hitch. "Safe and sound."

She chose not to reveal she'd intended depositing them all in Bud's apartment, not here at the location where she and Murphy had nearly been decapitated. 'Twas a trifling error. Mayhap there was a reason for such a mistake she wasn't privy to and at least the offenders were where they belonged. Behind bars.

***

Bud looked about him. The alleyway was dark, grimy and he was sure he heard rats scratching around in its murky recesses. The place made his flesh crawl and he couldn't fathom why Glory had brought them here. Unless this was one of those wonky moments she had talked about when her magic didn't go according to plan.

"Where are we?"

"This, dear fellow is me home." Murphy enlightened him. "And over yonder," he pointed into the dark corner where a sorry excuse for a cardboard box lay, "is where I rest me weary head at night."

Bud's lips thinned and the crease between his eyebrows formed a brooding slash across his forehead. He was appalled. He lifted his glasses from the bridge of his nose and pretended to inspect them closely. Pulling out a handkerchief he polished the lenses, giving himself time to compose his agitated thoughts and school his features. He was sure Murphy didn't want his pity.

Bud knew the tight feeling in his throat would go away. But, no matter how many times he dealt with those who lived in abject poverty, no matter what it had taken to put them there, it never got any easier to digest. Or understand.

Placing his glasses back on the bridge of his nose, he cleared his throat. There was only so much polishing one could do. "You live here?"

Why was he so surprised? Perhaps it was the feeling in his gut that hidden behind Murphy's dirty clothes and drunken exterior lurked an educated man with a conscience. A man few got the opportunity to meet.

Murphy scratched his hair, which, clearly, hadn't been washed in months. "Aye. 'Tis been me home for some time now."

Bud's lips compressed into a grim worried line. However, he

wasn't quick enough to hide his feelings.

Glory asked, "What's wrong, Bud?"

"Where's Murphy to live? He cannot stay here?"

"Oh 'tis a trifling matter."

Bud didn't think it was trifling and it showed plainly on his face.

Murphy nodded his head vigorously. "'Tis a trifling matter. New cardboard boxes aren't hard to find."

"Surely you want something better than a box," Glory's hand pressed against her chest. "Wait 'til you see Bud's apartment. 'Tis not as wonderful as Tree, my home." She pointed to the ratty cardboard. "'Tis better than that defeated thing."

Now why did she have to go and tell Murphy about his apartment. Bud hadn't planned on having a room mate, let alone one who was a drunk. Bud tried very hard to hide his consternation, but the old codger wasn't slow on the uptake and didn't miss a beat.

"To be sure. A man's home is his castle. I've been on me own far too long to be sharing with someone." His eyes brightened and he turned to Glory. "I have a hankerin' to have a castle of me own, girlie." He fashioned the shape of a house with his hands. "A small one maybe, with enough space to hold a bed with a soft downy pillow or two and a place to sit and eat. Perhaps there could be an extra chair for a visitor."

An acute case of guilt hit Bud fair and square in his conscience. Murphy's idea of a castle was a room with a bed, a couple of pillows, a table and two chairs. He was ashamed for worrying about Murphy moving in on his territory. Maybe this was why Glory had brought them all here. So he could see and understand where Murphy came from.

He needed to learn more compassion for those less fortunate than himself.

***

Glory rested a hand on the old man's dirty coat. Over the past few hours, Murphy had become her friend. She owed this man a great deal.

She owed him for her life. "You can have your dream, my friend," she said. "I'll see to it and more. We will find a way that will best suit us all." Then she raised her hand to silence them both. "But first, I need a few moments to harness the strength required to cast the Forget glamour over everyone at Oaktree Falls precinct. I'm tired, and 'tis late in the day." Glory was fearful her magic wouldn't work at all. The daylight was disappearing and she felt drained, lacking in the necessary energy to complete the entire process.

Oh Triumphant she intoned softly, if only you were here with me now. She paused, hoping her sister would appear and provide the answers to her questions. However, without direct permission from the King to leave the borders of the forest, her sister would be unable to help.

Whereas she, Glory, had permission to venture across into the Human Realm to clear rubbish from the outlying areas of the forest. The King insisted she learn the ropes of the Faerie Kingdom from the ground up. A decree was duly bestowed and she was given, with all the pomp and circumstance deserving a member of the Royal Family of Faerie, the highly embarrassing title, Her Royal Highness, Princess Gloriane, The Good For Nothing Faerie. Her only consolation was that at one time, Triumphant had briefly held the same title. Alas, her sister had been so good at her job she had cleaned up the forest so fast they'd had to promote her.

So far, all Glory had managed to succeed in doing was getting herself captured by humans, arrested for indecent exposure, falling dangerously in fascination with Bud, and accidentally befriending another who just happened to be drunk most of the time.

She was collecting humans. Somehow, she didn't think collecting humans was part of her position description.

She considered the two men as they in turn considered her. They were her friends. Her very *human* friends. Silently, she signaled for them to stand beside her before she began her glamour. As she suspected, when they joined her, she felt her energy pulse in waves around them and she rejoiced. Before it disappeared she swiftly incanted the words, the auras of her two new masters melding with hers, assisting, willing her to succeed. Far more swiftly than she expected, the surge of energy always accompanying a successful glamour presented itself in the form of a golden orb of light. It was as strong as it had ever been. Surprised, she studied it for a second or two. Mayhap it was even stronger?

Not knowing how long this new found strength would last she closed her eyes and imagined sending the orb of light via an invisible arrow to Oaktree Falls Precinct and its inhabitants. On arrival it would dissolve into a spray of golden mist, descend and remove all memory of Gloriane Niamah Firyani Faerie from the memories of everyone at the precinct.

There was no need to include Bud in the casting. He worked at the precinct and everyone knew of him. It would not matter whether they remembered they had seen him that day or not. She didn't remove the memory of Murphy either as he would be needed to ensure their prisoners were sent to jail where they belonged.

"All done," she exhaled in a rush. "I think?"

"Perhaps we should be taking a visit back to the precinct to see if the magic has worked," Murphy suggested.

"No. If they see me, they may remember everything. I can never go back there."

***

Alarm bells went off in Bud's brain. He understood the repercussions of her declaration. He took one of her hands and thread his fingers through hers, holding on, not willing to let her go. He was afraid she would vanish before he had the chance to tell her how he felt. He wanted her to stay longer. With him.

Recognition flared in her. A touch of pink colored her cheeks. She squeezed his hand and a sad smile tugged her lips downwards.

Glory shivered and it had nothing to do with magic and everything to do with having to leave the Human Realm. Of never seeing Bud again. Tears welled in the corners of her eyes, but they did not spill. Instead, she tilted her head this way and that to blink them away. She held his hand tight and her fingers cramped. She never wanted to let go.

Regret shimmered in every word. "I must go soon. But first, we will find a better home for Murphy."

"Take us back to my place then." Bud saw apprehension in Murphy's eyes, recognizing he too was not ready to part with Glory. "All of us. We'll have coffee, wash up and decide what to do."

"To be sure. A wee rest in the comfort of your home would be good for Murphy," the old man said. He rubbed a shaky hand over his creased forehead. "I confess I have a headache and a feeling in me gut that it won't be long before drink claims me again."

"Oh no," Glory told him. "We're going to help you as best we can to give up your desire for alcohol."

Murphy appeared doubtful, but with Bud at her side, Glory felt more grounded, in touch with her special gifts. His presence reinforced her belief that all was possible. He gave her a confidence she had only aspired to in all her years of training as one of the faerie.

How would she get by without him? Without Murphy too, who had saved her life.

Fighting the growing panic in her chest she uttered, "Yes. 'Tis a splendid idea. We will go to Bud's and decide what to do later. Much later. Do not worry Murphy. You're alone no longer."

Returning to Newberry Forest would come soon enough. From first light this morning, she had been fighting the inevitable. There was no way she could survive in outside of the Faerie Realm. Not unless she constantly stayed at Bud's side. And that was impossible.

He would be a prisoner in his own world and she could not, would not, place such a burden upon him.

As she prepared to take them all to Bud's apartment, Bud stayed her arm. "No. Let's walk. It isn't far and I don't want to attract further attention."

"There's only rats in this alley to see, and I'm sure they won't be tellin' anyone," said Murphy, obviously eager to experience more magic.

Bud looked to Murphy. Then he looked intently into Glory's eyes and gave the matter only a second's thought. "Have you the strength?"

"Aye." Glory nodded. "'Tis a funny thing but when you're touching me, I feel stronger."

Bud gently squeezed her palm and motioned Murphy to take Glory's other hand. "OK then. Click those heels like Dorothy of Oz and zap us out of here."

Not knowing why she should click her heels or who Dorothy was, she did so anyway, and uttered the magic words to take them to Bud's apartment. Now connected to her friends, the flow of energy flooded through and all about, swirling, arcing and encompassing them and within the twinkling of a dandelion's eye they were transported to Bud's living room. It was the quickest and easiest translocation she had ever experienced and equally as perplexing as it was exhilarating. This was definitely something to discuss with Triumphant once she returned home.

Murphy grinned like a Cheshire cat. "I'm thinkin' this zapping about is better than walkin'." He looked about, his voice immediately growing wistful. "This be a grand home you're havin' Bud. Mighty fine."

He wrung his knotty hands together and as if afraid of the answer, his voice lowered to just above a whisper. "Do you think, Glory me darlin', that with a dash of your magic I could have somethin' as grand as this?"

The longing in Murphy's voice brought a lump to Bud's throat. He looked about, seeing his home through new eyes and whilst there was nothing flash in his home, the furniture was comfortable, the carpets soft underfoot. He had money to buy books whenever the fancy took him. He could eat take-out every night of the week without wondering if there was enough money in his wallet. He could shower and change daily. He wanted for nothing and until this very moment, he hadn't realized just how lucky he was.

"I'll make us all a coffee while you work the details out with Glory." Bud left them to it, not sure he could trust himself to not look sorry in front of Murphy. Drunk or not, the old guy would still have pride.

Patting Murphy on the back, Glory led him to the window and indicated to the world outside with a sweep of a hand. "You can have better than this apartment my friend. You can have a real castle if you wish. With turrets and windows with views to survey all the land that comes with it."

Murphy shook his head. "What would I be doing with a real castle when I can't keep me own wife and children. No. Not Murphy."

Glory blinked in shock and her skin prickled. "You have a wife and children?"

"Aye. Once. A long time ago."

"Where are they now?"

A deep sadness filled Murphy's old eyes. He gazed out the window for a long time before he turned to her and spoke again. "'Tis a long story, I'm sure you'll be not wantin' Murphy to bore you with the details."

"Tell me. Mayhap I could do something to help." A witness to the sad slump of his shoulders and wistful eyes, she encouraged him to provide her with a clear idea of what he wanted most in the world.

"What is it? What do you really want, Murphy?"

Murphy rested his forehead against the clear glass and stared blindly out over the rooftops of the other buildings and into the distance where the southern perimeter of Newberry Forest was faintly visible.

Bud who had returned with the coffee and cookies, had heard most of their conversation. He whispered to Glory. "Leave him. He'll talk when he's ready."

Murphy was silent for what seemed like a long time and when he finally spoke his voice was hesitant, broken and barely above a whisper. "I haven't seen me family for ten years. Me wife, God bless her dear sweet soul, put her boot to me bum for being drunk once too often. Kicked me out she did, and told me not to come back until I was sober."

His voice trailed away and a sad expression creased his weary, lined face, making him appear even older than before. "Prior to the incident we had been happy. Very happy."

Glory rested an arm across his shoulders. "What incident? What could have been so awful to cause you to turn to drink for solace?"

Murphy's eyes glazed as Glory felt his thoughts return to a time past. Remembering.

"I had three children. Now there are only two because of me."

Glory failed to stifle a sharp intake of breath. Her heart skipped a beat. What did he mean? How could this be? Surely 'tis not true.

Before she could voice her concerns, he spoke, his lilting brogue so soft and broken she strained to hear each word. No longer aware of his surroundings and oblivious to Glory and Bud, Murphy recited his tale.

"I promised me darlin' wife I would collect the youngest from school one afternoon, but business got in the way. It was always getting in the way. I was in sales and in the middle of a deal so I was late arrivin' at the school. Me boy, Sean, waited and waited at the school gates for me, but he grew restless. Perhaps he thought I had forgotten to pick him up. I'll never know. He decided to make his own way home. It must have been only minutes later that I arrived to find him gone, and only a few more to discover he had been knocked down while tryin' to cross the very street we had warned him never to cross on his own. He was killed instantly."

Murphy shook his head and his voice broke completely, his sorrow woven into a wreath of despair in his aura as he continued to recite his depressing tale. "Me grief is inconsolable and the guilt within me is as deep as a bottomless ocean. Everyone says it was an accident, but I've never forgiven myself.

"I turned to the drink. It took the edge off me pain you see. Eventually the drink claimed more and more of me and me family saw less and less. Eileen–that's me darlin' wife–kicked me out. And rightly so. The strain was too much for her and the wee ones." He heaved a huge sad sigh. "'Tis a wise thing she did. They're better off without a drunkard draggin' them down into the gutter with him."

Tears began to careen down his cheeks and his shoulders shook with grief. "I haven't spoken about the incident in years." He wiped the moisture from his face away with the grimy sleeve of his old coat. "The drink keeps the memories at bay. Jus' where I like them." He lifted a hand towards Bud's liquor cabinet and licked his dry, cracked lips. "I'll be needin' a wee dram before long."

Glory shed tears of her own. Her heart cried for this man and for the loss of his precious boy, the loss of his family and for all the time lost spent in sorrow. She grieved for his other children, now without a father and for his wife who no longer had a husband. How painful it was for a human in this world. She held back a sob of her own and hugged Murphy even more tightly as he turned into her embrace and emptied his heart and soul onto her shoulder.

"You've been living with your guilt for a long time Murphy," Bud said eventually. "Have you ever tried professional help?"

The old guy shook his head and accepted one of the soft squares of white linen Glory conjured out of nowhere to dry their eyes. "Jack Daniels has been me confessor, along with Jim Beam and a few other persuasive friends."

Bud handed Murphy a coffee and led him to his favorite chair, gently guiding his frail frame down into it. "Rest up, Murphy. Take as much time as you need to collect yourself."

Glory picked her mug up and warmed her hands against the china. Even though the sun sat on the edge of the sky and it bathed the room with its last rays of golden warmth, Murphy's confession chilled her all the way through to her soul.

She took a tentative sip and tasted only sadness. Although completely out of her depth, she was already formulating a plan to reinstate Murphy back into the real world. For now though, she was happy to hand the situation over to Bud. His manner was both kind and professional.

"I'm a psychologist," Bud told Murphy. "If you ever feel the need to talk, please know that you can. Free of charge, no strings attached. I don't want you leaving here not knowing you can call me any time you want."

Fresh tears threatened to spill from Murphy's eyes. He hugged his coffee as if his life depended on it, his hands shaking like a leaf, the liquid in the cup dangerously close to spilling. "'Tis a wonderful day to be sure. This morning me only friends were rats nibbling on me big toes and the whisky bottle in me hand."

He shook his head as if he couldn't believe everything that had happened to him today and looked up at the two of them and Bud recognized hope in the old man's cloudy eyes. "No one has treated me so kindly in such a long time. 'Tis a rare thing, this kindness."

"Well, my friend," added Glory with genuine warmth and a tremulous smile. "You deserve the best. You've suffered and punished yourself for far too long. I have a special gift for you.

Whatever you want, I promise I will grant it if it is within my power. What would you like most in the world? That castle? A home like this?" She waved a hand around Bud's living room. "A million dollars? What? I can do this for you my friend, for you deserve it."

Murphy gasped. At a loss for words, he remained silent for a long time. Twenty minutes ticked by during which Murphy mulled over his all-important decision.

Eventually he said, "I haven't had enough to drink today. I'm becoming delusional." He shook his head as if to clear his thoughts and held out his now empty cup to Bud. "Do you think you could be putting a little of that whisky I see over there in this for me?"

Bud took the cup, knowing that if Murphy hadn't drunk anything since meeting Glory this morning, he would definitely be feeling the effects of withdrawal.

However, Glory stayed him with one hand. "Wait." Kneeling on the floor Glory rested a hand on the arm of the chair. Bud stood behind her and she could feel the strength of his support as he waited despite not knowing why.

"Tell me Murphy. What is your greatest wish?"

His aura flowed and ebbed around his frail body with a tentative touch of color that hadn't been apparent before and Glory knew what his request would be and she smiled on the inside.

His words were tentative and apprehensive. "More than anythin', more than life itself I want to be sober. To never want another drop of alcohol. I want to find me family. I want a second chance at livin'. A second chance at love."

"Oh, Murphy." Glory jumped to her feet. "What a wonderful request."

"Can it be done?" asked Bud, concerned Glory would not be able to achieve such a huge ask. He had thought for a minute Murphy might ask to have his young son returned from the dead and he wondered if Glory could actually do that? He didn't want

Murphy's hopes dashed, because he knew it had cost him dearly to reveal his greatest desires. It didn't bear thinking what would happen if Glory couldn't work her magic or if it was a request beyond her abilities. The old guy was too fragile. Too beaten up by what life had thrown his way.

"Oh it can. I'm sure it can. 'Tis a wish from the heart and Father always says a wish from the heart is greater than any materialistic request. He says that when the heart is involved, there is love and love is the greatest gift of all. Oh Bud, truly, 'tis the easiest wish to give and I will grant it gladly."

Murphy surged forward in his chair his face a picture of disbelief and hope blended together. "You can do it?"

"Aye, Murphy," Glory beamed at him. "I can."

And that was how Murphy became a new man. He stood apart from his new friends as Glory wove the magic that would set him free from the vicious demon of drink, and before their very eyes, Glory's glamour began to take effect. Years dropped away from Murphy, making him appear younger, healthier, and robust. The lines on his face disappeared and his red rummy eyes cleared, and once where there had been nothing but dull despair was a bright twinkling light of mischief. Even his hair lost its dull grayness, and shined with vigorous health.

It occurred to Glory that Murphy must have been an extremely handsome man in his earlier years, and that the glamour had helped him regain some of those looks.

"How do you feel?" Bud was dumbfounded.

Murphy licked his dry lips and paced to the mantle over the fireplace to stare into the wide mirror positioned there. He studied his reflection for a long time before another tear slid down his less weathered cheek.

Eventually he turned to face his new friends, gratitude in eyes shining back at them. "'Tis a miraculous day. For the past ten years the urge to drink has been me only true companion. I gladly give up me old life for now I have a new one and new friends as well. Not a single drop of liquor will ever pass these lips again. You have my word on that."

Both Glory and Bud believed him. Glory decked Murphy out in the finest of clothes. A new dark navy suit with a crisp white shirt beneath, a wallet in his pocket with money already in it, a pair of gold cufflinks and custom-made black leather shoes. The ensemble gave Murphy an air of sophistication that astonished Bud.

Before he left to find his wife, as a parting gift and to send him on his way out into the unknown, Glory silently wished him good fortune for the rest of his days and added a little something to enhance that luck; a winning lottery ticket of a few million or so. What he did with it was entirely up to him, but she already knew he would put it to good use.

"Remember to call me next week," called Bud as they waved goodbye from the apartment steps that evening, "You'll always be welcome in my home."

With a spring in his step, Murphy waved and went off in search of his past so that he might have a future. A future he would never have thought possible only a mere few hours ago.

The luck of the Irish truly did exist.

≈ CHAPTER 9 ≈

Alone. At last.

Soon Glory would be gone and Bud would be left with only fleeting memories of their short time together. In his mind's eye, he could see his future and he didn't like what he saw. It included him and Murphy as old men sitting in rocking chairs on a porch at twilight, trying to recall the time they were visited by one of the little people.

Would they eventually think it all a dream?

Well, heck! On impulse, he made a decision. He would make certain the dream was a damn good one. The moment the door closed behind Murphy he pulled his dream-girl into his arms and before he lost his nerve, he said, "I've been aching to hold you and tell you I believe you really are a faerie."

He kissed her, softly enough for his lips to moisten hers and deeply enough to leave his glistening imprint on her mouth. "I'm crazy for you."

Glory was in turmoil. She'd had ideas of her own including pretty much what lay unspoken in the smoky depths of Bud's eyes. She'd discounted those thoughts as foolish, wistful daydreams but it seemed they would be fulfilled after all.

She had expected a few awkward moments, a reminder from him that he still had two remaining wishes. Then he would release her and that would be an end to it.

So final. So definite. So intensely disappointing.

Now he was kissing the disappointment away and still she hesitated, employing a remarkable and unusual amount of self-control. Should she allow this to happen when it went against everything she had been taught? Her doubts, her fears held her captive only for a few seconds for when Bud's lips descended to claim possession of hers, she surrendered her doubts and decided she would remain in his arms for a few wonderful hours. She would reap memories to hold inside her heart. Memories to cherish when times grew difficult.

Yes, she was crazy. Crazy for being in Bud's arms. Allowing a human's lips to press against hers, letting his hands thread their way through her hair to cup the base of her skull and hold her there, while he took what she was so willing to give.

Heat built up inside her, melting into a molten bundle of need. She should be saving herself for one of her own kind. Except she couldn't ever imagine being with anyone else. "I'm crazy for you too, Bud."

He lifted his mouth from his exploration of her jaw-line to check the truth of her statement in her eyes. It was all there. Everything he could have ever hoped for. Passion lit her eyes to the deepest azure and a demand equaling his own consumed him as she brushed her lips against his skin.

It was the fierce grip of her hands against his back as she pulled him to her that gave him his answer. Releasing a deep, barely controlled moan he planted a hungry kiss on the slender nape of her neck. Bud plundered her neckline, first with his lips then with his hands.

Glory's palms smoothed up his arms, reveling in his tensile strength as each muscle contracted one after the other beneath her touch. Encouraged, she moved on, tracing a pathway of discovery to his neck and jaw. Murmuring a soft sigh, she told him how much she enjoyed touching him. How rough his skin was against her softness and how much he pleased her.

She pushed his glasses up and away from his eyes, until they perched atop his head. Her fingers traced a path along his eyelids, his warm brown lashes tickling her fingertips. Turning her hands over she brushed her knuckles down his cheeks, outlined his lips with moistened thumbs before finally slanting her head and placing her mouth once more against his.

"'Tis not permitted to do this," she murmured giving up all sanity and abandoning herself to her desires.

"Do you want me to stop?" Bud groaned his response.

She knew he would stop if she asked him, but she'd made her decision and she wouldn't turn away now.

"No." She moved wantonly against his long tall frame.

Sweeping an arm under her knees, he scooped her up off the floor and carried her down the hall, through to his bedroom. With her secure in his arms and with very little decorum he collapsed onto the center of his bed with her beneath him.

Laughter, a bubbly musical sound, filled the room. Glory stared boldly into his hot, smoldering eyes. "Teach me how to love you."

"I was hoping you'd say that." Then Bud proceeded to peel away what there was of Glory's itty bitty red dress from her shoulders and down over her breasts and hips, until it ended in a puddle beside her ridiculous platform shoes on the carpet. Only when she lay naked and ready for him, did he remove his own clothing and kneel between her legs, towering over her.

Glory had never seen a human naked before. She felt her eyes widen as all of Bud was revealed. Her mother had told her of such things, though she'd never seen one quite so... so... attentive. She had seen many a male faerie naked, but physical relations were always conducted away from others in the privacy of their own home or the solitude of the forest. Being a daughter of the King, she had not had the inclination to bed any of the suitors who were paraded before her in all their finery at court, except for a faerie prince who had spurned her and cleaved with another.

Her heart went rat-a-tat-tat against her chest as she viewed the spectacle before her. Never before had she seen an appendage of such magnitude. Indeed, all male faeries and their appendages amounted to no consequence at all after viewing Bud's impressive presentation.

Now here was something to crow about. "Mother never told me about ones like that." A mixture of disbelief and mischief danced in her eyes. "However will it fit?"

Bud chuckled and assured her it would, and her eyes followed his hands as they encompassed her waist, and she arched up, stretching her spine as his thumbs smoothed over the flat plane of her stomach before palming their way up her rib cage and over her breasts, spreading out to grip her shoulders. He pulled her against him and she felt the weight of his body as he eased them both back down onto the mattress.

"You're so beautiful," he murmured against her neck.

His words were like thick warm molasses oozing into her bloodstream, creating a sensuous pathway to her heart.

"Tell me more." She eagerly turned her head to his, searching for his lips. "Ahh," she sighed as they found their target. "Show me."

So he did. And more. Not only did his hands slide over the dips and hollows of her curves, his ever so talented lips trailed a path of discovery to all her secret little places and then possessed them with his tongue.

And that wasn't all he was doing. It was dawning on her that Bud had taken possession of her heart as well and she could see from his aura that his feelings for her were of a similar nature.

When he nibbled his way to… down there… her breath whooshed out in a rush. She dug her fists into his thick hair and bucked on the sheets beneath the wicked onslaught of his tongue.

"Oh. Oh."

Fiddledeedee! Mother had never told her about this either.

Great waves of... of... she didn't know what it was, spiraled through her until she couldn't think, couldn't do anything but react. "Oh Bud." She lost control altogether and her wings popped into being. "'Tis magic of another kind. Never stop."

But he did, and she thought for an instant she truly would go mad. Bud lifted his head to look at her wings and a huge grin spread across his face. Her eyes met the glazed intensity in his gray ones and she knew he was pleased at her lack of control.

"That was just for starters," Bud growled.

Her skin goosed and a strange tremor coiled in her. Slowly, ever so, agonizingly slowly he slid his finely honed body up her torso, their skin barely touching, teasing her with an anticipation that nearly sent her right over the edge.

His lips only a fraction from hers, he was like a coiled spring, the controlled tension in his eyes, drawn cheekbones, the way his teeth bit down on his bottom lip. He pushed his hips down to hers, his head and shoulders arched back, and he groaned from somewhere in his chest. As if he wanted to roar.

How she loved that sound. It drove her on, responding to its deep elemental call until she could do nothing but beg him to enter her. She lifted her hips to his, inviting him to discover her final and most important secret place. A place she could share with Bud. A place she had shared with no other. She protested when he leaned away and retrieved something from the drawer next to the bed.

"What is that?"

"Protection," he replied.

"Against what?"

"To ensure you do not return to your world pregnant," he told her.

Glory marveled at such a device and watched with interest as he rolled what he called a condom on. "I wouldn't mind having your child," she told him. "But mayhap, my family might object."

"I would mind," he told her. "I would mind because I would want to be involved in his or her life. It wouldn't be fair to you or to me." He returned to kissing her.

"Oh," she whispered as he gently eased the tip of his erection against her entrance. She was more than ready to cleave with this man. To know him in the truest sense.

He was patient and teased her by moving ever so slowly as he eased his way in stretching and filling her with his impressive appendage. She lifted her hips to accommodate him, allowing him to enter her fully, surprised at how little resistance there was. Wrapping her long legs about his hips she cupped his bottom with her hands and held on so tight she left imprints on his soft skin as he began to move rhythmically inside her.

"'Tis magic how it fits so. 'Tis truly a miracle of grand proportions."

Bud's features were harsher than usual as he filled her with long slow tortuous thrusts. "I knew we would fit. I knew we would."

His breath was hot against her skin, his eyes a stormy gray. With a light sheen of perspiration on his skin and desire in every movement, their passion took them where they needed to go.

Glory smoothed her hands down his back with lengthy strokes. She whispered heated words of love against his shoulder, in his mouth and in the thatch of warm honeyed hair on his chest. She told him how much she liked his hands touching her. She showed him just how much she loved feeling him inside her, by matching his thrusts as he moved rhythmically into her, encouraging him on and on and on.

And when she flew across an invisible barrier into a world of brilliant light, the promise of Bud's loving reached fruition. "Can you see it?" Tears shimmered brightly in her eyes as wave upon wave of luminescent silver pulsed through and around her, flushing her skin with rosy dew. It was more than physical. It was elemental. It rained down from the universe above. It was hot liquid. It was sparkling light. It was wonderful.

"No," Bud replied, breathless when only seconds later his seed surged its release into Glory in long urgent spasms. "But I heard the most incredible music."

As their breathing and hearts slowed, Glory lay wrapped in Bud's arms and understood what fulfillment meant at its deepest level. Every now and then Bud would drop a kiss on her lips, a shoulder, a breast. His hand would sweep possessively in the gentlest caress over the dips and curves of her body and she knew there was nothing more wonderful than lying beside the one you loved.

***

Like all faerie tales, their time was almost at an end.

"I'll have to leave at dawn. Will you release me, Bud?" She bit down on her lip, striving to stop it from quivering.

The words were whispered so quietly, so softly, Bud could have pretended he hadn't heard them. Fear rocked his world at the request so quietly given. Disappointment drenched him with unhappiness, but he would not deny or ignore her request.

Reluctantly Bud released a gruff, "Yes." He turned to her to bury himself once more deep inside the woman who had changed his life forever, wanting to stretch out the last remaining hours together. This time his loving was tender, precious and profound.

Breathless, he held Glory to him so she couldn't see his sadness and whispered words of love against her skin. "I don't know how or why it has happened, but I love you." *I don't want to let you go.*

Though Glory asked for release, he understood it wasn't something she truly wanted and that the request was acutely painful for her to ask as it was for him to agree. He wouldn't make it any harder for her than it already was.

From a reservoir of strength he didn't know he possessed, he brushed her cheek against his and whispered a hushed, "I will release you if that is what you want?"

He waited for her to say, no, it's not what I want, but she never did. He witnessed the pain in her eyes, but her lips remained closed to the words he so desperately wanted to hear.

Another thought had come to him in the night, but he had held on to his request for as long as he could. Now the desire was too strong to deny and the time too short for him not to ask.

"Glory?" He fingered her long wild locks of hair.

"Hmmm," she purred and snuggled more closely into him.

"Will you do something for me?" His heart kicked in to a faster beat. He was about to ask for the one thing he'd only ever dreamed about. A secret dream he'd held inside his heart for most of his life and never expected to realize.

Glory pushed herself upwards, pressing a palm against his chest. "What is it Bud? You know if it is in my power I will do it."

"I want to fly without the aid of a parachute. All my life I've dreamed of flying along the coastline with the ocean on one side and land on the other. I've imagined it so often that at times I've thought it was actually happening only to wake up and discover it was all just a dream.

He knew he was rambling, but now he'd started he couldn't stop. "Take me flying so I can see the sun rise. I want to fly as you do, through the air, darting this way and that with the wind in my hair and the freedom to choose where to go without restraint, unencumbered by ropes and strings. Can you do that for me Glory? Can you take me flying before you go home?"

Tears welled in Glory's eyes. "How can I say no to such a plea. Flying it is then. Without encumbrances," she assured him and her mouth twisted into an impish tilt despite her sadness. "None at all. And when we get back I would ask something of you."

"Anything," Bud promised rashly. He could deny her nothing. "Name it."

"Make love to me again. The last thing I want to remember before I leave this world are your hands on my skin, of you moving inside me, the sound of your voice as you make love to me. Shower me with kisses to remember you by."

Bud's palms smoothed down her back, all the way to her rounded bottom. One hand paved its way back up to end in a fisted tangle in her hair. He pushed his hips up to hers and pulled her head down until his lips brushed against her rosy kiss-swollen ones.

"Why wait?" He tugged at her lower lip, fighting against the deep sadness welling inside, clenching his stomach into tight knots.

Glory looked towards the windows. "No time left, my love. If you wish to catch the sun rising we must go now."

A moment of panic held Bud immobile. No! Please God, not yet. Why had this wonderful, exciting woman-faerie-creature come into his life if not for some special reason?

Regret soured the bittersweet anticipation of flying. He brushed his knuckles gently against the soft silk of her cheek. What a wonderful gift God had given him in Glory, even if only for the agonizingly short time they'd spent together.

Tears threatened to blur her vision. He sensed her despondency. A melancholy to equal his own.

"Come," she said. "I'm about to take you on an adventure you'll never forget." She pulled away from the safe harbor of his arms, stood beside the bed and offered him her hand.

Bud's fingers entwined with hers and he arose but, when she immediately began to incant a glamour, he stopped her. "What about clothes?"

Glory chuckled softly and ran a fingernail lightly down his torso, her eyes following the movement. "No encumbrances, remember."

Bud looked horrified. "I meant no parachute. People will... ah...

see."

"No they won't. They won't see a thing."

"You can do that? You can make me invisible."

"And more."

Bud wasn't convinced. What did she mean and more? Baring his private parts to the citizens of Oaktree Falls wasn't on his list of fantasies. "It's cold out there." There was a chill in the air and he'd bet a month's wages it was frosty outside this morning. He had no particular desire to freeze his doodacky off. Whipping his glasses off the bedside table, he planted them firmly on his face. If he was going flying, he wanted to be able to see where he was going at least.

But Glory wasn't listening. Instead, she was vocalizing the final words of her glamour and waving her free arm through the air in some mystical pattern.

First came a loud buzzing and a sensation of lightness in his head and body. He almost felt dizzy when the full power of the glamour took effect, making him feel as if there was no substance to him at all. Along with the weightlessness came the discovery his feet no longer touched the floor. In fact, both he and Glory were no longer in his bedroom, but suspended high above the land on the wild coastline of the ocean several hundred miles from Oaktree Falls.

It was still dark, but all along the horizon were signs it would be only minutes before the sun would begin spreading its embracing warmth and light out across the vast expanse of sea, rolling fields and cliffs over which they flew.

"How do you feel?" Glory called to him, as she swooped through the air, his hand in hers. "Is this what you wanted?"

How did he feel? Overawed. Unencumbered and totally free. Strangely, he couldn't feel the cold so perhaps his doodacky would live to see another day after all. "Incredible. Intoxicating. I feel like Peter Pan and you're Tinkerbell."

"I'm flattered. Tinkerbell is one of my best friends."

Bud laughed. "That doesn't surprise me." Bud snatched an all too brief kiss from Glory and then they soared up, up towards the soft voluminous clouds above.

Freedom. He didn't have wings as she did, but he was weightless and all he had to do was follow her lead. As the sun began its ascent Bud learnt how to fly. With warmth on his face and wind in his hair, he dipped, rose, swooped, and swirled through time and space. A joy he'd only known in his dreams, he experienced a curious sense of rightness, of being where he should be, as if it was predestined. When this morning was over he would never be able to recreate these experiences except in dreams. Savoring every image, every single moment, he tucked them away in the center of his heart as if they were precious gems.

His life was permanently altered and he didn't know whether to laugh or cry.

As he flew alongside Glory, Bud acknowledged he was hopelessly and irrevocably in love. "Promise me I never will forget you Glory. Promise me you won't place a glamour on me to forget these memories."

Glory, her long tresses flying out behind her, didn't hesitate. "I promise. A promise once made by the faerie can never be broken."

"Not just flying. Of our time together. All of it. Don't erase any of these moments from my mind."

Glory placed a fist against her breastbone and then touched it to his heart. "I promise. Faeries' Honor."

≈ CHAPTER 10 ≈

Glory's sadness would haunt him for the rest of his days. The unshed tears as they brimmed at the edges of her extraordinary eyes had just about been his undoing. Her departure left him feeling empty and hollow, as if someone had cut out his heart and shredded it to pieces.

Releasing Glory was the hardest thing he had ever done. Two horrendously long days after she had returned home, all he thought of, all he dreamed of, was Glory.

Glory, with her long blonde hair threaded through his fingers as she lay next to him in his bed.

Glory's hushed tones as she lay beside and beneath him.

Glory, the only woman he would ever love.

Everywhere there were reminders, evidence of her existence. She had not been a hallucination.

She *was* real.

He was *not* crazy.

He tossed and turned each night beneath the rose covered duvet. He rested his head where hers had been on the rose covered pillowcases, understanding why star-struck fans refused to wash a cherished item of their hero's clothing.

Her scent was everywhere. Her special blend of eau de Morning Glory enveloped him in lightheaded memories. He tended the clinging vines flowering profusely across the walls, dutifully picking up any fallen petals and scattering them daily in the local park. He wondered absently why they and her sheets had not disappeared when Glory had left but he took care of those too. And all his clothes too. He was a changed man.

She was in his bed, the kitchen, the hallway, and the living room. No room had been left untouched by her presence.

Most of all Glory lingered in his heart.

When he closed his eyes, there she was, large as life. As real as the air he breathed.

"Damn it all!" Bud shouted in the privacy of his apartment. "Why did she have to go?" Never would he forget the pressure of her lips on his, of her soft breath as she uttered words of love when he entered her. His hands, his lips, his heart remembered but he worried the memories would fade and dim. He wanted to remember her forever.

Even now, he found it difficult to believe how incredible, how exciting, how achingly passionate their union had been. He'd asked God if he could meet a woman who loved flying as much as he did and, hey-presto, Glory had flown into his life.

"You give on one hand and you take back with the other." He shook his fist at the ceiling, imagining the heaven above. "Why?"

God didn't reply. All Bud heard was the beat of his own empty heart.

Work was an effort. Every day he forced himself out the front door. He smiled and offered sympathy and encouragement to those in need. On the outside, he was calm, unflappable Bud. A man equipped with the skills to counsel others. On the inside, there was a constant ache, which refused to go away. He was a hollow shell of the man he used to be.

The compulsion to spill his worries with someone was strong. Someone who knew Glory and who would believe his story and not think him on the brink of insanity.

Before Murphy left to find his new life, Bud had arranged for him to check in once a week with an update on his search for his family. To let Bud know how his new life was going, but he was not expected to call so soon.

Bud didn't know how to contact him. He'd even tried returning to the alley, Murphy's former home, to question those loitering in the area. No luck there.

When Jack called and suggested a day of parachuting Bud quickly said yes. It was better than going stir crazy staring at the apartment walls.

On his first jump, he encountered something he would never have thought possible. His favorite pastime paled into insignificance after flying with Glory. Parachuting would never be the same.

Over a whisky in a bar later that afternoon, Bud spilled his heart out to his best friend, leaving out the small but important fact that Glory was a faerie.

"Phone her," Jack commiserated while ordering another round of drinks.

"I can't." Bud gritted his jaw. Glory's living arrangements included several branches and a tree trunk. They didn't need phones to communicate with each other.

"Why not? Give me your phone. I'll call her."

"No." Bud coughed as he thought up an excuse. "She doesn't have a phone."

Jack snorted. "Get outta here! Everyone has a phone." He patted his own iPhone tucked in his leather jacket pocket.

"I tell you, she doesn't have one."

"Why not?"

Jack's words were beginning to slur. Bud put down his drink. It looked like they would be taking a taxi home tonight. "She's old-fashioned." He cringed. It was a lame-brained excuse if there ever was one and heck, he couldn't even make it sound like the truth.

Jack wasn't so drunk he couldn't spot a lie. "She didn't strike me as old-fashioned. That little number she was wearing the other day was almost see-through. Old-fashioned women don't wear see-through dresses."

"Get your mind out from under her dress," Bud muttered. "Only I'm allowed to look."

"If you don't go get her somebody else will." Jack waved his hands in the shape of a woman. "She has attri… atr… treats."

"Glory only has eyes for me." Bud insisted. So, why did he sound so uncertain? "Her treats are mine. Not yours."

"Then what's the big deal?" Jack didn't wait for a reply. He pointed a finger at Bud and issued an order. "Go get her!"

"I can't." Bud was beginning to regret telling Jack anything.

His best friend laughed. "Right. Wait until you're sober."

"No. I can't go see her."

"Why not?"

Bud shrugged his shoulders.

Snorting rudely, Jack exclaimed, "Don't tell me you don't have her address?"

Bud shook his head. "Not exactly." His eyes dulled for a moment before an idea struck. He perked up immediately. "I know the general vicinity." How did one tell which tree housed a faerie and which did not?

Jack's expression was comical. He tilted his chair backwards onto the two back legs and peered over his glass at him. "Didn't anyone teach you that the first thing you do when you meet a foxy lady besides finding out whether she's single is to get her contact details? I can't believe you got neither." A thick mass of jet hair fell forward to hide the frown on Jack's forehead, giving him a rakish appearance. "I don't believe it."

"I don't expect you to."

Jack gestured to the door of the bar. "Stop moping, get out there and find her. Retrace your steps. Where did you first meet?"

All these awkward questions. They were giving Bud a headache.

He wondered if it was wise to tell Jack any more. "At the precinct."

"See." Jack slapped a hand down on the table between them. "That wasn't so hard. Is she an officer?"

Bud bit down on his bottom lip. His brain said no, don't tell him, but his mouth apparently had other ideas. "She was arrested for indecent exposure."

Bud couldn't help but laugh at Jack's incredulity. "Indecent. What?"

"You know. No clothes in a public place. That kind of thing."

"How?"

"Just like everyone else I guess. One item at a time."

Jack shot him a dirty look. "And you said she was shy." Jack leaned forward the chair landing with a thud back on all four legs. "Why did she take them off?"

Now this was where Bud came unstuck. He couldn't tell Jack why. Could he? Nah. No one would believe him in a million years. He reckoned a little white lie wouldn't hurt about now.

"She was at a hen's night." The cogs in Bud's head were spinning too fast for common sense to catch up. "Things got a little out of hand. The next thing you know, she found herself being booked for indecent exposure."

Jack rocked back in his chair again. He was your classic bad-boy knock-em-dead kind of guy. His mouth stretched into an outright grin.

Bud knew he was never going hear the end of it. "It isn't funny."

Jack exploded into laughter and the locals in the pub turned to look in their direction. "Yes, it is."

"It's not." He wished he could tell his friend everything. About Delaney turning into a frog and how he'd discovered Lacey bound by cobwebs. About the transformation of Murphy and, most of all, about Glory and who she really was.

Who would believe him? Glory's true existence would have to

remain his and Murphy's secret for the rest of their lives.

"Glory is a faerie." Astonished, Bud clamped his mouth shut, not believing he'd said the truth out loud.

Jack laughed deeper, harder and longer. Tears streamed like a waterfall down his cheeks.

"I tell you she is. That's how she flew into my life. She has wings." Bud tried to stop his mouth from moving. He was beginning to sound like Murphy. Then a light bulb went on in his head and he grinned. He could tell his friend anything. It didn't matter what he said because Jack would think it was the alcohol talking. "Big gossamer ones. She can fly too."

"Yeah. And I'm the tooth faerie."

"And that's another thing. Did you know the tooth faerie is male?"

***

Newberry Forest – The Glory Tree
"Come now dearest. All this crying isn't good for you." Triumphant cradled Glory in her arms as her sister poured her heart out. Glory buried her head against Triumphant's shoulder and did not see the dawning look of horror and fear in her sister's eyes.

Glory had touched the lips of a human. In fact, if she was hearing things correctly, Glory had touched more than this human's lips.

Triumphant didn't have a clue what to do or say. For the first time ever, she was unable to offer a solution or aid her beloved sister. She had never touched a human. Never been in love. She didn't understand how Glory could have been so foolish.

As far as she knew, no faerie had ever broken a single one of the Twelve Golden Rules set down by the Ancients over five centuries ago. Ever. The code of conduct for a faerie or the wisdom of the Ancients was never questioned. A flicker of fear curled up her spine. Triumphant was truly afraid for her younger sister.

"Come now," she soothed, running her hand lovingly down the length of Glory's silken locks. "Dry those tears and tell me everything. Remember what mother always says. Share your problems and they will be halved."

"No one can halve this problem for I am already split in two. My heart has a jagged crack in it and it's leaking out all over the forest floor. I miss him so."

Glory palmed away the tears from her cheeks and collapsed into a chair Tree had so kindly fashioned for her comfort. She leaned back against the soft cushion of leaves and pressed a damp hand against her heart. "Bud has released me but I sense his unhappiness and it goes as deep as my own."

Glory reached out to take her sister's hands and pressed them against the center of her chest. "We are joined somehow. What he feels, I also feel. If his heart cries, so does mine. Can you feel him? He's as sad and lonely without me as I him. What am I to do Tri? What am I to do?"

Triumphant had never heard of such a thing. It pained her to admit she didn't have any answers. "This is not something I can easily answer. I believe we should speak with mother."

"Nay." Glory was horrified. "She will tell Father."

"Mayhap she will lessen the blow for you."

"Tell them I'm unwell."

"I will not lie to them Glory."

Glory sniffed good and loud. "'Tis not a lie. My eyes are swollen, my nose is leaking."

My heart is broken.

***

The Glory Tree was worried. Never before had his mistress been so unhappy. He could feel her desolation; her deep, deep sadness. He was a sensitive tree who appreciated his namesake's kindness. She always treated him with the respect deserving of one as old as he. She tended his roots, branches and leaves with the utmost care.

What could he do to ease her pain? How could he make things better for the one who cared for him so well? Tree wanted to pick her up in his branches and cradle her, rock her until her tears evaporated and sleep soothed away this new, foreign disquiet.

The Tree of Triumphant suggested filling Glory's rooms with her favorite flowers. Taking up the suggestion, Tree filled his entire body with Morning Glory and golden roses until he overflowed with scented blooms. Tree even went so far as to deck them among his branches, but alas, his mistress continued to cry.

His fellow neighbor, The Tree of Bluebell, sent feelers out to neighboring trees and music was suggested. The Tree of Glory immediately requested The Tree of Exquisite Notes play songs for his mistress.

He did all of these things and more out of love, but it was to no avail. Glory continued to cry. The clouds gathered above, and grew in proportion to the heaviness of her heart. Joining in, they dropped big wet tears of liquid onto his leaves and drenched his roots.

Tree was as water logged as Glory. Sighing under the weight of the oppressive rain he was at a loss as to what to do next and considered contacting the most revered of them all.

The Tree of All Knowingness.

This venerable advisor to the Great Ancient Ones lived at the epicenter of the Faerie Realm and had existed for several thousand years. The Book of Truth stated it had always existed and would always remain, collecting and storing history, ready to gift wisdom to those who cared to ask or listen.

It had existed long before there was a forest to name, or before the faerie came to live amongst their branches.

But before Tree could send a request to the Tree of All Knowingness, he received an urgent message via the Faerie Chain.

The leaves were whispering on the south side of Newberry

Forest. Birds were atwitter with curiosity as they sheltered from the weather in their nests. To the human ear, the noise would have been put down to ordinary forest sounds, but the forest inhabitants were sensitive to the changes in their atmosphere and these sounds were not any of the usual ones.

What The Glory Tree heard in the message alarmed him enough to contact Triumphant.

There were humans behaving strangely not far from the Faerie Portal and if something wasn't done soon they might well slip into the Faerie Realm by accident.

Triumphant sent one of her sentry out to ascertain what the commotion was about, and attempted to soothe Tree by saying it was probably nothing and to remain calm.

'Twas uncommon for humans to be outdoors during a heavy downpour. They generally preferred hiding out in their dark airless boxes, in their concrete cities.

Triumphant awaited word having already decided she would not alert Glory to this curious occurrence. She was apprehensive, certain it would be that Bud person.

What would she do if it was?

When her sentry reported back, her worst fears were realized. There were two human males in their midst, acting strangely and calling for Glory. As Captain of Faerie Sentry, it was Triumphant's duty to investigate. Marshaling her defenses, she forced herself to speak calmly to her troops to stay close but to remain hidden and to keep watch but take no action before she herself headed out to the portal as well.

Oh, Glory! What have you done?

≈ CHAPTER 11 ≈

Later that afternoon, Bud could have sworn that as he and Jack darted from tree to tree, the branches moved aside to allow the rain to pelt them from the sky above. Creeping about in the woods in the heavy rain, the leaves provided little, if any, shelter and Jack didn't think it was fun. His sense of adventure seemed to have deserted him.

"What the hell is wrong with you man?" He slicked back his soaked hair, looked up at the towering branches and huddled with his back against a large trunk for shelter from the downpour. "No one lives here."

Bud huddled next to him, his fist holding his jacket closed at his neck. "Glory does."

"Yeah right." Jack shoved back a branch laden with water that seemed closer than it had been a second ago and peered into the dim interior of the woods. "Somewhere in here lurks a faerie. By all accounts, there's a whole passel of them."

Bud no longer cared if Jack believed him or not. "Glory does live here and I'm not crazy." He surveyed the trees in front and around them. "If only I knew which tree she lived in."

Jack stared glumly at Bud, a cynical eyebrow cocked in question. "Back at the bar I thought your rambling was a simple case of you being drunk. I'm cold, wet and I'm beginning to think that counseling all those down-and-outs has addled your brain."

"My brain isn't addled."

"I'm an idiot for agreeing to venture into Newberry Forest with you. I'm a sucker for a sob story but this is ludicrous!"

"You'll see," Bud said, not deterred in the slightest.

"I'm concerned for your mental welfare. That's why I'm here. No other reason would possess me to wander about in this weather to watch you commune with nature."

Bud wished he hadn't brought Jack along for the ride. "Faeries do exist and I'm going to prove it to you."

Jack tried another tack. "You wouldn't want Glory to see you looking like a drowned rat. How romantic is that? Let's come back tomorrow once the rain has stopped." He swiped away moisture on the face of his watch. "The taxi isn't going to wait for us forever."

Bud cupped his hand to his mouth and yelled Glory's name several times. The dense wood swallowed up any sound.

Jack stared at Bud as if he'd suddenly grown a set of antennas and who would blame him.

"Who goes there?"

Jack looked at Bud. "What did you say? Who goes where?"

"I didn't say anything. I thought it was you."

They both stood silent. Listening. Nothing.

"That's a relief," muttered Jack.

"Who goes there?"

"There it is again." Bud grinned and pointed toward a natural clearing. "It came from that direction."

"It's probably a forest ranger," Jack scowled. "Wondering why two idiots are creeping about Newberry Forest in the rain."

"Speak for yourself," Bud said. "I'm not an idiot."

Jack mumbled something unintelligible under his breath.

There was a buzz and a rattling of leaves above them. Suddenly a branch bounced violently, sending a fresh spray of water over them both. Nothing could have caused it to bounce like that unless someone or something had knocked it.

Both men watched intently as the branch slowly settled back to stillness.

Jack was clearly freaked. "Bud. Let's go."

But Bud was walking forward into the clearing. "They've come for me."

"Oh they're coming all right. Men in white coats if you don't stop this asininity right now."

Bud grinned. "I thought you were the fearless type?"

"I was. I am."

"Well, then. What are you waiting for?"

"I'm waiting for you."

In Bud's opinion, his friend looked as if he wanted to run. In the opposite direction.

A woman's voice caused them both to jump. "This is private property. Please leave."

Bud knew this was nonsense. Newberry Forest was public domain. "I can't leave. Not until I've found Glory."

"Glory who?"

"Princess Gloriane." Bud could have sworn the trees were leaning closer and closer towards them, blocking out the brooding clouds above.

Crowding. Listening intently.

Jack wrapped his arms about his broad chest and stamped his feet on the ground. "I'm not interested. Faeries don't exist. Neither do enchanted forests. This is all nonsense. Come on Bud. Let's go."

But Bud wasn't listening and put an index finger to his lips to quieten him when the female voice spoke again. "Who requests her presence?"

Bud took a step forward. "I do. Bud Chandler."

"And the other one. Does he too wish to see the Faerie Most Royal?"

"No!" Jack declared. "I don't."

"This is Jack. My best friend." Bud gripped Jack by a leather-clad elbow and dragged him forward. "He doesn't believe."

"That's right," Jack said, having recovered his voice. "I don't believe."

***

Tree had been correct, Triumphant acknowledged. The humans were far too close to the Faerie Portal for comfort and 'twas imperative they did not accidentally slip into it. Humans did not belong in their world. Especially the one clad in skin hugging leather called Jack. He possessed the aura of a hunter. Wet to the bone, he oozed raw animal power. Power begging to be unleashed. She shivered, her movement sending a spray of silver droplets onto the men below.

Triumphant flew from her vantage point, landing several feet from the men and made herself full size and visible to Bud only. "What gives you the right to ask to see one of the faerie?"

Bud was startled at her sudden arrival in human form. "You must be Triumphant."

Jack's tone was one of being pissed. "I'm anything less than triumphant."

"No. Not you." Bud gestured to the woman standing in front of them. "Her."

Jack frowned and looked to where Bud pointed. "Who?"

"Triumphant."

"I can't see anything remotely happy about any of this."

"No. Not that kind of triumphant. Triumphant, Glory's sister."

Jack shook his head and closed his eyes. "All right. You've had your fun. Let's go."

"You really can't see her?" Bud pointed at Triumphant. "That woman there, dressed like one of Robin Hood's merry men, except in this case she's a merry woman."

Jack slapped both hands over his face. "I don't see anyone and I don't believe any of your story."

"I was like you once. But now I believe."

Bud couldn't take his eyes off Triumphant. She was shorter than Glory, but only just and dressed head to toe in a figure hugging forest green jacket and tights. Perched atop her thick blonde hair sat a ridiculous pointy felt hat, just like one he'd seen in one of his childhood books. Her long tresses exploded out from underneath and all around, cascading down her shoulders in a riot of curls. Hooked over her shoulder was a pouch containing arrows. In her hands, she held a bow. "You're not thinking of using that on us, are you?"

Triumphant reached over her shoulder for an arrow, studied it intently with pursed lips, then blew against the quiver. "If necessary."

Heaving an irritated sigh, Jack muttered. "Use what?"

"She's got a pile of arrows and it looks like she knows how to use them."

Jack rolled his eyes. "Oooh, I'm scared."

Triumphant's eyes glinted in the dim light and she cocked the arrow to the bow.

"No!" Bud put out a protective hand. "He didn't mean it."

Jack looked all around him. "What's she going to do?"

"Use him as target practice," Triumphant enlightened Bud. She raised her bow and eyed Jack in her sight.

Bud took a step closer to the woman who resembled Glory so closely and placed himself between her and Jack. "That's unfair. How can he defend himself if he can't see you? Jack stay behind me."

"You're crazy." Jack hissed at him. "Can't see a thing except rain and leaves and a demented friend."

Bud shot him a *watch-it* look over his shoulder. "But you heard her didn't you?"

Jack was prepared to lie. "I didn't hear a thing."

"Liar," Triumphant accused. "All humans are liars."

"We are not!" Jack exclaimed hotly and stepped up beside Bud.

"To whom are you talking?" Bud asked Jack with an arch to one brow.

Jack snarled. "You know who."

"But I thought you said you couldn't hear her?"

"I know. I know." Jack rolled his eyes. "I'm prepared to admit I heard something. It's probably hypothermia and a mild case of delirium. I don't want to meet faeries. I want to go home, have a whisky, hop into a warm bath and forget I ever agreed to let you drag me along to this infernally wet forest."

"Enough!"

The command rang out through the forest and even Jack shut up. For a second. Then he opened his mouth again. "Enough. Yeah. Right. I've had enough. If you want to stay and talk into thin air Bud, then that's your prerogative. I'm leaving. I'm heading home and I'm going to wait inside, under a concrete roof until the rain stops. Just like all other sane Oaktree Falls citizens."

He turned and marched away, shouting over his shoulder. "Are you coming?"

"I'm staying." Bud had found one of Glory's kin and he wasn't about to chicken out now he was so close to seeing her again.

Jack continued to stalk back the way they had come. "Damn fool," Bud heard him mutter. "I'll send the taxi back for you in an hour." Then he was gone.

Bud turned his attention back to Triumphant. "Can you take me to her?"

Triumphant stuck her chin out and peered down her nose at him. "I cannot."

Disappointment welled within Bud. "Why not?"

"Humans are not permitted to enter the Faerie Realm."

"Why not?"

"'Tis against the rules."

"They're silly rules."

Triumphant's lips twitched. Bud could have sworn she was amused. "Every rule is set down for a reason."

"Well, what is the reason I can't enter your world?"

Silence ensued. Bud saw momentary consternation flicker in Triumphant's eyes.

Mulling the question over, as if uncertain how to answer, she finally admitted, "I don't know the reason."

Relief coursed through him. He would see Glory today. "Take me to her."

"I cannot."

"Why not? Cast a glamour and take me there."

"'Tis not possible."

Jeez! "Surely you must be able to do something?" He hadn't meant to sound so impatient or rude but some of Jack's irritation had rubbed off on him.

Triumphant was clearly annoyed by his shift in attitude. Her knuckles tightened around the arrow she still carried in one hand. "I can do anything I want."

"I need to see Glory. I need to know how she is. Is she well?" He pressed his hand against his heart. "Is she as sad as me?"

"Well?" Bud asked, after several seconds of tense silence.

Triumphant placed the arrow back in the pouch and slung her bow over the same shoulder. "Glory's heart is drowning with sadness."

"Then you must let me help her."

"My duty is not to you. I serve Glory, my family and the forest."

"Then you won't help me." Bud's heart was in his throat, his disappointment acute.

"I cannot."

Jeez! He was fed up with the cannots. "She's unhappy." He patted his chest. "I can feel her unhappiness here. It will help lift her spirits to see me."

"'Tis true her spirits would be lifted," Triumphant agreed. "'Tis also true I cannot do what you ask."

"I thought we'd cleared that little matter up."

"Those are the rules."

Bud was beginning to feel weary. "Please?"

"I don't know the reason behind why you shouldn't enter my world, but I do know there is a very real danger you will never be able to return to your own world if you do."

Bud didn't hesitate. "I'll take my chances."

"You're prepared to venture into our world knowing you may never be able to return to your own."

"I am."

She leaned forward, as if interested in his words and amazed that he dared to take such a chance.

Bud decided Triumphant was warming to him. Her fierce expression had softened and a spark of indecision clouded her unusual violet eyes. He was beginning to believe there was a possibility he would see Glory again. He smiled, his white teeth flashing, animating his features and enlivening his eyes.

***

To Triumphant, his aura brightened and as she studied him, she realized something else. The relentless rain of the past few days had all but petered out to a light drizzle.

Glory had stopped crying. The trees crowded less, standing taller towards the break in the clouds. A promise of soft blue sky peeked through along with a small ray of sunlight, reaching down through the treetops, bouncing from branch to branch until it reached the forest floor.

The ray of light poured over Bud, illuminating him, as if in welcome. What portent was this? Triumphant didn't know what any of this meant but knew it to be significant. The sun did not shine so benevolently upon a human for no reason at all.

"As Captain of the Sentry, I must regretfully inform you that you are not permitted entrance to our world, but as Gloriane's sister, my feelings are torn. I feel for you both. The pain is real. I can see that. But truly, what good would it do you both? Eventually you would have to leave and the pain would be no easier. Indeed, in all likelihood, 'twill be greater. There can only be more tears."

"You are right sister dearest. As always."

Startled, Triumphant and Bud twirled to witness Glory materialize beside them.

Bud sucked in a huge dollop of oxygen. "Glory!"

"Bud!"

"No!" Triumphant stretched out her arms when she realized what her sister was about to do. "Glory! No!"

But it was too late. Glory was already in Bud's arms and their lips were touching in the most intimate of ways.

Embarrassed by such a scandalous display of affection, Triumphant averted her eyes. What could she do? She loved her sister dearly, but she had never failed in her duty before.

The murmuring of the two lovers filled her with fear for her sister, but she also experienced a curiosity she had never known and in that moment, the image of Jack nimbly jumped center stage into her minds-eye. In that unwelcome image, he was kissing her as Bud was kissing Glory.

Deeply, openly, wantonly.

Shocked beyond all measure, she broke her perfect track record, communicated to her Sentry to say nothing to anyone and translocated to her home, her mission of protecting Glory a total failure.

Bud's entrance to the Faerie Realm was now up to Glory and if anyone were to ask, Triumphant would say she had seen absolutely nothing.

Not a thing.

≈ CHAPTER 12 ≈

Bud's fingers linked with Glory's. Hands down at their sides, their faces almost touching, she gazed adoringly into his eyes. His breathing quickened and he leaned in to kiss her. Glory blinked rapidly and cleared her throat. She backed away. "Nay. Let's not." She looked over her shoulder. "There are eyes everywhere."

Bud was as anxious as a boy on his first date. All he had thought about for the past few days was being with Glory. Now here he was, in another world, with her just a kiss away, and she was saying no. If he leaned forward just a fraction, his lips would touch hers.

Glory saw Bud's eyes darken. Saw his intent and desperately wanted those wonderful lips on hers. Conscious he was in her world now, she was acutely aware Triumphant had done an amazing thing by retreating when she should have refused to allow Bud into their world.

She also knew they were being watched by Triumphant's sentry.

"Not here," she whispered, her fingers dropping away from his. "I've provided enough fuel for gossip within the forest without allowing more to develop. There are eyes everywhere."

Pushing the knowledge that her parents, if they didn't already know, would learn about her flagrant violation within the hour, she turned and began to walk into the forest. "Come." She waved to him to follow her. "We will retreat to Tree."

Bud looked all around but couldn't see anything or anyone. Unseen eyes watching him kiss Glory wasn't his idea of a good time and he realized his selfish desire to see her again held serious ramifications for Glory. "I didn't give any thought as to how this would affect you."

Glory lifted an index finger to her lips as a signal to speak softly. "'Tis I who brought you here, not you. There's no time for regrets. We must enjoy your visit to my world while you can. You will not be able to stay long I'm sure."

"So when do we go through the portal," he asked.

Glory laughed. "We're already through it."

"We are!" Bud looked around him. Was it really as easy as that?

Having landed on the other side of the portal in a world so similar to his own, surely he should have felt some sense of discomfort at the very least. There was none.

"I didn't feel anything. Everything looks the same." He touched the bark of a tall oak, the petals of a delicate primrose, the frond of a dark leafy fern. His hands patted his own torso in a searching motion. "I feel the same. I'm still the same height? I thought I would only be a few inches tall."

"'Tis the Faerie Glamour," she said. "Everything is not always as it seems. Vibrations in this realm are finer, the life spans longer. As to size, we are smaller although it does not appear to be so."

Bud's rain-soaked jeans and jacket, which had stuck to his skin only minutes before, were already beginning to steam dry from his body heat. Peeling his jacket off, he slung it over a shoulder with the crook of one finger, and ambled along behind Glory, happy for her to lead the way. "It's warmer too."

"Why do you think we wear so few clothes?" Glory winked saucily at him.

He grinned. "I'm surprised you're wearing anything at all. I thought you said faeries didn't wear clothes."

"They don't. Then they do. We're a contrary lot and are free to dress as we please in the forest. Except when at court. Then we must be clothed in our finest."

Glory wore a skimpy lightweight shift that looked as if it had been spun with gold. It's scooped neckline dipped so low in both the front and back that nothing was left to his imagination. The hem barely skimmed her taut buttocks. Deliberately he slowed down so he could catch delicious glimpses of rounded flesh. His fingers itched to touch. Propriety and the knowledge there were spying eyes hidden amongst the branches kept his hands at his sides.

A rush of need arose within him. The craving to bury himself deep inside this glorious woman and tell her how much she had changed his life forever was almost overwhelming. "Where are we going?"

Glory turned to face him. She looked as if she wanted to throw herself into his arms, but to his frustration, she didn't. "To my home. The Glory Tree."

All the trees looked the same to him. They had trunks, branches and leaves. "How far is it?" How the hell did one live in a tree?

"'Tis over yonder." She pointed to an enormous oak that must have been as old as the forest itself. Awed, his neck rocked back as he looked at the height and breadth of Glory's home.

The roots of Tree, as she called it, stretched its tentacles out in a large circumference, wending and weaving across the earth's floor before tunneling beneath the ground. Its trunk grew wide, strong and tall. The branches and leaves reached out with health and vigor, announcing, if anyone was in doubt, that it was an important tree.

Glory walked over to stand beside the trunk, and patted her hand gently against the bark. "Tree. I introduce to you my human friend, Bud Chandler." She gestured to Bud to join her. To Bud, it seemed Tree acknowledged Glory by sending out waves of reciprocal love.

Denial was uppermost in his mind. His imagination was working overtime. He could believe in the existence of faeries. But trees with emotions and thoughts? No. Surely not? Bud also sized up the comforts of living in a tree. As far as he could tell, there weren't any. He wanted to make love to Glory, but if there were eyes watching and only a grand old tree for shade, he couldn't see that being a possibility.

How did one get privacy around here? How could he make love to Glory with the world watching on? Unconsciously, he rubbed his butt as his imagination planted virtual splinters in his skin. It appeared any up close and personal time would be out of the question.

"It's a beautiful tree. Magnificent."

Glory beamed. "And thoughtful too."

A thoughtful tree. "How?"

"He shades me when it's hot. He makes me a bed of the softest leaves to sleep upon, and treats me with respect. The Glory Tree is one of the more senior trees of the forest. There are only a few loftier than he."

Bud stood beside Glory looking up into the thick canopy of leaves and branches and tried to ignore her heady scent. "I'm grateful you're well looked after. But I don't understand how a tree can do all that you say?"

She placed both hands carefully against the rough bark. "I'll show you. Rest your hands like this against Tree's trunk."

Was it hug a tree day today? Bud complied even though he felt a little foolish, but when she instructed him to watch, he watched. He couldn't have said where the magic began or where it ended. One second they were standing outside Tree, and the next they were standing in a living room, of sorts.

Light streamed in through irregular shaped windows, knotholes, and the room he found himself in appeared to be round. Chairs fashioned from wood and seats padded with silken leaves were located by a large window on the far side.

There was an abundance of climbing roses and trumpet shaped

flowers growing inside the room. They were everywhere, hanging from the ceiling, spilling over furniture, carpeting the floor beneath their feet. Just like his bedroom at home. Sort of.

"Where are we?" He moved to an irregular-shaped window knowing he wasn't going to be comfortable with what he would see. He looked out, only to stagger back seconds later. His mouth gaped foolishly. "We're inside your tree." Not just inside either. They were way, way high up, almost to the top of the great trunk. He took another look out the window. It was difficult to glimpse the forest floor below for all of Tree's leaves and branches. He peered down at his hands and torso. This meant he was tiny. How could that be?

Glory clapped her hands capturing his attention. "'Tis so clever of you to notice. Let me introduce you to Tree."

Bud's eyebrows twitched but he said nothing. He was too astonished to think.

"Tree. Bud Chandler is my guest and no mention of what goes on between us is to pass down to even the smallest of your branches, leaves or roots."

She paused, waiting for a moment. Bud heard nothing, but he understood she was communicating with Tree. He caught himself beginning to believe Tree could talk. Oh brother! Information overload. Bud felt a sudden need to sit down.

As his thought passed through his mind, Tree placed a seat behind him. Apparently, Tree could read minds as well. Bud sank gratefully into the makeshift chair. If Tree could read minds, then already, it would know what else was on his mind.

As if in answer, Tree immediately formed what looked suspiciously like a bed in the corner of the room. Bud blinked twice and looked again. "Oh no!" he exclaimed. "Oh no!"

Glory literally flew to Bud's side, worry creasing a line across her brow. "What is it? What's wrong?"

Staring over Glory's shoulder, Bud tensed when Tree began to reassemble the leaves into what looked suspiciously like a hammock.

"Tree can read my thoughts."

Glory laughed. "Nay. 'Tis not possible. You're human."

"I swear it can read my thoughts."

"How so? 'Tis a puzzle indeed. What is it you thought?"

The hammock behind Glory rocked rhythmically, backwards and forwards, backwards and forwards. "Never mind."

Bud dragged his attention away from the swinging hammock and gripped Glory by her forearms. "Are you certain no one can hear us except Tree."

"I have instructed Tree so. Nothing of what happens here will be revealed to any of the faerie. Tree is my private sanctuary."

"Can you instruct Tree not to listen to us as well?"

Glory frowned. "'Tis not something I've ever asked of it."

The notion that every thought could be heard by Tree, especially if they did get the chance to use that hammock, was a far more effective deterrent than any cold shower.

A loud lip-smacking sound came from the corner and the hammock swung wildly as its pace increased.

Bud pointed at it. "Look at that. I think Tree has a warped sense of humor."

By the time Glory shot Bud a puzzled glance and turned to where he pointed, Tree had rearranged his leaves yet again, this time into an innocent leafy couch.

Bud was certain he heard Tree snicker.

"Mayhap the trip through the portal has affected you." Glory placed a hand on his brow.

Her touch was warm, soft and caring. "No," he croaked. "Tree can read my thoughts." Bud was in trouble. Big trouble. "Is there a chance you could instruct him not to watch as well as not listen? I want to kiss you but I'd prefer to do so in private."

"Oh Bud. You are funny. But if it makes you more comfortable,

I'll ask."

Glory looked up into the cavernous heights of Tree. "Please refrain from listening to Bud and I while we join together. It makes Bud uncomfortable. Instead, be our eyes and ears on the outside world. Keep us informed of approaching visitors and do not allow entrance to other faerie for now."

Glory waited a few seconds in silence and then nodded. "Tree likes you."

"How do you know?"

"He is grateful to the one who dried my tears and put gladness back in my heart."

She didn't elaborate. Both knew the sadness would be back. Right now, they had each other. Right now, there was happiness to be explored.

Sinking to her knees, Glory knelt in front of him and placed her palms on his thighs. "I am grateful also."

Her hands reached up, cupped Bud's cheeks, and traced a path with her thumbs over his lips, relishing each dip and curve. She remembered with startling clarity their teasing gentleness. She recalled their seductive powers. He angled forward and their lips connected and exultation exploded within her. They were together again and 'twas a miracle beyond words.

'Twas as if the kiss washed away all doubt, all memory of their differences. When Bud opened his arms, Glory entered the circle of his embrace and as his strong lean arms enveloped her, she knew a sense of belonging and although she didn't know how or why, she knew this was meant to be. Their joining had been ordained from the very beginning of time. It must have been for no one could possibly feel as she did right now.

"Make love to me," she murmured, their kiss deepening.

Savoring. Devouring. Absorbing. It seemed as if she drowned in sensation after sensation. She heard her own protest when his lips left hers, but when the assault on her neck and collarbone began she begged him to continue. "Oh, Bud. More."

Glory waved a hand and Bud's clothes disappeared. That was more like it. Skin to skin was best. She heard Bud's sharp intake of breath and pulled away to gaze into the softest, warmest gray blue eyes. Lifting his glasses off his face, she hooked them on a willing branch.

He whispered. "I've missed you. I love you. I ache for you."

Glory placed a palm flat over his heart, pleased at its acceleration. "You need ache no longer."

But that was before she pushed Bud further back and sat astride him, resting her knees either side of his thighs. She whipped off her shift and leaned forward, and rubbed the tips of her breasts against Bud's chest hoping to create a different kind of ache inside him.

"Make love to me. Show me how much you love me," she whispered, and then softly sucked his bottom lip into her mouth.

Bud gathered her up in his arms and carried her to the hammock Tree had provided. "Your wish is my command."

Bud stared at the hammock which had begun to swing rhythmically, backwards and forwards as if they were already in the throes of making love.

"Tree makes it for me each night," Glory explained. "Though, 'tis not every night there are roses as well. Tree is most thoughtful."

Bud thought Tree most cheeky, that's what. "Are you sure he isn't listening?"

"I sense he is guarding us and looking outward. He won't listen. We're safe until dawn."

Twilight was approaching and soon night would descend upon Newberry Forest, swallowing up what was left of the day. Bud knew Jack would have sent a taxi back as promised to collect him, but that time was long past. Jack would be worried and the knowledge was a new burden Bud carried on his shoulders. He would have to return to the real world and explain his disappearance to his friend who very clearly refused to believe.

Soon.

Tonight he would remain with Glory in her world and rediscover the delights and fulfillment of being with the one he loved. Besides, he had no clue in how to return to his world without her help.

The hammock was a whole lot more comfortable than Bud envisaged. He didn't know how Tree had done it. The leaves were the softest his skin had ever touched. Shrugging away any lingering thoughts about tomorrow and what it might bring, he said, "I've always wanted to sleep in a hammock, although never one made from branches and leaves."

"'Tis most comfortable." Mischief twinkled merrily in Glory's eyes and she pursed her mouth into a coy pout. "There will be no sleeping in this hammock tonight. Not if I have my way."

"My darling," Bud placed her on the bed of leaves and eased himself gingerly into it, hoping nothing sharp would poke any of his private parts. "You can have your way as many times as you like. I'm willing, but who knows how long my body will last."

Glory rubbed her cheek against his, enjoying the texture of rough against smooth. Her hands linked behind his back and she pressed herself against him, skin-to-skin, cheek to cheek. "We are in the Faerie Realm now. Everything is possible."

With Glory in his arms, he felt he was where he should be and did not feel out of place, as perhaps he should have done. Until meeting her, he hadn't known he could feel or care about someone so deeply. He caressed her soft porcelain skin with a tender restraint. He held her face between his palms and stared into her eyes and told her without mincing words just how much she meant to him. "I love you Glory. I barely know you but my heart knows and loves you."

Glory's eyes glowed with pleasure. "I love you too."

Thirsty as a dry sponge, his heart greedily accepted her love until it was full, and when he thought it could hold no more, it continued to expand until it spilled out with abundance and joy.

Love willingly given.

Love willingly received.

Then Bud showed Glory exactly how much he loved her.

He began with her mouth. Seeking. Exploring. Plundering. He progressed from one end of her body to the other, showering her with kisses, drowning her with displays of love.

Eventually, Bud had to breathe. Raising his head, he registered Glory's languid azure eyes. "Are you OK?"

"I feel all tingly." She ran her hands across his broad shoulders and down his defined biceps before sneaking over to trace their way down his torso, around to his back and down over his butt. She cupped his firm backside and wrapped her legs about his hips and locked her ankles together. "Got you," she whispered against his mouth.

"Right where you want me," he added and without waiting to be invited, he eased into her and began a series of slow rhythmic thrusts, his eyes never leaving hers. The hammock rocked too and fro as Bud thrust again and again increasing his pace and gathering momentum until, together, there was only one place to go.

Heavenward.

***

Glory peeled off the rose petals stuck to various parts of her anatomy and giggled. "You didn't know that could happen, did you? Neither did I."

Bud lay alongside Glory, one hand caressing the length of her back, the other crooked beneath his head as he watched in fascination as she divested them both of the rose petals that had fallen over them like confetti at a wedding. He winked. "We should do it again to make certain it wasn't a fluke."

Glory purred like a cat as she responded to his hand meandering over her stomach. "I love the way you think."

Their lovemaking had been intense and adventurous. At the apex of their climax, the hammock had swung so wildly, it had flung them both into the air. Their minds and hearts engaged in the pleasure of joining, neither had been aware they had left the hammock until both were suspended mid-air. As the euphoria had subsided, Bud laid a final lingering kiss upon Glory's inviting mouth and brushed the soft, damp tendrils of hair away from her face. Only then did he realize there was no hammock supporting them.

'Twas difficult for Glory to understand how or come up with an explanation as to why they remained suspended in the air without a glamour being cast. It was a first for her. She understood how she had flown and managed to stay airborne. But Bud? That was a conundrum.

Upon realizing where he was, the shock had sent him plummeting like a stone back into the hammock. Fortunately, Tree was strong or his branches and limbs could have broken. As Bud landed onto the leafy hammock with Glory still in his arms, they noted the entire room was littered with rose petals.

Plucking them from Bud's skin, Glory sighed and took a moment to apologize to the wild roses and morning glory growing throughout her home before they took umbrage and began to form thorns in defense of such treatment.

Immediately new buds formed on the vines and roses and Glory took heart. "My apology is accepted." She pointed to the new flowers. "Buds for Bud," she declared and exploded into gales of laughter before collapsing back into the safe warmth of his arms.

Bud wasn't mystified at his unexpected flight around the room. He assumed and still did that it had been Glory's doing. "It just keeps getting better and better."

Glory propped herself up on one elbow hearing the wonder in his voice. "What does?"

Bud tightened his grip around her waist and pulled her back down. There was no way he was going to let her go before he had to. "You and me. Together."

With her head resting on his chest, she tilted her chin upwards and he bent his head down to hers and kissed her forehead and she snuggled in and they drifted off to sleep.

***

Tree stood resolute, strong in will as well as in stature.

Tree guarded Glory and Bud the human and tried hard not to listen. But the heart of Tree warmed as he sensed the love shared between his inhabitants. He was pleased they liked his gift of bedding before he once again turned his senses outward.

His mistress's secret was safe, and he was as excited as a young sapling upon its first meeting with the golden orb in the sky above. The time was almost at hand, just as the Ancients had foretold.

<h1 style="text-align:center">≈ CHAPTER 13 ≈</h1>

Glory thrust a tatty book under his nose. It appeared to be made out of petrified cabbage leaves. "Fruit of the Forest Medley or Wild Mushroom Salad."

"The Fruit Medley." Taking the book, Bud stared at the language written on each leaf written in faerie. Why did he have the oddest feeling he should be able to read the words, and just when he thought he could, the writing shimmered and became indecipherable?

Turning the book over in his palms, he checked the spine for a title and a past memory was reawakened. His heart skittered in his chest. "This book. What is it?"

"'Tis the complete Recipe Glamour Book of Cooking."

Bud's eyes lit with interest. "Does this mean you have others similar to this one?"

"Any faerie worth their weight in primroses has a book of glamour for every occasion but every faerie has one of these. Other glamour books are presented to us on the day we graduate."

"Graduate from what?"

"Our apprenticeship. A faerie is always learning. Creating recipes is but a short and simple course and completed early in our training. A faerie lost in the forest needs to know how to forage for food."

"What about other apprenticeships?" He wanted to know. "Are they easy to complete as well?"

"They should be." She rolled her eyes and pulled a face. "I must be honest. I possessed a tendency to drift off in the middle of my lessons. I was always being sidetracked by one thing or another. I still am." Glory's cheeks were rosy. "If I'd learned the art of evasion, Sergeant Delaney would never have captured me."

Bud lifted a tendril of wayward hair from her cheek. He tucked it behind one ear before tilting her chin up to meet his gaze. "I'm glad you're not perfect. We never would have met if you had."

Glory blushed an even deeper shade of pink. "'Tis true. My life is richer for knowing you."

"Mine too." Bud wanted so much to always be a part of her life and the impossibility of it left him agitated and downhearted. "Just how old is this book?" Some of the leaves fell to the floor. He picked them up and tucked them back into place. "I'm sorry. The pages are all mussed up."

"'Tis nothing I can't sort out later. As for the age of my book, I don't know its age but it's much older than me as it belonged to another before me. They are handed down from faerie to faerie. Mine, I know, is very old."

Just how old was Glory? Maybe she read his mind because she answered his question without him having to ask. "'Tis but a mere two hundred and forty years since I was born."

Bud inhaled moisture into his lungs and coughed savagely, his eyes watering. When it was possible to speak again, he jokingly gasped, "My God! I've made love to an older woman!"

During his coughing fit he had come to a horrifying realization. Glory would still be alive long after his bones had turned to dust in the ground and he was but a faint memory to those left behind.

Reaching out, he tugged her, bowl and all, into his arms. More pages from the glamour book still clutched in one hand fell to the floor.

He grinned. "I prefer mature women."

"I'm older than you but in this world I'm considered young. I'm not so mature or I wouldn't keep making foolish errors of judgment."

"Don't negate yourself. I love you for who you are. No one is perfect."

"Triumphant is perfect," Glory said. "In every way."

He could see she really believed that. "In your eyes, perhaps. But in mine, you are the one who is perfection."

She responded with a sigh and a wistful smile. "You're so good for me." Kissing him lightly, she twisted in his arms and gestured for him to rescue the pages from her glamour book from off the floor. "You make me feel like I could do anything."

He kissed her. Soundly. "You can." Reluctantly, he released her, scooped up the loose leaves and handed them over. "Can I look at your other books?"

Glory hesitated. Some of her books were not handed down but were created for the individual and therefore were very private. They were to be shared with no other. She argued with herself that Bud already had touched one and the sky hadn't fallen. She peered out a knothole just to ensure the sky was still there. Everything appeared normal, so she placed the recipe book in her empty cooking bowl and another even tattier and torn one materialized in her free hand.

"Here." She figured she was safe giving him this one even though a sense of unease overtook her. She shrugged it off as Bud carefully opened the fragile pages. What harm could it possibly do?

Besides, Bud couldn't read the words for he was not of the faerie. Some of their laws were silly indeed and she would tell Father exactly that next time she was summoned to court. She had the awful feeling it would be soon, and there would be a whole lot of explaining to do and penance to undertake.

Bud leafed through the book, caressing each page as if it were a precious thing. He looked up and smiled and her knees took to knocking.

"I love old books," he said. "My father collected them. They're in my mother's library. In fact, I'm almost positive there's one similar to this on her shelves."

"'Tis not possible. This is a book of personalized glamour. No faerie would part with one of their books." She hefted the huge bowl from under her arm. "Fruit Medley you said?"

Bud nodded absently, his attention captivated by the book in his hands. "I think you're wrong. Dad told me it was centuries old."

Despite Bud's assertion, Glory was confident he was wrong and dismissed the notion immediately. "So my books are more interesting than me."

Bud flipped the pages closed and gently placed the large volume on her kitchen table. "When I get home I'm going to find it and prove to you that it is. It was important to Dad, and now I want to know why?"

Bud pointed to her open wardrobe on the far side of the room. "But right now I'm more interested in those."

Glory looked, although she didn't need to. "Oh. Those."

"What are they?"

She rolled her eyes. "Just what they look like. Wings."

"Why are wings hovering in your wardrobe?"

"'Tis but several sets of training wings."

"Training wings?"

"Faerie wings do not appear until we reach adolescence." She walked over and fingered the tattiest pair with a wistful smile. "Until they do, we use training wings. That's what these are. I'm sentimentally attached to them."

"How incredible." Bud had followed. He fingered the gossamer like things. "Who would have thought? What about those ones?"

Both stared at another set of wings suspended mid air in the wardrobe. Bud reached in, lifted them out and held them up before him. He thought he had seen everything and that nothing else would amaze or astound him, but these did.

Gold thread was woven into the sheer gossamer wings. They glistened in the light filtering through the knotholes of Tree. So soft and fragile in appearance he could see clear through them. Half afraid his coarser touch would cause them to disintegrate he let them go and they remained suspended in the air in front of him.

"These are my most Royal Wings. I wear them for formal occasions only. Only those of direct royal descent have wings with gold. You can touch them. They won't melt. They're stronger than they look."

"How do they go on?" Bud once again hoisted them high in front of him, his arms outstretched. They were as light as they appeared.

"There are magic words." Glory quickly recited them once. "You say the words three times and on they go. 'Tis a simple procedure." Seeing the assessing look in his eyes as he inspected them, she giggled. "It won't work for you. You're not of the faerie."

He looked up and smiled. "I prefer flying without wings."

Laughing, Glory pointed out the obvious. "Once not so long ago you would never have thought such a thing."

"Except in my dreams," Bud acknowledged, and released his hold on her wings, leaving them to hover on their own once again. Bud stole a quick kiss and grinned. "Making love to you is what I prefer most of all. You're the only delicious person-faerie I've ever met. The *only* faerie I've ever met."

He tweaked her imperial nose and pretended a light heart. "Want me to show you how wonderful I believe you are?"

Glory fluttered her long lashes. "As soon as you've eaten. You'll need all your strength to keep up with me."

Bud winked. "I'm fit and healthy. I think you'll find you'll need extra energy to keep up with me."

"Alas, I was referring to sending you home. 'Tis harder to pass back through the portal than to come through it." Unable to hide the sadness creeping in, it made a mockery out of her cheery smile. Their gazes met and locked. Soon, memories would be all they had to warm their nights and brighten their days.

Glory cleared her throat and spun on her feet, breaking the moment. She would enjoy her time with Bud no matter how short it was. "I'll be quicker than a flea on a cat. I just need to get a special ingredient from the pantry."

Bud let her go, knowing her quick exit was so she could collect herself. There was no pantry in Tree as far as he could see and he was sure a glamour was all she needed to conjure her *special ingredient* for their breakfast. He ached to call her back, pull her into his arms and voice what his heart wanted to say. *Come with me. Come with me back through the portal.*

It was futile of course. She would never survive in his world and if he were to remain here, his family would be beside themselves with worry. There were his patients too. Many of them just beginning to open up to him. He couldn't leave them in limbo knowing their growing trust in him could be destroyed in seconds. For some, their very lives depended on his constant presence. Abandoning them was not an option.

With Glory absent, he turned his attention back to the still hovering royal wings. He chewed on the inside of his right cheek as he tried to recall the exact words Glory had recited earlier. He mumbled several words under his breath. He shook his head knowing they weren't the right ones. He tried again, testing each word, rolling them carefully over his tongue, a crazy nervousness swirling in his stomach. This time he spoke aloud.

"Wings be light, wings be airy.

Place yourselves on this royal faerie."

The wings vibrated as he spoke and seemed to sparkle. The golden thread began to emit a strange glow. He felt his eyes grow big and round in surprise. His eyeballs darted in their sockets towards where Glory had gone and then back to the wings.

He repeated the rhyme. Heck! The wings were shimmering, beginning to flex and flutter lightly and they were gravitating towards him. He took a step back, suddenly wary. But he couldn't help it. He wanted to know if the spell would work on him even though he uttered, "Poppycock! You're no faerie." It wouldn't work he was sure of it.

Just in case, he recited the rhyme a third time.

The wings disappeared. Where the heck had they gone? "Glory," he called out. "Are your wings with you?" Jeez! The words coming out of his mouth defied rationale. With no reply forthcoming, he looked to the left and then to the right. An uneasy feeling churned in his stomach. Twisting his head round he peered over his left shoulder. The wings were definitely behind him. He whipped full circle, expecting, no, praying they would be hovering mid-air.

Nope. They were gone.

And he knew exactly where they would be and he couldn't believe he had successfully completed a faerie glamour. He wasn't a faerie. Had coming through the portal changed things?

"Wings. What are you up to?"

Once again, he felt foolish. He was talking to Glory's ceremonial wings. Had she not just said only a member of the royal family could wear them? He spun a third time, feeling increasingly more like a dog chasing his own tail.

"Oh please, no!" he exclaimed far louder than intended. His head darted from side to side as he assessed just how bad the situation was. Breathe he said to himself, reverting to the spiel he gave to clients when they needed calming. *Breathe deeply. Clear your mind. Breathe in. That's it. Breathe out.*

He tried this for a few seconds, and the oxygen did help to clear his head. A little. But then it began to fill with a jumble of wild, crazy notions, and he dug deep to find his common sense in an effort to not give credence to them.

Excitement flowed through his veins. If he had wings, perhaps he could fly as well. Gripped with a sense of daring he considered the possibilities and before he even knew he was going to do it, a rhythmic rhyme filtered from his subconscious and spilled from his lips.

"Fly on high with ease and care.
Fly Your Highness through the air."

The familiar buzzing, the same sound he heard when Glory recited a glamour began to fill his head and he vibrated, from within.

He repeated the rhyme two more times and miraculously, the wings began to flap. Slowly at first, but as they swooshed through the air he could feel their inherent power. Before he could even begin to think of another instruction, up, up, up he went.

He had lift off. The wings, opened and closed, flexed and stretched just like he'd seen butterflies do.

He was flying. He was weightless. The possibilities were endless. It was the weirdest sensation. He found himself undeterred and eager to continue. As if the wings sensed his keenness, their pace picked up and the excitement grew within him. *Jeez Louise!* He was flying all by himself. The wings beat faster, sending him hurtling round and round the room.

He knew the speed was attributed to the churning excitement roiling in him, but he was unable to control his feelings as he went faster and faster until everything was a complete blur. He was growing dizzy and disoriented and found there was little enjoyment in flying at this speed. He attempted to slow down. Any second now he would break the sound barrier.

"Wings stop!" he commanded with more than a hint of panic.

What a huge error of judgment those two words proved to be. Tree must have been keeping an eye on him for when Bud fell like a stone from high up in its cavernous heights, the hammock swung out and caught him before he ended up plastered on the floor like a wet dish rag.

And that was how Glory found Bud. Swinging wildly back and forth, half in and half out of the hammock with a hundred broken heads of morning glory, as well as a collection of rose petals scattered over him and her royal wings still firmly attached to his back.

Hair disheveled, glasses askew over eyes as round as apples, he carried an aura of absolute disbelief. The bowl, filled with her Fruits of the Forest Medley, slipped through numb fingers, sending strawberries, blueberries, blackberries, diced apple and nectarine onto the floor. Sticky juice puddled in a pool at her feet.

"How?" Never could she have imagined such a thing. She was speechless.

Consternation cut deep frown lines on Bud's forehead. "You're the one who should know that?" He combed shaky fingers through his hair, dislodging more flowers, and they fell about him like confetti onto Tree's floor. "I only repeated what you said."

"Three times?"

"Three times."

Glory pressed a hand against her breastbone. "'Tis a miracle."

"One minute I was safely on the ground and then next I was whizzing about Tree like an out-of-control demented bat."

His analogy made Glory giggle. He certainly did appear demented. She could not in any way comprehend how Bud could possibly have got her own personal glamour to work for him. She stifled back another giggle.

The hammock swung gaily. Bud growled, "What's so funny?"

"You are. If we had cameras in this world, I'd take a shot of you right now."

"How about taking a shot at getting me out of here?"

"Nay." She crossed her arms and lifted her chin in a show of defiance. "I think not."

"Why not?"

"Tell me how you got Royal Wings to fly." She wanted to figure out how he had accomplished the glamour. She could have understood it a trifle if he had managed to get her training wings to work but the royal ones? How could this be?

Once the Royal Wings were on, she knew Bud would be telepathically connected to Father, the King, and if there had been doubt before, there was no doubt now. Father knew there was a stranger in the forest.

"I have no idea why they worked for you," she admitted. Naturally, Bud would be unaware of being linked to Father. How could he know, Glory surmised, and as Bud watched her, his soft gray eyes glinted with something else, something intimate. She knew she had to get those wings off him before he transmitted thoughts no girl ever wanted their father to know.

However, Bud had already begun to chant the glamour to fly again and before her very eyes, he took off like a bumblebee in a garden full of flowers. It was the funniest thing she had ever seen. She forgot all about being afraid of Father as unexpected bubbles of laughter welled up like a spring from her lips.

Collapsing back onto a chair Tree kindly provided so she could view the entertainment in comfort, she rocked back and forth racked with the hilarity of the situation, until she clutched her sides in pain from laughing too much. "No more."

"I've no control," Bud yelled as he zoomed about Tree. "How do you direct these things?"

Unfortunately, before she could reply, he zipped out a knothole and into the forest. Instantly her laughter was replaced with trepidation. Bud was flying in the forest. Out in the open. Away from her and Tree's protection.

She flew out after him.

She needn't have worried. He was flying between Tree's

branches like that demented bat he'd mentioned earlier, but Tree was kind enough to move out of harm's way each time Bud looked as if he was about to crash into one of its branches

"Good Tree," she murmured.

Stark naked, Glory sat upon a limb perched high above the ground and truly enjoyed the moment. 'Twas a pity Bud had put his clothes back on. The sight of seeing him flying naked would have been ultimately satisfying.

"I'd be enjoying this," he called out as he zoomed past Glory for the ninetieth time. "If I wasn't so afraid I'd hurt something."

"Do not be concerned. Tree is quite safe."

"It's not Tree I'm worried about," he yelled as he zipped past once more. "It's me."

'Twas as well the rain had stopped. Her wings on Bud were creating a light breeze as he flew past each time sprinkling her with moisture but not enough to cause discomfort. "You don't look afraid. 'Tis excitement I see in your eyes."

"Excitement!" Bud shouted from the far side of Tree's outermost branches. "What you see is sheer, unadulterated terror!"

"I don't believe you. 'Tis a tale you are telling. You love to fly. I've heard you say it and I know it to be true." Swinging her legs back and forth, Glory searched her memory for a glamour to remove her Royal Wings and land Bud safely at the same time. Conjuring a book of glamour, she leafed through the pages, knowing it was probably a waste of time.

"Can you see anything?" Bud called out.

Glory shook her head, the edges of her lips pulled downwards into a glum expression. She stared blankly at the book. There would be nothing written in its pages on how to remove wings from a human. She would have to create a special one.

It was early dawn. The air was full of chirping birds and flapping wings as Bud unsettled the air about them. They left their nests to see what all the fuss was about and squawked raucously at him from a safe distance among the branches of other trees. The sound was deafening, and it seemed as if they were laughing at his plight.

He was beginning to feel nauseous. "Come on Glory," he called out as he zoomed between two thick branches. "This is no longer funny."

"How did you get them to stop before?"

He whizzed around Tree once more. "I asked them to. If I do that again," he circled around Tree once more then reappeared, "I'll probably kill myself." He whizzed by again.

"Fiddledeedee!" Glory clapped her hands, a relieved smile upon her lips. "'Tis simple. Instruct Royal Wings to slow down. Say it three times."

Instruct them to slow down. How stupid could he be? Heck! He should have known that. He didn't hesitate for a second. "Royal Wings slow down."

Immediately, his speed began to decrease and relief surged through his veins. He eyed the terra-firma with an obscene reverence. He'd never loved the sight of the ground so much. He would get down on his hands and knees and praise its beauty when he landed.

"See." Called Glory and clapped her hands once more. "'Tis easy." Still, she was puzzled. What was it about Bud that enabled him to use faerie glamour so effortlessly?

The Faerie Chain would be gossiping about what they had seen and it would be another story to explain to Father. Her list of misdemeanors was growing at an alarming rate. A nervous gurgle sounded in her throat and she clasped a hand to her neck. It was time Bud went home. All laughter died on her lips and sudden sadness clouded the all too brief happiness in her eyes. Her handsome Bud would soon be with her no longer.

"Oh Bud," she whispered for her ears only. "How will I survive without you?"

Flying much lower to the ground, at a safer and more controlled speed Bud could see everything now instead of one long blur. With the ability to focus on Glory sitting on her branch above, and after flying past for the umpteenth time, he witnessed the shift from happy to sad in her iridescent eyes.

The change had taken only one complete circle of Tree and it seemed to him he could hear Tree sighing. *Soon. Soon. Soon.*

"Why did this all have to happen?" He muttered to God above. "Why? Would it not have been better to ignore my wishes? Don't get me wrong, I'll never regret meeting Glory, or having this experience of flying. They're wonderful gifts but now my memories will be filled with what I can't have. Heck! I wish I was footloose and faerie free!"

It only took a second. Bud witnessed the sudden horror in Glory's eyes, saw both her hands cover her mouth as she stifled back a scream but it was all too late. Too late to do anything but fall, for his wings had evaporated into the ether.

Down, down, down he went, like a boulder on a cliff face, rolling and bouncing it's way to the ground. The only thing to prevent serious injury was that he was already near the forest floor when it happened. The rain softened grass was still firm enough to jar his bones and rattle his teeth. He knew he would be covered from head to toe in bruises tomorrow.

He was only human after all.

***

Picking his bruised bones up off the ground, Bud told himself he was lucky not to have broken anything. He rotated his neck from side to side, placed a hand behind his neck and tilted his head back and looked skyward searching for Glory. A pervading feeling of doom leaked insidiously into his gut and began to eat an enormous hole in it.

He'd been speaking to God when he'd asked for someone to fly with and he'd got what he wanted. Having questioned God's motives, it appeared God had acted upon his latest request. Bud shook his head as if it would make order out of the jumbled chaos that was once his mind but all he felt was a sharp pain in his skull.

The inner connection he'd only been half aware of with Glory was gone. What had he done? What would he do now?

Standing for several long agonizing minutes, he listened for something, but the forest was eerily silent. Where only moments before there had been the raucous chatter of wildlife, now there was an eerie silence.

He peered up into Tree's branches. "Where is she? Where is our Glory?" Tree remained quiet and unbending.

Then another sound broke through the weird silence. A woman moaned, but it wasn't coming from above. Renewed hope zinged through his veins. He raced around Tree's expansive trunk in the hope that perhaps, all was not lost. And there she was. Lying on her back, holding her head in her hands. Because she was naked, Bud quickly ascertained there weren't any obvious signs of broken bones or open wounds.

"Thank you God. Thank you, thank you." He dropped down beside her and brushed her golden, tangled mass of hair away from eyes dulled with pain. "Are you okay?"

"My head hurts. Why won't the pain go away?"

"You fell from Tree."

Glory rubbed a palm across her brow and squeezed her eyes shut. "I did? Why was I up a tree?"

"Don't you remember? You were watching me fly."

Glory groaned. "This is no time for jokes. My head feels as if it's been split in two with an axe."

"Can you sit up? I had your Royal Wings on. Remember?"

She held out a hand so he could help her up. "Royal Wings?" Then she gasped, her hands flying to her body. "Oh my!"

"What is it? Where are you hurt?"

"Where are they?"

"My wings? I don't know. They've gone."

Glory appeared confused. "Gone? Where?"

"Back into Tree I suppose?"

Glory was looking at him oddly. "Where are my clothes?"

He didn't like the horrified tone in her voice. There was something unnatural about all of this. "Your clothes?"

"In case you haven't noticed, I'm not wearing any." She moved to cover her body with her arms. "Where are they?"

"Faeries don't wear clothes most of the time." Now why was he telling her something she already knew? "Come on Glory. Stop joking with me."

Glory glared at him, as if he'd suddenly developed two heads. "Faeries! Did you fall from the tree too?"

A large leaf wafted down from Tree's branches to land at her feet. She picked it up and covered the apex between her legs.

"No, I fell from the sky." He shrugged out of his jacket and placed it over her shoulders.

"Thanks." She dropped the leaf and slipped her arms into the sleeves and zipped it up. "The fall must have loosened something inside your skull. Or mayhap it's me? Why am I talking like this?" She lightly thumped the side of her head with the base of her palm a couple of times. She winced. "Did you just say you fell from the sky?"

Bud's jaw clenched, but he managed to speak without revealing his frustration. "That's correct."

Glory held her head in both hands. "Yeah! Right! And I'm the tooth faerie."

That was when Bud realized Glory was suffering from partial amnesia.

≈ **CHAPTER 14** ≈

Bud cupped his hands to his mouth and called for Triumphant several times, walking about the glade beneath Tree's branches searching for any sign of Glory's sister.

"Anyone would think you were the one with the bump on the head." Glory trailed behind him, nursing the swelling near her temple. "And who is this Triumphant anyway?"

Bud swiveled suddenly and Glory slammed into him. Steadying her, he tilted her chin and searched her eyes for recognition. Nothing. Damn! "She's your sister. Surely you remember your own sister?"

She blinked and chewed a fingernail. "I have a sister?"

"How is it you remember me but not your family?"

In his field of expertise, he had encountered amnesia once or twice, but he was limited when it came to a faerie that thought she wasn't one.

"I don't know." Glory looked upwards and winced. "Was my sister up the tree as well? Mayhap she is hurt too?"

Bud cupped Glory's cheeks in his hands, his thumbs brushing her soft skin. "She wasn't with us."

"If she wasn't with us then why are you calling her?"

"She's Captain of the Faerie Sentry. All I have to do is call and she will come." He hoped. It had worked before.

Bud resumed his search of the glade. He called Triumphant's name over and over as he searched under leaves, lifted branches, and pressed his cheeks against the trunks of other trees and peered into ridiculously small knotholes.

"This is absurd." Glory planted her fists on her hips and stamped her feet. "You're crazy."

"I'm not crazy." He'd heard that phrase even more than usual of late.

"Why would you think such an idiotic thing anyway?"

"Because you told me you were one of the faerie."

If Glory couldn't remember who she was, she also wouldn't remember how they had met either. First and foremost, she was a faerie. He would not, could not deny Glory her heritage, no matter how tempting. If she discovered he had never tried to assist her in regaining her memory, she would never forgive him. Even if at this stage in the scheme of all things crazy, she thought him delusional.

He choked back the bitter urge to laugh. Perhaps this was a dream and it was him who was off his rocker, for no matter how loud or how often he called, Triumphant didn't appear and with each second ticking by, Glory was acting more and more as if it was he who had the problem.

He bent down and lifted the large frond of a fern. "Can we discuss this later? Right now, we have to find a way out of here."

The look of abject horror on Glory's face stopped him in his tracks.

"What is it?" He dropped the frond and grasped both her forearms. "Tell me. Are you all right?"

"Am I all right?" Glory exploded with irritation. "What do you mean we have to find a way out of here?" She tugged away from his grasp and stuck her hands in the pockets of his jacket. "Don't tell me we're lost."

"Of course not." He hoped the lie didn't sound forced. Newberry Forest had looked different in the heavy rain. Plus he'd had one too many drinks. Now he was no longer certain just how far into the woods he and Jack had ventured.

But then help came from an unexpected quarter. "Bud." A voice echoed in the early morning air. "Where the hell are you?"

Hiding the relief racing through him Bud grinned and cupped his hands either side of his mouth and yelled, "Over here. We're over here."

Help was at hand, although it was not from Triumphant. Jack had returned to the forest to look for him. No doubt worried when Bud hadn't turned up for the taxi last night.

He grinned. "See. We're not lost."

Glory cast Bud a disbelieving glare. "I hope that deep voice doesn't belong to my sister."

Biting back laughter, Bud said, "That's Jack. You've met Jack."

"Jack." Glory rolled his name over a few times. Her eyes brightened. "Oh yes. Your best friend. Right?"

"Right." How odd she should remember Jack, but not her own sister. The whole thing had him bamboozled.

The best course of action for now would be to visit a doctor to check that bump on her head then get Glory home to his apartment and map out a plan from there. They could both take a hot shower and find something for Glory to wear. It stood to reason, if she didn't believe she was a faerie, she wouldn't be zapping up clothes any time soon.

After that, he was going to knock back a stiff drink. Anything alcoholic would do.

Jack burst through a stand of trees prepared for the worse. Under one arm he carried a first-aid box and under the other a blanket. "Fuck me!" As eloquent as ever Jack strode over, his anger and relief plain to see. "Where the hell have you been? I've been up half the night searching for you after you didn't turn up for the taxi. I was about to call in reinforcements you dumb oaf."

Here we go. More explaining to do that no one would believe. "I was in the Faerie Realm."

Jack rolled his eyes and turned to Glory. "Have you been out here all night too?"

Bud swore he could see wheels turning in his friend's head. He would be mentally assessing Glory's disheveled and barely clothed state. Daggers of irritation flashed in Bud's eyes and he shot them at his friend. *Get your eyes off her. She's mine.*

Jack spotted the swelling on Glory's head and concern flashed in his eyes. "You're hurt." He reached out to touch the bump.

Glory winced and stepped backwards. "I fell from that tree there." She pointed to Tree accusingly.

Jack looked upwards. "How the hell did you climb up there? And more importantly, why?"

Bud agreed it was a hard tale to believe. The lowest branches of Tree were at least twelve feet above them and the gnarled roots provided no purchase on which to climb, unless one possessed a ladder or a trampoline. Or magic.

Bud grinned and flapped his arms. "Wings."

Glory audibly groaned. "Toadstools and rats droppings!"

Jack tsked. "I thought a rain-soaked night in the forest would have cured you of that nonsense."

"'Tis a pity I can't remember any of it." Glory said to Jack. "I'm certain 'twas eventful." She flourished a hand down the length of her torso. "Was I drunk too? Is this why I can't remember where I put my clothes?"

Jack snorted and his laughter rang loudly in the forest. "It must have been one hell of a night. How is it you're both so dry when you've spent the night out in the open?"

Bud winked and patted Tree's trunk with affection. "Magic."

"You're not going to give up are you?" Glory was clearly pissed. She tapped her bare toes impatiently on the ground.

He wasn't going to lie to her. "No. I'm not."

Jack handed him a blanket, opened the first-aid box and went into first-aid mode. Pouring clear liquid from a bottle onto a square gauze pad he dabbed the inflamed area and prattled on asking a litany of questions. "How do you feel? Do you have a headache? Is your vision blurred? What day of the week is it? What year are we in? Where do you live? What's you're phone number?"

"There's nothing wrong with me," Glory insisted. "Ouch! That stings." She started to answer his questions in quick succession. "I can see very well. Sharp and clear. And it is…?" The fingers of both hands flew to her mouth. Alarm flared in her eyes as comprehension dawned. "I don't remember what day it is?"

"I wouldn't worry about that," interrupted Bud. "Remembering members of your own family is far more important. Name some of them."

"I don't know." The last word came out as a wail. "I don't remember. Anything! Only that you say I have a sister called Triumphant. I don't remember her or what she looks like. I don't remember climbing that darned tree. I don't even know my last name." Frustration turned her eyes to an iridescent azure.

"Your last name is Faerie." Bud pointedly ignored Jack's barely controlled grunt of skepticism and hugged Glory's shoulders and pressed a soft kiss against her hair. "Your last name is Faerie. Don't worry my love. Everything will come back to you soon. These things don't last long."

Jack's sarcasm was evident when he said, "Listen to the expert. He knows about these things."

Missing the inference altogether, Glory all too logically pointed out, "I assume you mean Bud. How can I trust a man who sticks his eyeballs in knotholes and looks under leaves and shrubs for members of my family? 'Tis sheer madness."

Bud knew Jack was waiting for him to respond. Well, he wasn't going to because he already knew Jack refused to consider any of it was true, and it was also apparent he had conveniently chosen to forget all about meeting Triumphant last night.

Nothing was going Bud's way. "Believe what you want? Just get us out of here. Do you have your Harley, or is there a taxi waiting?"

"I borrowed my brother's car. I said I'd have it back by mid-morning so we'd better put our skates on."

"What about my clothes?" Glory looked down at Bud's jacket, her long legs bare and revealing goosebumps. It wouldn't take a rocket-scientist to work out she had nothing on underneath. "I can't go into town dressed in practically nothing."

How quickly things change Bud thought. He offered her the blanket Jack had brought with him and both men turned away to give her some privacy while she wrapped it around her waist like a sarong.

"That will have to do until I get home."

Jack winked at him. Now you get to find out where she lives was the silent message from his friend.

Just as quickly, Glory blinked and declared, "I don't know where I live either. I'm homeless." Then she brightened. "Of course you'll know," she said to Bud and looked expectantly at him.

Bud completely understood the pathetic look Jack shot him. He narrowed his eyes at his friend, and ignored the *I-told-you-so* glare his friend was sending him.

***

"Remember what the doctor said. Plenty of rest, lots of fluids and hopefully your memory should return before too long."

"I'm not an invalid Bud. I walked halfway round the forest with you while you looked under every leaf. I'm fine."

"It's my fault you are in this state," he insisted. "Making things easier for you helps assuage my conscience."

There were still things so faerie-like about her. For one thing, she weighed lighter than a feather and secondly, she still used the phrases 'tis and mayhap. There was hope her memory would return soon.

"Don't move a muscle," he ordered, when she attempted to get up from her spot on the couch. "Relax. Take it easy." He lightened his tone. "I'm here if you need anything."

A look of longing filled her eyes and she ran a moist tongue over her dry lips. "I wouldn't mind a pot of tea. Something herbal if you have it."

Desire licked like lightening through him, but conscious of her concussion, Bud leaned forward and placed a light kiss on her forehead and ignored the fire burning him to a frazzle on the inside. Before he threw caution to the wind and devoured her on the spot he sought out the tea, certain he'd seen some in a cupboard his mother had left behind a few months back.

While doing so, he formulated a plan. What was needed above all was patience. He was anxious for Murphy to make contact as he'd promised. Bud needed him to look after Glory while he searched for that book in his mother's bookcase.

It was a tiny book, the writing almost illegible, but he was positive it resembled the one Glory had shown him. He was also going to need a magnifying glass. In her world, her books were the right size for them. In his, the book was the size of a small piece of Lego and the pages, although not cabbage leaves, were fragile with age.

Satisfied with his plan of action, he placed the drinks on a tray and carried them out to the living room, only to discover his faerie princess had succumbed to sleep. He placed the tray on the coffee table and went to his bedroom for the duvet. He was bitterly shocked to find that all traces of Glory's magic had gone from his room. No roses, or clinging vines and no duvet!

"Here's hoping your memory returns soon," he whispered after covering her with his old duvet he'd found folded in his wardrobe.

***

The days while they waited for Murphy to contact them were the longest of Bud's life. Glory was suffering from cabin fever and it was becoming increasingly difficult to keep her at his side. He was fearful that if she left his side, she would die. He wasn't about to risk finding out.

Two days after losing her memory, Murphy phoned Bud to let him know how he was getting on and to elaborate at length on the wonderful fortune to have graced his life since being cured of the drink.

When Bud relayed his news to Murphy and asked if he could help, the old guy came knocking at the door within thirty minutes of ending their call. He was sober, dapper and brimming with good health and humor. The glamour Glory had crafted for Murphy appeared to be strong and true. Thank you God.

"'Tis a sad day to be sure when a faerie loses the magic." Murphy looked down at the very put-out Glory and scratched his thick thatch of hair that also seemed less grey.

Glory glared at Murphy. "I do not require a babysitter. In case you haven't noticed, I'm an adult."

"Do you not remember me?" Murphy's lilting voice was laced with concern. Sitting down next to her, he lifted one of her hands and clasped it between his.

Confusion flared in Glory's eyes and a new crease formed between her eyebrows. "Should I know you?" She did know him, she was positive. A dark image of two evil youths popped into her head and then another of Murphy and she….

"Nay!" She sprung from the couch as if it had suddenly morphed into a bed of hot potatoes and backed away from Murphy as unwelcome images danced elusively in her still throbbing skull.

An anxious Murphy blinked his wise old eyes and turned to Bud. "You'd be right me old fellow. This Glory is not the one I met a few days ago."

Murphy asked Glory again. "Do you not remember attirin' me in a new suit and sendin' me on me way. Completely sober I might add?

Ah Glory girl, 'tis a fine 'ting to see the world through eyes not colored by the drink. And miracles be praised, I found a winning lotto ticket in me pocket."

He winked and drew himself up as tall as he could, which wasn't much as he was vertically challenged. "'Tis a rich man you're lookin' at. A man of substance. Rich in spirit with a bank balance to match."

He patted his hand over Glory's once more. "Don't you be worryin' your pretty head at all. You'll be your true self before too long I'm sure."

"I tried the releasing spell last night," Bud informed Murphy. "It either no longer works, or won't until she believes she is a faerie once more."

Murphy made several tutting sounds with his tongue. "Would you like me to give the magic a try, dear fellow?"

"That's an idea." Bud knew it wouldn't hurt. "You've already touched her so go right ahead."

"Mayhap you've both forgotten I've thoughts and opinions too," Glory was clearly exasperated. "I'm not a toy you can pass around to play with."

Bud shrugged his shoulders. "I know you think we're crazy, but wouldn't you do everything in your power to help if I had been hurt or lost my mind."

"There's nothing wrong with my mind." Glory rolled her eyes. "But I *am* worried about *your* mind." She inclined her head towards Murphy, her mouth pursed in irritation. "You might as well try. Hopefully it will convince you both that you've lost your marbles."

Murphy didn't hesitate. He recited the glamour immediately. Bud crossed his fingers behind his back, waiting for something, anything to happen.

"Have I gone yet?" Glory's sarcasm was unmistakable.

"No." There was an edge of sadness to Murphy's voice. "And no wings in sight."

"Thank heavens," Glory groaned. "Now can we forget about this and get on with finding out who I am through normal channels."

"I don't know what normal is anymore," Bud admitted. "I'm not even sure I want life to be normal again." For now, he forced the attention away from himself and Glory. "Murphy. Have you managed to find your wife?"

"To be sure. And the children." He paused, opened his mouth and then shut it, not saying anything. The light in his eyes dimmed somewhat. "What grand lads me boys have turned out to be. Mrs Murphy has done a fine job in raisin' them."

"I'm glad they've turned out well. Do you think there's a chance of reconciliation?"

"I don't know. I haven't approached them yet. I've been watchin' from afar. 'Tis a man aquiverin' in his boots you're lookin' at. What if she says no? What if me sons grab me by the seat of me pants and kick me right back into hell."

"The world is full of *what ifs*. Do it Murphy. If there is one thing I've learned over the past few days it's to take risks. You have a chance to restore your link with your family. Do you want to wonder for the rest of your life whether they would have welcomed you back or not? Surely, it's better to know either way. Take control of the fear. Don't let it control you."

A small smile played on Murphy's lips. "You have a fine gift for words, and when I hear ye say it I believe it to be possible."

Bud looked over to Glory who was listening intently to them both with a frown on her brow and confusion in her startling clear eyes.

"Take the chance Murphy," Bud insisted. "Before it's too late."

≈ **CHAPTER 15** ≈

Bud searched high and low for the tiny book on his mother's shelves. It had fascinated him for most of his childhood. Just when he'd nearly given up ever hoping to find it, his fingers encountered something tucked away behind a large volume intriguingly entitled, Myths & Legends of Newberry Forest, Oaktree Falls & Surrounding Plains. He grabbed that one too, pausing briefly to wonder why he had never seen it before. He knew his father's collection of books intimately, or thought he had.

He recalled his father's voice as he informed him that one day, when he was old enough, the small book would belong to Bud, and he would become its caretaker. His father it seemed had been a caretaker of secrets. What had he known? The tiny book had remained tucked away, forgotten and collecting dust on an old bookshelf.

Until now.

***

Murphy and Glory sat side by side on the couch sharing the larger volume on Myths and Legends between them. Bud sat opposite in his favorite wingback chair inspecting the tiny book with a full sized magnifying glass.

He'd suffered the bark of hilarity from Glory when he'd shown her his find and even Murphy's eyebrows rose upon seeing the postage-stamp sized book in Bud's palm.

The pages were old, yellow and fragile. The words so small they were almost impossible to read, even through the magnifying glass. They were written in an ancient language so dissimilar to his own. Again, he felt as if he should know their meaning. Methodically, with the aid of a pair of tweezers, he leafed his way through from beginning to end and then he started again.

One painstaking page at a time.

Lost completely in his own world of concentration, he was startled when Murphy let out a cry of excitement while bouncing on his behind on the couch, treating it like it was a trampoline.

"Would you be lookin' at this?" He jabbed a forefinger at the page on his knee. "'Tis all here. Right under our noses. According to this book, faeries have inhabited Newberry Forest for nigh on two thousand years."

Glory bounced from Murphy's momentum and nodded. "'Tis interesting reading, but surely you don't believe it? 'Tis just a fable after all." Her eyes glazed over as a dreamy expression took over. "A wonderful romantic fable."

Murphy winked at her. "Me darlin'. I don't just believe. I know it to be the absolute truth."

Murphy spoke with such conviction. Happiness glowed from his eyes. She didn't have the heart to negate him. He truly believed she was a faerie. As did Bud. Even now, as they poured over these silly books, muttering words making no sense at all, she could see they were both serious and intent on finding something to help regain her memory and turn her back into a faerie.

She was in love with a crazy man. She knew it to be so, just as 'twas clear how Bud felt about her. Despite her lack of memory, she knew his heart beat surely and steadily within his chest and that it overflowed with love for her. His feelings were genuine and it was the only certainty she knew right now. He was a lifeline and she was clinging to it hoping everything would all make sense. Soon.

If only she could remember where she had met Bud? Murphy

said it was at Oaktree Falls precinct. When she'd asked why she had been at the precinct they'd both mumbled incoherently about a citizen's arrest. Then, when she'd suggested returning to the precinct to help jog her memory, both had looked worried and hotly exclaimed, "No!" They also refused to explain why.

It was all so confusing. She needed some of that coffee Bud had made earlier. "I'll get us a drink," she muttered and left them to it.

No need to encourage their delusions. 'Twas no need at all, for there were stranger ones going on in her head and she was beginning to think there was some truth to their words. Things were knocking on the closed door of her memory, but the door was weighty and refused to budge more than a smidgen at a time.

Where was Jack? He hadn't believed a word of Bud's story. What she needed was a sane person to drum some sense into those two weirdos in the living room.

Putting the cups on the tray alongside some chocolate chip muffins Bud had bought on the way home from his mother's, she made a plunger of coffee.

'Twas impossible to say how long it had taken to make the coffee, but surely it had only taken a maximum of five minutes, yet when she returned to the living room, something significant had clearly occurred in her brief absence.

Murphy was reading aloud to Bud with barely controlled excitement. Bud looked as if ten thousand watts of high voltage electricity had surged through him. Glory deduced he must have run his hands through his hair a hundred times for it all stood on end, spiked into a hundred exclamation points. He'd pushed his glasses high on his brow and rubbed his eyes with his fists and muttered in apparent stupefaction. "Say what?"

"'Tis true," Murphy insisted. "'Tis right here in this book." He read directly from the page. "Up until five centuries ago, man and faerie lived side by side in harmony. It is said the faerie openly shared their secrets with the inhabitants of Oaktree Falls and the surrounding villages, often inviting humans to visit their world via a Faerie Portal.

"Not long after the summer solstice in the year 1432, the peaceful existence of Newberry Forest and Oaktree Falls was completely and irrevocably shattered. An Ancient One, a teacher of magic called Silversleeves, opened his mind and heart to a woman from the small village of Oaktree Falls and began to teach her the ways of the faerie. It is reported her name was Rosebud. Increasingly, they spent more and more time in each other's company. Before long, the great teacher found himself in love with his pupil and it appeared the love was reciprocated.

"Their love was like no other and crossed the boundaries more deeply than had ever been done before. They wished to marry but a physical union between human and faerie was unheard of. Their request to do so placed the entire countryside in turmoil. Arguments broke out. Human against human. Faerie against faerie. What once had been a joyful community was now sullen and divided in opinion. It is reputed other Ancients met with the King of the Faerie and the villagers with their elders. Leaders of both parties held a formal gathering in a glade near a great tree known as the Tree of All Knowingness. This tree is purported to grow at the epicenter of Newberry Forest although no human since has ever been able to locate it.

"Silversleeves and Rosebud were present at this gathering, their love visible to those that had eyes to see, as they pleaded their case. The arguments for and against went on until the moon slipped away and the sun rose on a new day. Eventually it was proclaimed the lovers could not marry or continue their union. Their fate was sealed by the shake of hands between human and faerie.

"To prevent a situation such as this occurring again, a decree was written and signed by leaders from both sides. No mortal could marry or enter into a relationship with one of the Faerie. Inconsolable, Rosebud clung to Silversleeves, refusing to relinquish her hold on him. Her fingers had to be prized from his and she was dragged kicking and screaming from his arms and all the while, she cried *I will always love you. I will love you through time. I will love you until this world ends and a new world begins.*

"When Silversleeves finally relinquished his hold on Rosebud, he spoke and a hush fell over the forest. His words although softly spoken were heard throughout the entire countryside. Many say they heard his voice from as far as a hundred miles in every direction. It is recorded he said, *I will never forgive any of you for your great unkindness and your narrow minds. Never.*

"There is evidence Rosebud retired to a solitary life behind the walls of a convent. Nothing more could be found about this historical figure. It was as if she had not existed at all after her entry into the convent. As for Silversleeves, he never forgave those who separated them. He became a hermit, disappearing deep into the forest for increasingly longer periods of time, refusing to have anything to do with anyone. He grew wild and unkempt. On rare occasions when spotted he was said to pace beneath branches, his eyes burning with malice. No one dared venture too close to him, not even the most ancient of the Ancients. Unresolved anger gnawed like a festering boil in his soul until one day that anger and wrath exploded in a binding curse upon both human and faerie alike. The curse severed the bonds of faerie and human forever.

"For the faerie it was certain death to remain in the human world. It was now impossible for humans to gain entrance to the Faerie Realm unless expressly invited by one of their kind, where once they moved freely between each world."

Murphy looked up, his voice rough and dry. "'Tis also written that the curse exists to the present day and none have been able to break it." Murphy flicked the pages back to the beginning. "This book was published in the early 1930s."

The heavy tome slipped from Murphy's knees to the floor and he looked over to his friends. There were tears of regret in his eyes for he understood too well the implications behind such a revelation.

***

Bud was numb and shivered as the stark reality of their situation sunk in.

Down, deep inside his soul, he had been harboring hope? Hope that he would find a way in which he and Glory could be together. Forever. If this myth was true, then there was no chance for either of them.

His heart shattered into a million fragments.

One by one, Bud picked up all the pieces and meticulously put them back together. Watching Glory as she slept later that night helped ease his pain somewhat, but it was only a temporary comfort.

He knew she was concerned for him. He also knew she was beginning to remember things. Little things that in her present state made no sense to her at all. Before long, she would remember everything and then she would return home. Without him.

She had sensed his despair. He had seen the knowledge in her eyes, and by some kind of osmosis, he knew she shared it also.

Never had he loved her more.

Never had he cared so deeply or been so sad.

***

Just after midnight, Bud wandered into the living room. Careful not to wake Murphy who slept on the couch, he picked up the book Murphy had been reading from earlier and moved to the far corner of the room and flicked on the reading lamp.

He turned to the bookmark where Murphy had stopped reading and continued from there. Within minutes, he was unable to contain his excitement. Switching the main light on he shook Murphy's shoulder. "Wake up. Wake up."

"'Tis no need to shout, me dear fellow. Murphy can hear ye loud and clear." The old man rubbed his eyes and squinted against the harsh artificial light.

Bud perched on the edge of the couch and shoved the book in front of Murphy. "Read this."

Eyes still blurred with sleep, Murphy squinted at the words on the page and began to read softly. "A footnote to this myth lies mysteriously cloaked in riddles. Historians are divided on its meaning but it is widely accepted there will come a time when a window of opportunity will be granted from the heavens above and during this time it will be possible for the curse to be broken."

Murphy looked up at Bud as he read the last words aloud. "Love is the key."

≈ CHAPTER 16 ≈

Convinced he and Glory were the combined key, Bud and Murphy attacked the tiny glamour book with renewed vigor. Throughout the remainder of the early hours, they struggled with the strange language, and searched the internet for sites on ancient text and myths.

Eventually, just as the sun began to rise, Murphy and Bud, through a process of elimination and guesswork, held a handful of glamours that made sense. They hoped.

By mid-morning Bud was psyched and ready to test a few. Once more, he headed for Newberry Forest, but this time he took Murphy and a still protesting Glory with him.

He could hardly believe it had been barely two weeks since Glory first burst into his life, tipping his world upside down and turning it inside out. He felt as if he'd known her all his life.

Glory flicked out a large red and black checked blanket on the grass and smoothed the edges. Murphy placed two large hampers in the center, sat down beside them, eased off his shoes and wiggled his toes.

"Mighty fine idea," he beamed and inhaled the fresh scent of clean air and pine.

"Truly," Glory agreed and picked through one of the hampers. "I love a good picnic. As for the reason we are here in the forest, I want you to know I'm tolerating you both, but not believing any of it." Making her choice, she held a sun-ripened strawberry high over her lips, tilted her head back and sunk her teeth into the plump fruit. Juice dribbled down her chin.

Bud watched her devour it and his body spontaneously reacted. Reaching out, uncaring of Murphy's presence, he fingered the juice from Glory's chin and placed the strawberry moistened finger in his mouth and sucked, slowly and deliberately. His eyes held hers and a whisper of seduction tilted the corners of his mouth upwards.

Glory blushed bright pink but didn't turn away. Instead, she took another strawberry and with a teasing glint in her eyes, devoured it.

"Uh hum," Murphy coughed. "Maybe I should be takin' meself off for a walk?" He winked and focused on the food basket, the items inside a gift to his new friends. Bud had protested that it was too much, but Murphy had replied that there was plenty more where that came from and insisted it was only a wee gift considering the new life and friendship they had given him.

Bud forced his focus away from Glory. He hefted a bottle of champagne out of the basket and two long stemmed glasses. Murphy was already drinking freshly squeezed orange juice and didn't bat an eyelid when Bud popped the cork. In fact, it was he who had bought the bubbles.

"Have you lost the urge altogether," Bud lifted his glass to indicate his drink to Murphy.

"To be sure, I have. In its place I have found urges I thought never to feel again." He winked at Bud. "I'm sure you'll be catchin' me drift."

Glory changed the subject. "I know we were here yesterday but I do feel this location is so familiar. I sense I should know it well."

"You should." Bud was hopeful she was remembering more. "This is your home after all."

"'Tis easy for you to say. But I need proof."

"I'll show you." Bud was already tipsy. Champagne on an empty stomach would do that to you but he needed fortification to perform the glamours he and Murphy had come up with. There was every possibility he would fail and Glory would think him a total and absolute idiot.

Standing, he took his notes from his back pocket. "When I repeated the glamour to wear the royal wings it worked for me. I'm hoping I can do it again."

"What? Wear my wings?" Glory scoffed. "You know, I'd really like to see that?"

"Being sarcastic doesn't suit you. I've a glamour to send you back to the Faerie Realm."

Glory was affronted. "Is this an elaborate way to say you want me gone?"

"You're deliberately misunderstanding me."

Glory shrugged. "I'm not going anywhere. I may not remember the details but I do know my place is with you. I feel that I loved you before. I'm sure I do now."

Her admission that she loved him was both uplifting and saddening. "Your place is with Tree and Triumphant and your family."

Glory studied him for a few seconds, glancing momentarily to Murphy and back. "You're my family Bud. And Murphy too."

Bud was developing an ulcer. He was sure of it. No amount of alcohol would diminish the gut-wrenching agony of being separated from Glory. Even though she was convinced she was his, he had to let her go. Grateful for the dulling effects of the champagne, he said, "You cannot survive here. You *must* return to your world."

"Go to it boyo," Murphy said sympathetically. "Get it over and done with. This wee girlie is not herself and prolonging the agony of parting won't make it any easier for either of you."

Glory strongly protested. "I am myself. I just can't remember my last name."

"If this works," Bud said, "you will remember everything."

"Rats and toadstools! Just get on with the show and then we can enjoy the rest of this lovely picnic in peace."

Bud turned away so she couldn't see the misery spilling from his heart into his eyes. The pain in his chest acute he began to recite the first verse he and Murphy had transcribed. A loud buzzing began in his ears, as if he'd suddenly developed tinnitus. A terrifying thrill grew within him. There was something happening. He could feel it. He repeated the words a second time.

The buzzing in his ears increased until he had to block them with his hands. A vibration started deep within his belly. His legs shook and he couldn't decide if it was the magic or his fear. He took a final look at his beautiful Glory and uttered the words a third time.

Just when he thought he could no longer stand and would collapse to his knees, the vibration eased and was replaced by a loud popping sound.

Glory shrieked with alarm. "Great leaping lizards! Where did he come from?"

"The spell appears a trifle wonky," added Murphy. He poured champagne into an empty glass. "You look in need of a drink, boyo." He offered it to Jack who had suddenly appeared at their picnic. "If'n you don't mind me sayin', you look a trifle pale."

"Where did he come from?" Glory's face was leached of color. Her hands were pressed to her breastbone and her mouth gaped while the dark pupils of her eyes swelled to the size of the strawberries she had eaten only minutes before.

Jack sat on the picnic rug between her and Murphy, his eyes glazed with panic. He was completely naked, except for a skimpy towel wrapped about his hips.

Silently and with a shaking hand he took the champagne offered and knocked it back in one gulp.

Murphy, calm as a cucumber, said, "Such a waste. Champagne, dear fellow, is to be savored, not tossed back like it's your last. Here," he proffered the bottle. "Try again."

Obediently, Jack held out his glass for Murphy to fill. However, that was the closest he came to following instructions. He slugged it back again. Sparkling liquid caught in his windpipe and he coughed, sneezed and swore explicitly.

Glory covered her ears and Murphy admonished him for swearing in front of a faerie princess.

Bud was stupefied. Unable to believe he had just conjured up his best friend, straight from the shower no less, he was currently speechless. The magic had worked. In a roundabout kind of way that was.

Water dripped from Jack's freshly shampooed hair onto wide bare shoulders and ran in rivulets down his defined chest which Glory seemed to be fascinated with if the size of her eyes were anything to go by.

Bud finally found his voice. "It worked." If he'd tried the glamour a minute earlier there might have been no towel at all around Jack's hips. What timing. "Kind of."

The second glass of champagne must have worked some of its magic on Jack, for he began to form words that were unrepeatable before saying, "Send me back. Whatever it is you did, undo it. Now!"

Glory jumped to her feet and stared at Jack in horror. "'Tis true. Oh my! 'Tis all true."

"None of this is real," Jack protested. "I will not believe it. It's a free country and it's my right not to believe."

He held out his glass for more champagne. "I must be dreaming," he reasoned. "I'm a figment of my own imagination." He grinned and took a swig of liquid. "I'm not really here at all. And neither are any of you."

"If you say so." Murphy saluted Jack with his glass of juice. "Murphy's me name."

Jack held out his free hand. "Pleased to meet you. Jack

Diamond."

"Likewise." Murphy shook Jack's hand.

"So," said Jack, getting into his so-called dream. "What's happening? Why am I here?"

Murphy enlightened him. "'Tis an experiment."

Not enlightened at all, Jack inquired, "What kind of experiment?"

Glory added her tuppence worth to the conversation. "Bud is attempting to send me back to the Faerie Realm."

Jack chuckled. "Of course. It makes sense now."

Glory wasn't amused. "It does? How?"

"These kind of things always make sense in dreams. It's when you wake up that you can't make head nor tail of them."

"True," agreed Murphy. "Dreams are a mystery to be sure."

"If you don't mind." Bud interrupted. "This is serious. I'm about to try another glamour and need some quiet."

"Of course. Sorry about that mate." Jack held his glass out to Murphy for another refill then saluted his friend. "Go for it. Glamour away."

"Please don't, Bud," Glory tugged on his arm. "What if it works? I want to stay with you."

Glory's touch was just what Bud didn't need. He would have to release her first before reciting the next glamour he and Murphy had come up with. However, he hauled her into his arms, and said the words he didn't want to say. "I can't Glory. You won't survive out here. You must go back."

"But I love you."

Bud smoothed his knuckles down her cheek, cupped her chin and gazed into liquid eyes now pooling with tears. "I love you too. And that is why I'm sending you home."

"I don't want to go. Not yet." Glory clung to the only human she would ever give her love to. There was no need for him to cast another glamour. Her memory was returning and she knew the way home. She guessed Jack's sudden arrival in their midst had been a trigger.

"All this emotion is embarrassing," Jack mumbled and turned his head away to give them some privacy. Murphy did the same and in unison, their jaws dropped. Jack whispered to Murphy, "Can you see them?"

Murphy nodded and winked at him. "To be sure. All three."

"This dream keeps getting crazier and crazier." Jack stood and checked his towel for decency's sake. "Jack's my name," he said and held out his hand to what appeared to be the leader. "Welcome to my dream."

The leader, haughty and severe, peered down at Jack's hand and then cast a glance to Glory and Bud. He didn't move. Jack's hand dropped away.

"Daughter!" The stranger boomed and everyone jumped. "I trust you have good reason to be in the arms of that human."

Glory spun in Bud's arms. "Father!" Glory blushed the brightest pink as her memory returned in full. "Mother! Triumphant!"

"Unhand my daughter!" the King boomed. He pointed a long finger directly at Bud. "I have a mind to turn you into a petrified tree for all eternity. Release her this instant."

"No!" Glory stood defiantly next to Bud. "Father, no!"

Bud wondered if Glory had ever said no to her father before. The King looked as if he was about to explode. His Queen, Bud supposed it was she, placed a hand on his forearm, her expression one of silent warning. It seemed he took heed of her warning, for his next words were less fierce but still stern and unforgiving. "Give me one good reason why not."

Glory raised her hands and shrugged. "I love him."

In Bud's opinion, King Aloysius did not appear to be as shocked as he made out, even if his enormous wings were buzzing with what

Bud supposed was irritation. The fear in the Queen's eyes was genuine enough. She would be concerned for her daughter as only a mother could be.

As for Triumphant, she stood silent but resolute at her mother's side, an arrow cocked in her bow, ready to shoot should anyone make a move of violence towards them.

The Queen spoke to her husband. "Our Glory must have good reason for her actions. Do not judge hastily dearest."

Glory was ready to defend Bud, but he could not allow her to do so alone. It was his fault she was in this mess. "It's my fault. Do not blame your daughter."

"Of that I have no doubt." Glory's father's tone oozed disdain.

"No. It's mine," Jack interrupted. "This is all just a dream. My dream. So there's no need to turn anyone into anything. I'll wake up soon and all this," he waved his arm about, "will be over."

Jack certainly hoped he was right. Because the faerie in the forest from last night stood right next to the so-called King, dressed this time in faerie finery with wings glittering rays of rainbow light.

Hers was the voice he had heard. And he remembered her name too. Triumphant. He wished he didn't.

"The fault is entirely mine," Bud interjected. He reached for Glory's hand, threading her fingers through his and gripping tightly. They stood so close, their arms melded together, as if one. Bud was reminded of the myth they had only just discovered last night of Silversleeves and Rosebud before they were parted forever.

Glory was defiant as she listed all her misdemeanors over the past few days. "'Tis no human's fault I'm here with them. They try to take my blame but I cannot allow it. 'Tis I who was careless enough to be trapped in the human world and 'twas Bud who freed me to return home. 'Twas I also who bought Bud into our world." She gulped, not certain they had known that piece of information. "There is no-one to blame except me."

Raising her linked hand, she rested her knuckles against Bud's cheek. "Truly, he is kind, gentle and loving. More than most faerie I know."

"There is no freedom when a human's hands are on you." Her mother's eyes held an indefinable sadness.

"Bud will release me anytime I ask. These humans, Bud's friends, Murphy and Jack, are my friends also. I know you can see their auras and their hearts. They're here to send me back to you for they know I cannot exist in their world for any length of time."

"Some of the blame lies with me also." Triumphant turned to her parents. "I turned a blind eye when Glory brought Bud into our world? I should have reported it but I didn't." Her eyes were downcast as the King frowned at his daughter. "I will relinquish my post as Captain upon our return."

"We'll discuss this later, daughter," the King was gruff, but his eyes gentled. "Let me hear the truth from this Bud person." The King looked Bud square in the eye, the kindness evaporating swiftly into one of suspicion. "No untruths. I will know by your aura if you lie."

Bud wondered if that was true. "The love I have for Glory is denser than this forest." He swung his free arm in a wide arc and sought a way to explain how he felt about their daughter in a language they would understand. "Our love is planted in the ground beneath our feet, all the way to the center of the earth. It reaches up to the stars and beyond. We are bonded in a way I cannot begin to explain. She is my life."

Surprised at the ease in which he slipped into the eloquent speech of the faerie, he continued. "My heart beats for Glory alone." He placed their linked fingers over his heart and stared adoringly into Glory's eyes. "It overflows when I see her smile. It beats within my chest with a love unparalleled and equally matched."

He dragged his gaze away from Glory, back to the King. "I

willingly release her back to her world, though it pains me to do so, and when she leaves, a part of me will go with her. I will never, ever forget her or our time together."

Tears careened down Glory's cheeks. Uncaring of her father's censure, she threw herself into Bud's arms. "I don't want to leave you."

Bud murmured against her hair, "You must. You know you must."

The harsh features of the King softened to concern. Worry created a crease between his eyebrows. He reached out a hand. "Come daughter. This Bud is right. You cannot tarry. Dry those tears and say faretheewell."

"But why Father? Why?" Glory implored.

"'Tis Faerie Law."

"You're the King. You can change the law."

"I cannot."

"You mean you won't."

Queen Celandine reached out to her daughter. "My darling Glory, some things are not easily changed."

"History repeats itself," Bud murmured. Desperation drove him on. "Is there a way to change that law?"

"If there is, I know not of it." The Queen spoke softly, gently, as if she regretted having to give him that answer.

"Human and faerie are not permitted to form a pairing," the King declared. 'Tis written in the Twelve Golden Rules."

"They are silly rules." Glory almost stamped her foot in frustration. "Who made them?"

The King coughed and turned bright red. His wife patted him on the shoulder. "I believe 'tis time to confess, husband."

"A King has no need to confess anything, wife. I will not be bullied into upsetting the Faerie Realm which has existed happily for the past five hundred years under such laws."

"Father," Triumphant intervened. "Surely, we can do something."

King Aloysius held up a hand to silence the questions. "I wish I could. The Rules are sealed within the heart of the council. An agreement was reached between both human and faerie to live this way. I fear, even if this law were to be rescinded, 'tis the curse created by Silversleeves, the great Ancient One, which binds us so tightly. Many have tried to sever the curse he crafted and all have failed."

"So it's true. Love is the key," Murphy spoke softly, as if to himself.

"Aye," agreed the King, upon hearing Murphy's words. "I see the love in my daughter's eyes for this Bud. His love is pure. I see the linking of their aura and know their lives have been entwined. Still, the bonds of the curse are not broken. What can we do? Glory must return with us to where she will be safe. Her place is with us in Newberry Forest."

The King had clearly decided to take his wife's advice and explain further. "When I first heard there was a human in the forest I thought perhaps Bud was the one to break this confounded curse." He spoke directly to Glory now. "I could have stopped you then, but I did not. I have known at all times exactly where you were." He glanced to Triumphant and back again. "There is nothing I don't know about my kingdom. Nothing."

The King grew quiet, his anger and arrogance gone and his Queen took up where he left off. "Your birth, Glory, signified great change in the lives of the faerie thus the reason for your name. Gloriane. It means glorious one. The tears from heaven signified great changes. We welcomed you into our lives with the joy only a parent can understand."

"We welcomed you with joy *and* trepidation," the King clarified.

"Truly, daughter," Queen Celandine continued. "We believed you would be the one to break the curse Silversleeves created."

Sympathy glowed in eyes the same color as Glory's. "Alas, 'tis not to be. We have seen your love and know how deeply it runs, but the curse remains unbroken. Now 'tis time to come home, child." She smiled wistfully. "I have missed you sorely."

Glory was flabbergasted. "You knew where I was? All along. Right from the very beginning?"

When both her parents nodded, she turned to Triumphant and looked to her in askance.

"I did not relay a single word to them sister dearest." She had long ago placed the arrow back in the pouch resting against her shoulder blade. She fisted one hand and placed it over her heart. "Faeries Honor. Did I not tell you Father would know?"

"Your sister is loyal indeed," agreed the Queen.

Acceptance accompanied the ache in Glory's broken heart. She turned to Bud, and then to her friends. "What can we do? Murphy? Jack? Help me please?"

"'Tis shame I am feelin'. Great shame to admit Murphy cannot help the one who changed me life." He bowed his head and scuffed a shoe on the grass.

Jack challenged the notion that this was not a dream. "I know of nothing to help you either," he admitted. "I wish I could wake up then it would be all over."

The Queen appeared amused. The King frowned. "'Tis not expected for humans to know the answer to a centuries old faerie curse. It does my heart good to know there are those in your world, Bud, who still believe in us."

He stepped forward and reached out a hand to his daughter. "Come. We can no longer tarry. Other humans are entering the forest. Soon 'twill not be safe for us here in this form."

Glory linked her free hand with that of her father's. With one half of her in the human world and the other in the faerie, she felt torn in two. Why should such choices have to be made? 'Twas all so unfair. Accepting the fact that Father was right, she took one last sad imploring look at Bud, and raised his hand to her lips, then leaned in and whispered "Faretheewell my love. I will never forget you. The sun may rise and the sun may set, but my memory of our time together will remain in my heart forevermore."

Releasing her hold on him, she stepped away, to ensure there was no chance he could touch her again. "Release me now so I may go."

Bud's heart twisted in his chest but he knew prolonging the inevitable would do none of them any good. He nodded and recited the releasing glamour for the final time and within one moment and the next, The Royal Family of Faerie were gone, leaving Murphy and Jack to pick up the jagged shards of Bud's broken heart.

≈ CHAPTER 17 ≈

It took only a few minutes for ominous clouds, heavy with the threat of rain, to congregate above Newberry Forest where once there had been nothing but the bluest of skies, and even less time for them to unload their grief on the citizens of Oaktree Falls and the surrounding districts.

Bud stood at his living room window, watching the torrential rain cascade down the glass in front of him. It was so heavy, visibility was virtually zero. He could no longer see Newberry Forest or even the rooftops of the buildings closest to his apartment.

The grayness of the day hung as heavily in his heart as it did in the sky. Resting his forehead against the cool glass, he heaved a long breath of regret. He knew, with certainty that the rain was connected to the depth of Glory's sadness, just as it was his own.

He wandered aimlessly for days about his apartment, refusing the urgings of Jack and Murphy to rejoin the world. The idea he could have done more plagued him day and night. There was silence in his small apartment, but the noise in his head could have rivaled that of a jet engine.

Sleep proved elusive. His bedroom was an empty shell without Glory to fill it with her joyful, bubbly presence. He moved himself onto the couch in the living room, spending both day and night pouring over the little glamour book and deciphering each spell in the hope it would reveal something new. Anything that would indicate what was required in order to break Silversleeves' curse.

He found nothing.

Not a damn thing!

***

The Tree Most Royal

The forest floor was waterlogged and moisture was beginning to seep into the interior of all the trees in the forest. "If this rain continues Newberry Forest will have to be renamed Newberry Swamp." King Aloysius squelched the width of the throne room for the thousandth time. "The entire valley will flood if Glory's spirits do not lift soon." He turned to his wife. "Is there no inkling of hope the tears will stop?"

Queen Celandine wrung her hands together, her knuckles white. "No inkling whatsoever." She turned to her eldest daughter. "Do you know of anything to cheer your dear sister's heart?"

Triumphant tapped her bow against her lips. Something she'd been doing often of late. "I have not ceased to search for an answer. We have but one last avenue to try."

The King stopped his pacing. "Pray do reveal your thoughts, daughter. What avenue is this?"

"I should like to consult the Tree of All Knowingness. If there is a solution, mayhap he will be kind enough to bestow a knowing upon us."

The King spun on his toes and a huge smile spread across his face for the first time in days, smoothing his lined brow, and easing the worry away. He cupped his daughter's cheeks and planted a kiss on her upturned nose, then turned to his wife. "My darling have I not said before, what a clever daughter our Triumphant is?"

Queen Celandine clasped her daughter's hands in hers. "She is extremely clever as well as beautiful."

King Aloysius rubbed his palms together. "Indeed. Indeed. Go immediately, daughter." He paused. "Take Glory with you. In fact, we will all go. A touch of nostalgia has touched me. It has been a long time since I have paid a visit to the Tree of All Knowingness." He smiled lovingly at his wife. "The place has special meaning to your mother and I, daughter. 'Tis where she agreed to be my wife."

A wistful smile softened the Queen's heart shaped face. "'Tis an excellent notion. I should love to accompany you and mayhap visit with our old friend and brother, The Guardian of All Knowingness."

King Aloysius nodded. "'Tis decided. We will prepare immediately to leave at first light."

Triumphant hesitated. "I fear Glory will not agree to accompanying us, Father. She still refuses to leave the comfort of Tree."

"She will go if she believes there is promise of an answer to her grief." King Aloysius peered down at the damp floor beneath their feet and over to the equally wet walls of their home. "We need her to stop this crying before 'tis too late for us all."

***

The Tree of All Knowingness stood surrounded, at a respectful distance, by a circle of smaller equally important trees. The area was known to all faerie as The Knowing Circle and was tended twenty-four hours a day by an Ancient One, aptly named The Guardian of All Knowingness.

With the utmost regard deserving of a tree so ancient and important to all faerie, The Royal Family approached its presence, bowing in respectful silence to the Guardian reclining nearby under the canopy of a large leafy branch.

The only awareness they had of his recognizing their presence in the Knowing Circle was the slight nod of his head before he placed a volume of Faerie Folk Lore into the folds of his long voluminous crimson robes and arose to greet them.

"Father sent word," Triumphant whispered to Glory. "Of our intended visit."

"'Twas no need." The Ancient One clearly had the hearing of a bat. Age had not diminished any of his senses. "We knew you would come."

"We?" Glory, her eyes red and swollen but dry for the first time since parting from Bud looked around for another Ancient One.

"Why the Tree of All Knowingness and myself of course. The Tree knows what has been and what is to come."

Hope lit a small fire in Glory's heart. "Mayhap 'twill know how to break the curse."

"Truly," nodded the Ancient One. "But 'tis also a wise tree who knows some truths are best kept veiled in mystery."

Glory peered up into the tree's magnificence in awe. "'Tis a wondrous sight to behold. My spirit delights to be in the presence of so great a tree." She acknowledged the Guardian. "And you too, of course, Uncle."

Her Uncle nodded, a small smile tilting the corners of his mouth upwards. He kissed his nieces on their foreheads, ruffled their hair with affection and ushered them forward with a hand behind their backs towards the greatest tree in the forest. "Tree recognizes your respect and requests you approach."

As both sisters took a step forward, he turned to Queen Celandine and King Aloysius. "How good it is to see you both again." He clasped the Queen's hands in his and planted a kiss on her smooth cheek. "You age well my childhood friend."

Queen Celandine blushed. "You never change. Flattery still runs thick in your veins Albertus."

Albertus chuckled. "'Tis the knowingness. It recognizes your need to be praised."

"And me," King Aloysius declared with warmth. "Do you not have praise for me also?"

"Your head is swollen enough already, brother mine. We do not want that crown of yours to fall off its already precarious perch." He laughed and tugged his brother, the King, into his embrace and slapped him heartedly on the back. "Enough with the formalities. It warms my heart also to see you." He looked to his brother. "It gets lonely out here sometimes. You should visit more often. There is much wisdom Tree wishes to impart and I would enjoy sharing your company for a while." He grinned, a mischievous glint in his eyes. "There's only so much quiet an Ancient One can take."

They all knew this to be a huge joke. King Aloysius laughed loud and long. "Your love of isolation is legendary, Albertus. There is no-one better to tend to and impart the knowledge the Great Tree chooses to share."

"Yet you are free to visit or stay with us at any time," Queen Celandine reminded him. "But you rarely visit."

"It's been very wet of late and the Great Tree wished for me to remain here for now. He knew you were coming."

Glory now standing near the Tree of All Knowingness heard the inference. She blushed. "I should have been born a water sprinkler. The tears arrive even before I know they're on the way."

"I gather this is why you're here. Tree told me you were coming to ask him a very important question."

Glory's eyes welled, but fear was uppermost in her heart. "What if the Tree of All Knowingness has no answer to my dilemma?"

"Do not be afraid child. Tree always provides an answer. What you do with the truth he imparts is up to you." He gave Glory a nudge. "Go now. You too Triumphant. Tree wishes to speak with you also. Rest your palms against his trunk. Be silent and listen. Open your hearts and the answers will come."

He backed away, beckoning King Aloysius to follow him. "Watch over your children, my Queen. I have something I wish to discuss with my brother."

Queen Celandine bowed her head once, slowly as if considering her response. A small smile played on her lips but there was concern clouding her eyes. "For you, anything."

Glory held a hand out to Triumphant. "Come. It will be good to have you at my side."

Triumphant threaded her fingers through Glory's. "I confess, I'm curious," she said as their uncle and Father moved away to speak privately. "But also nervous. I had not expected to receive a knowing."

"We cannot predict our future paths," their mother said. "I know not why he has asked to speak with both of you. 'Tis a rare privilege and few are ever given such an opportunity as this." She nodded at Tree. "He waits for you. I will remain nearby."

Tree was so tall, so regal in stature, his vast branches reached almost to the heavens. It was as if the uppermost tips stretched all the way to God.

A direct link, Glory thought, mayhap to the earth he protected below as well.

Silence descended upon the forest around them as the two sisters stood side by side and pressed their palms against the rough bark of Tree. Triumphant closed her eyes and Glory followed suit. The silence about them unnatural. Not a whisper of air rustled a solitary leaf, nor did an insect or animal move or utter a sound. The Tree of All Knowingness was about to impart wisdom and all the forest was agog with suppressed excitement.

For the longest fifteen minutes the sisters stood, side by side. Waiting. Listening. Hoping.

Trying as hard as she might, Glory learned nothing and her spirits began to sink into the murky depths of despair from whence they had only just arisen. Unusually quiet, she lingered lest she disturb her sister's communion with Tree. Just when she had all but given up hope, warmth flooded through her fingertips, up her arms and spread like thick warm tree sap throughout her entire body. She felt languid, warm and at peace all at once. She felt Tree's love as he placed an invisible mantle over her shoulders, cloaking her with its protection. A deep sense of wonder filled her heart.

Then Tree began to speak, his message for her alone. *There is a way.* Tree's energy thrummed through her veins as it imparted wisdom and it was as if her world expanded to include the universe and everything it contained. *You have done your part in shining your light and breaking down barriers no other has dared since Silversleeves cursed this land. The next step is not yours to take. You must be patient.*

Tree's voice faded from her mind. She clung to the deep love emanating from its presence. *Take heart,* he whispered his words now faint. *All is not lost.*

Maybe that was the case, but Glory was lost in the world of comfort she had garnered from Tree. She did not witness Triumphant's excitement until her sister literally plucked her away from the great trunk and began to twirl with her and sing.

"I know what to do," Triumphant sang. "I don't understand the reasoning of it, but 'tis a simple assignment."

Glory stared balefully at her sister, refusing to allow another single seed of hope in her heart to germinate. She didn't know if she could survive having her heart broken all over again. "You know how to break the curse?"

"Nay. 'Tis not my part in the scheme of things." Triumphant laughed and so did, it seemed, the wildlife in the forest around them as they began once again to chatter and fill the air with a noisy, excited hum.

"Then what is your part in all of this Tri?"

"I'm not certain of the why, but I have been given an assignment by the Tree of All Knowingness and you are not to interfere."

Glory was puzzled. Her shoulders slumped and her mouth wobbled. "I don't know why Tree spoke to you but he spoke to me too." What in the world could Triumphant do to help? "He told me I must be patient."

"And we all know that works for you!" Triumphant slung an arm around her sister's shoulders and hugged her warmly. "Do not fear, sister dearest." Then she echoed the exact words spoken by the Tree of All Knowingness that sent Glory's hope soaring. "All is not lost."

≈ CHAPTER 18 ≈

Bud stood in the middle of the clearing and stared up into the sprawling branches of Glory's tree while Murphy and Jack took shelter under two large black umbrellas, their faces a mixture of puzzlement and cynicism.

Bud gave no heed to the rain drenching him or the wetness of the bark chilling his skin. He closed his eyes, breathed deeply, held his breath and attempted to calm his roiling mind. He rested his palms against the damp trunk. "Tree. If you hear me, will you pass a message to Glory for me? Tell her I'll never stop looking for a way for us to be together. Tell her I love her."

Warmth spread like honey through his fingertips and palms, then moved up his arms to radiate throughout his tall frame. He could almost see steam rise from his body and Bud was sure he could feel Tree's effort to respond. Hope surged in his chest, talons of anticipation curled around his bruised heart. "You can hear me. I know you can."

In the silence, Bud thought he heard Tree intone, *Tree hears Bud's words*. A part of him hoped Glory would appear, but he knew it wasn't likely. He didn't wish to create havoc or add to her sadness by constantly turning up in her life, reminding her of their love, then having to leave. He just wanted her to know he would never give up. Ever.

Leaves rustled, disturbing his concentration. The sounds of the forest grew louder and birds chirped more raucously as they flit deftly through and around the branches. Crickets sang as loud as an orchestra. A small squirrel with a bushy golden tail, the size of Bud's mother's feather duster, darted past his feet and shot up Tree's nearest neighbor. It chattered, its button nose twitching while peering down at him from a branch, droplets of rain glistening in its fur.

"What's the commotion?" Murphy asked and the squirrel darted further up, sending a sprinkling of moisture onto Bud's upturned face. "'Tis uncommonly noisy even for a forest."

But Bud didn't have time to reply. Triumphant emerged from a dense stand of trees and walked into the clearing. She glared at Jack. "Not you again."

"I was thinking the same about you." Jack was clearly not pleased to see her.

Triumphant's fingers twitched and Bud wondered whether she fought the impulse to draw an arrow and aim it at his best friend once again. Instead, she said, "I have a message for Bud."

"Why are you here?" Bud asked Triumphant. "Is Glory unwell?"

Triumphant's smile softened with genuine regret, which he wasn't prepared for. Then she said something that totally had him reeling. "You're to come back with me through the Faerie Portal. Now!"

It was clear she expected no argument from him. That didn't stop Jack from protesting for him. "No!"

Triumphant's chin jutted and she looked down her nose despite her being shorter than all of them, even Murphy. Her expression morphed into one of disdain. "I'm puzzled by the Great Tree's request but it seems you're all invited." She signaled with her arm. "Come. The King awaits your presence at court."

Never before had she seen such happiness in a human. The joy in Bud's gray eyes was both humbling and gratifying, but it was Jack's expression of horror she enjoyed the most as the Faerie Portal opened and all three humans found themselves inside the Faerie

Realm.

***

King Aloysius squelched across the floor of the antechamber. "How could I have not known?" He flung his hands in the air and paused before his Queen. "'Tis a mystery."

"Mayhap it was meant to be. Though, 'tis a shame so much pain has been endured over the centuries as a result."

The King gripped the forearms of his wife and pulled her into his embrace. His large hand cupped her face and he looked into the kindest, gentlest eyes he knew. "What to do? What to do?"

"When the time comes, as in all things, you will know."

"How can you be so sure, my dearest?"

"Because you are shrewd, wise and in possession of a good heart. I would never have accepted your offer to Cleave with you within the Knowing Circle otherwise. I love you well and know the past decision regarding Silversleeves was not made lightly. I also know your past actions have been plagued with regret all these years."

Damp wings unfurled and fluttered lightly, spraying a myriad of droplets about the room. Queen Celandine wiped the shower of moisture from her cheeks and nose and hid a knowing smile, for she was wise also and knew how to reassure her husband and restore his pride when needed.

***

It took seconds for Triumphant to translocate all of them into the hallowed halls of King Aloysius and Queen Celandine's ancestral home, The Tree Most Royal. They stood before two guards who protected the entrance to the throne room with garlanded spears.

The sound of a trumpet heralded their arrival.

"Who dares enter the Throne Most Royal," one of the guards bellowed.

Murphy blocked his ears.

Jack dug a finger in his ear, waggled it about and replied blackly,

"Certainly not I."

Bud ignored the question altogether and charged forward only to be thwarted by crossed spears.

Triumphant moved to the front and pushed back the spears with the touch of one finger. "The Most Royal Triumphant requests an audience with her Father the King."

"And what of these humans?"

"What of them?" Triumphant replied haughtily.

"Do they also request an audience with the King?"

"We do," Bud spoke up. "All of us."

"Aye," agreed Murphy. "All of us."

"I don't mind staying out here," muttered Jack.

"Let us all through." Triumphant shot Jack an amused glance then focused on her younger brother and assumed her Robin Hood pose.

Herald stepped back and placed his spear at his side. He signaled with the nod of his head to the other guard to do the same. "I bow in deference to one so lofty."

Triumphant raised her imperial nose a notch or two in the air. "'Tis well you know your position in the scheme of things." She rose on tiptoe and planted a light kiss on the young guard's cheek and signaled to the others to follow.

Once more, a voice rang out. "Stand back. Make way for the humans. Make way for the loftiest sister of all."

Triumphant kicked her brother in the shins. "Behave, or I'll have you demoted."

"That was Herald?" Bud thought he looked all of twelve.

Triumphant looked to Bud. "You know of my brother?"

"Glory mentioned him. She said he was a youngling?" And over a hundred years old.

"He's in apprenticeship to the Captain of the Guard."

Bud looked about him. "Is his Captain here?"

"'Tis I of course," Triumphant informed him with a hint of irritation. Her imperial nose pointed a little further toward the inner caverns of Tree's interior. "I hold many important positions for I am the Ascendant Faerie of the Realm."

There was so little Bud knew about Glory and her family. His heart in his mouth, they entered the King's throne room. He walked behind Triumphant with slow measured steps toward the King who sat upon a throne at the end of the long narrow room. Bud looked over his shoulder to ensure Jack and Murphy were behind him. Reassured by their presence he continued his progress forward. Maybe that was why they were here. To bolster his courage.

There were faeries everywhere and if he wasn't mistaken, all were dressed in their royal finery. Bud peered down at his faded denim shirt and jeans. They would have to do. Jack, as usual, was encased head to toe in black leather. Only Murphy, dressed in a pair of designer jeans and a white starched tailor-made shirt, was suitably attired for such an auspicious occasion.

It appeared the whims of faerie went from one extreme to the next wearing not a stitch of clothing one moment, and resplendent in full ceremonial dress the next. And what a display of finery it was. Layer upon layer of the finest silks glistening in a range of iridescent colors, none of them earthy, as he would have expected. Then there were the wings. They were everywhere. Gossamer, gleaming gold and silver with intricate patterns of the forest woven into them.

If Bud didn't know better, he'd say that Jack was frozen with fear. On the other hand, his reaction to Triumphant was interesting and needed exploring further, but now wasn't the time. Jack "Daredevil" Diamond was a man who, with a wink and a nod, could have any woman he wanted. Yet, here he stood, surrounded by a bevy of astonishingly beautiful faeries and not interested in any of them.

As for Murphy, he was relishing the opportunity to participate in such a spectacle. Bud supposed the old guy's Irish heritage helped him accept such things much more readily than his you-live-and-then-you-die friend.

Bud searched the room for Glory, forgetting all about questioning his sanity or reason. His heart leaped into a rapid rat-a-tat-tat in his chest when he spotted her. His lips parted and he silently mouthed her name. "Glory."

She stood at the foot of the raised dais near the throne to the King's right. She offered him an uncertain smile and he knew she was as puzzled as he in why he was here with Murphy and Jack.

His heart continued to pound against his ribcage. A sudden case of nerves produced a fine sheen of perspiration across his brow. Triumphant had brought them all here to the world of the faerie. He did not know why and he dared not hope. Not yet.

His beautiful Glory was dressed in a slip of luminous silky pink. The color of pale marshmallows, he thought. One of the more demure items he had seen her wear, it hung in a dozen handkerchief points about her calves. The wings he'd worn when he'd accidentally taken flight were attached to her back. When their eyes met, the wings opened suddenly and she bit her bottom lip and glanced nervously towards her father to see if he'd noticed. If he did, he didn't show it.

Bud thought she might be holding her breath. He focused on the circlet of blooming roses crowning her thick blonde hair in profusion. Metallic things twinkled in her hair. Tabs from cans and Lacey's buttons. A rosy blush on her cheeks accented the fine porcelain of her skin, enhancing the dark circles beneath her eyes. Bud thought she was the most beautiful creature he had ever seen.

Why were they all here? In the King's court no less? What was so important he and his friends were invited to the Faerie Realm, when by all accounts it was forbidden?

Bud noted the apprehensive exchanges on every faerie's face

except Glory's. They were afraid of being touched, of being entrapped by him, Jack or Murphy.

It wasn't only Bud wondering why they were there. Most in the room were wondering the same also.

***

The King placed a hand on Glory's shoulder to prevent her leaving her position beside him. "Remember daughter, your part is done."

"Not all." Queen Celandine mirrored her husband's action and placed a hand over her husband's other hand resting on the arm of his throne. "There is the small matter revealed to you by The Guardian of All Knowingness."

Glory looked to them both, her eyes narrowing. "What does the news Uncle spoke to you about have to do with Bud?"

Aloysius placed a finger against his lips. "All in good time, daughter. All in good time."

The King instead turned his attention to Triumphant and the humans who stood expectantly before them. "Triumphant," the King spoke loudly, so all in the room could hear. "'Twas bringing these humans through the portal what the Great Tree advised?"

"Truly Father. Plus, I'm to remind Bud of something he appears to have forgotten."

Bud's eyebrows rose. He looked questioningly at Triumphant and it was as if the rest of the court leaned in to listen. "I have?"

"Indeed." Triumphant signaled Bud to step closer to the throne.

Stepping towards her, Bud forgot for a moment he shouldn't touch anyone and reached out. "Tell me."

Triumphant jumped backwards, her palms raised defensively to ward him off. A united gasp of horror hissed throughout the room.

"Did you see that?" he heard someone say.

"The human nearly captured our future ruler," came a horrified whisper to his right.

Bud's hand dropped away. "I'm sorry. I forgot. Forgive me." He spoke to the King. "What is it you must tell me?"

"Yes," the Queen spoke. "We are all agog with anticipation."

"There must be an extremely good reason to bring the humans to my court." The King appeared to be fighting the urge to dispel them immediately from the room and probably the forest as well. "Pray tell us everything daughter, and then I will relate my tale also."

Triumphant focused on her sister. "Did you grant a rare gift to this human? Or did you not?"

Puzzlement crossed Glory's features. "A rare gift? Is love not the rarest gift of all?"

"'Tis so dearest sister. But love 'tis not the gift I speak of. Pause for a moment, for I am certain 'twill come to you."

***

The room fell into a hushed silence. Weak from grief, Glory's mind was muddled. Not an unusual occurrence, granted, but still, what was it that had propelled her sister to bring Bud and his friends, her friends too, into their world when she had been so set against it only a few days ago?

She dared a glance at Bud who was focused on her with such trust, acceptance and most of all, love. She could not fail him now. Before anyone realized what she was about to do, she left the King's side and walked to Bud and held out a hand. Bud immediately took hold of it and cupped her palm to his lips and then rested it against his cheek. He mouthed *I love you.*

An audible series of gasps erupted in the throne room. Wings whirred frantically, but Glory no longer cared what anyone thought. She held out her other hand, palm outwards to silence the babble.

"I have given Bud my heart. What more is there to give?" That heart was jumping like a cricket in her chest, but his presence and touch clarified things for her, made her feel stronger. More grounded. She was where she should be. With Bud.

"The rare gift," she prompted Bud as the seconds ticked by. She had an inkling of what it might be but didn't want to put voice to it in case she was wrong. "Do you remember?"

There was a crease of worry on Bud's brow. The longer Bud held her hand, the more in tune with him she grew and gradually her thoughts cleared and a light glowed in Glory's eyes, causing them to appear almost iridescent. She smiled a glorious smile and her voice rose as her excitement grew. She gripped Bud's hand even more tightly and lifted it to her lips and placed a kiss on his knuckles. "I remember."

"Daughter dearest," her mother broke the unnatural silence in the room. "I am relieved to hear this."

"Aye," the King cleared his throat, his voice husky and unusually hesitant. "Now mayhap we will get somewhere."

"Nay," Triumphant said, with warning. "'Tis Bud who must remember."

"I'm a tad curious meself," Murphy added softly from his position just behind Bud's right.

Jack who still didn't appear to believe this was really happening, drawled, "The suspense is killing me." He assumed a studied pose with his leather-clad arms crossed over his chest and a defiant tilt to his chin.

"I'll give Bud a hint," Glory said. She tilted her head to Triumphant. "Surely I can do that?"

Triumphant appeared uncertain. She shrugged. Glory turned her focus back to Bud, willing him to remember. "You recall our first meeting."

Pushing his glasses up onto his forehead, Bud rubbed an eye with the base of his fist. "You mean at the precinct?"

Glory nodded. "'Twas where I gave you a gift for helping and believing in me enough to repeat the releasing glamour."

"You did?" He appeared puzzled for only a short sweet second and then, a grin to equal Glory's spread across his face. "You did."

Everyone leaned in a little closer. Glory's heart was in her mouth. "What was the gift?"

"Three wishes," he murmured with wonder. "You gave me three wishes."

"And how many have you used?" She knew the answer, but did Bud? How could she forget something so vital? Excitement bubbled like a brook through her veins. With one wish left, mayhap he would ask for her hand. Then Father could not deny them, for a wish once promised by the faerie, must be granted. No questions asked.

"I remember." His cheeks flushed a ruddy pink. He still hadn't told her what his first wish had been. What the heck was the second one? He searched for the answer and quickly found it. "Oh Glory. If I had remembered, I would never have been so careless." He cringed, recalling his wish to be footloose and faerie free. It was a miracle she hadn't died or suffered permanent memory loss. He had almost destroyed her ability to return to her world. She would have been trapped in his world, doomed to a life of unhappiness.

He pressed her hand against his mouth. "How could I have been so careless?" Feathering the fingers of his other hand down the side of her cheek, Bud gazed regretfully into her bottomless azure eyes. "I'm so sorry."

Glory turned into his palm and placed a swift light kiss there. "I know you would never deliberately hurt me. 'Tis as well my magic is weak, or my memory might never have returned."

One wish left. There was so damned much he could wish for and he knew what he wanted most to use it on. But would it be the wisest choice? There was no room for error. "What if I get it wrong? What if the magic from the last wish isn't strong enough to last?" Responsibility came with heavy burdens. One wrong word and all could end in disaster.

One right move and everyone would be cheering, slapping him soundly on the back, and offering to shake his hand.

"All is not lost," the King called out from his throne. "We are placing our trust in you, hoping that you will use your remaining wish wisely. Before you make your decision I feel now would be the time to reveal to you, and everyone else assembled here today, a knowing I received from Albertus, my brother, the Guardian of the Tree of All Knowingness. Mayhap it will aid you in making the best decision for all concerned."

King Aloysius raised his arms to soften the chatter that had erupted throughout the room at his announcement. He surveyed his loyal subjects, recognizing all with a slight nod of his head, ensuring he had everyone's attention, knowing what he was about to reveal could change all their lives in the measure of a single heartbeat.

"The Guardian of All Knowingness has disclosed a truth, which I must confess has had my wings all aflutter. The news, I feel, must be revealed to you all. The way we live our lives in Newberry Forest may be forever changed from this day forward. Indeed, 'tis at the Tree of All Knowingness's express request that I reveal to you a secret, well-guarded since Silversleeves placed his curse on faerie and human alike several hundred years ago. But first, I have a secret of my own I must reveal."

≈ CHAPTER 19 ≈

King Aloysius stood silent, surveying everyone in the room, ensuring he had their full attention before continuing. "Before the human," he looked to Glory and corrected himself. "Before Bud, makes his third and final wish, I would ask all to listen carefully, for future relationships between human and faerie depends upon what happens today in this room."

He indicated Bud with the wave of a hand. "You have already noted the peculiar attachment our daughter has for this human."

"He's enjoying this," Glory whispered an aside to Bud. "But there's something in his demeanor that tells me he is both afraid and excited." A light flush touched her cheeks and she squeezed her fingers against his. "I know we are destined to be together. I don't know how, but I know 'twill happen."

King Aloysius began to recite his tale, a gleam in his eye, and an air of mystery in the telling. "Silversleeves created a strong and powerful curse, so strong that no faerie or human has been able to break it. Many have tried. All have failed. Including me."

"Silversleeves disappeared deep into the forest not long after and has not been seen by anyone since, although rumors exist that he resides in a charmed cave near The Tree of All Knowingness itself. No one has been able to confirm or deny this. If the Great Tree itself knows, it is not telling."

"As for Rosebud, the human…"

"We know this story," Bud interrupted and was rewarded with a stern frown from the King. "She was taken to a convent, never to be heard or seen again."

King Aloysius nodded his agreement, his eyes assessing, his lips pursed in thought. "So, the tale has spread to the human world. 'Tis as our legend relates the tale." He shrugged. "We never questioned what happened to her. Rosebud was human. Our concern was for faerie alone."

He cleared his throat again, his expression one of regret and uncertainty. The King spoke directly to Glory but loud enough for all to hear. "Mayhap, it was meant to happen this way? Mayhap not? Who knows what the three Fates had in mind when all this started."

Queen Celandine's touch on his arm was one of reassurance. "My husband has wrestled daily throughout the centuries with his conscience. Believe him dearest, when I tell you his decision was not made lightly."

Glory had never seen such a look on Father's face before. It was if he was, ashamed. "What decision is this?"

The King appeared even more uncertain as he revealed his truth. "'Twas I who cast the deciding vote to separate Silversleeves and Rosebud permanently."

Glory choked down on a startled cry, a hand flying to her chest as if to steady a wildly racing heart. "'Tis not so."

"'Twas I who was instrumental in causing this curse that keeps the faerie and humans apart." An extremely apologetic King declared. "Do not look at me so, daughter. I have wrestled with my decision and many times wished I could go back and change things."

Glory's vision blurred. She felt anger build within from her heart outwards. Her wings, which she'd managed to keep under control whooshed open and shut, her anger evident in their color. Bud was alarmed. He could see that the court was too, as collectively they all took a step backwards. Then Glory's wings turned a dull red. He had no idea what that meant but he figured it wasn't good as several of the assembled faeries stepped even further away.

"How can this be? I don't understand."

"We lived in a world of constraints, of old-world Faerie Law. Few disagreed with the decision back then. Nearly all thought it for the best."

Queen Celandine spoke up in defense of her husband. "'Twas a decision not taken lightly. I was also there, and although it was not for me to pass judgment, I never agreed with the final decision. Though once made, I abided by it." She encompassed the room with a sweep of one hand. "As we all have. 'Tis Silversleeves' curse that compounds the problem."

The red in Glory's wings intensified. Bud squeezed her hand and tried to calm her agitation. "Do not blame your father. Your mother is right. He did what he thought best. We all make choices. Some are good and some are bad. Like my second wish."

"What I don't get," Bud addressed the King, "is what does this have to do with my wish? Why have you brought my friends and I into your world, when by all accounts, it's against Faerie Law?"

Glory had been thinking the same thing. "I'd like to know the answer to that also."

The King inclined his head to his Queen. "We named you for a special reason. When the skies opened and drenched us with tears upon Glory's birth a Knowingness was also bestowed upon us." He strode to Glory, picked up her hands and held them loosely in his. "We have always been aware you were an extraordinary gift to us. To all faerie."

Bud considered King Aloysius's statement. What did he mean by such a declaration? Glory looked to Bud, and then back to her father, confusion in her eyes, the red in her wings fading to a dull washed out pink

The King elaborated. "On our visit to The Guardian of All Knowingness my brother revealed a Knowing to me and I was made aware of my second error of judgment. I was too precipitous in bringing Glory home from the human world. I should have been more patient. According to my brother, the window of opportunity is now. If ever the curse is to be broken, now is the time."

He gently squeezed Glory's hands then released them, stepping back and speaking to the entire assembly still listening intently to every word. "The angels in heaven are listening, ready to trumpet the success or failure of the next few hours. I must give you the information handed to me and then the rest is up to Bud. Our future is in this human's hands."

"Bud!" Glory gasped and her expression lit with hope.

Bud felt the immediate weight of responsibility settle on his shoulders.

"This gets more diabolical by the minute," muttered Jack from behind.

Murphy elbowed him in the ribs to be quiet and mumbled. "I don't want to be missin' a single word."

Bud was grateful to have the support of his friends behind him. "How can it be up to me?" Fear and hope competed for space in his already too jammed-up brain.

King Aloysius was aggrieved. "An extremely important detail was left out of the legend and it concerns the human, Rosebud. 'Tis true she was sent to a convent, never to be heard of again, but what happened behind the walls of her self-imposed prison was a well guarded secret. Eight months after she was separated from Silversleeves, Rosebud gave birth to a son. A changeling."

"A son," Glory breathed in a hushed voice.

"A son!" Bud exclaimed hotly. "What has this to do with the curse?"

"A changeling. With the blood of human and faerie combined." The King appeared mortified.

"Was the child healthy?" Triumphant asked. "What became of it?

Did it survive?"

"Aye. The child survived and thrived behind the walls of the convent. He was nurtured and loved by Rosebud until her death when he was but fifteen human years. After that, the nuns continued to care for and educate him. The secret was well kept. No one in the world outside the convent suspected a thing and on the day after his eighteenth birthday, he left the convent with the blessings of the nuns under an assumed name, to begin life anew in the village of Oaktree."

"Then faerie and human can survive together." Glory spoke clearly. "'Tis possible." Her earlier anger forgotten, a tentative joy sparkled in her eyes and her wings returned to gold.

"But only if we break the curse." Bud tempered Glory's happiness.

She wasn't so easily deterred. "We will find a way."

"Not we." The King clasped Bud by the shoulders and a commotion of horror broke out in the room to an almost deafening level. "You will. You are the one to break the curse. Only you can do so."

"Father!" Triumphant cried. "What are you thinking? Touching a human!"

"Nay daughter. Not just any human."

Bud looked deep into the King's iridescent green eyes and it seemed to him it was as if he could see his past, present and future. What great cataclysmic happening could induce the most royal of faeries to touch him? He had a terrible feeling he should already know the answer.

Then the King announced his final and most astonishing revelation.

"The blood of the faerie runs strong and true in this man's veins. This is Bud, descendant of Rosebud and Silversleeves. 'Tis, mayhap, why my daughter's magic does not last the way it should on you."

A commotion broke out in the room, everyone talking and shouting at once. At first, it was the babble of outright skepticism, and then as the shock settled, it was the babble of incredulity, wonderment and finally capitulation and acceptance.

If the knowledge had come from the Great Tree and its Guardian, then there could be no doubt as to the truth of King Aloysius' heart-felt words.

"I don't believe it!" Jack exclaimed hotly. "What a load of hogwash!"

"Quiet," Triumphant warned. "Or I will draw an arrow."

"Fine." Jack retorted and pulled out a pencil from his jacket. "Go right ahead."

"Not that kind of draw you idiot." Triumphant's eyes flashed with anger.

"Triumphant!" The Queen scolded. "'Tis no way to speak to a guest."

"It wasn't my idea to invite him."

"Please forgive my daughter," Queen Celandine smiled warmly at Jack and shot her daughter a clear reprimand. "I've never known her to be so rude. These are unique times and I feel this revelation has unnerved her as it has us all."

The King took up the conversation once more. "And by the look of this young man," he heartily thumped Bud on the back, "he needs a chair and time to accept this news. Tree," he commanded. "A seat for Bud. Great, great, great, great grandson to Silversleeves the Ancient One."

Bud collapsed gratefully into Tree's dutifully made chair. Glory collapsed down next to him, picked up his hand and held it against her thigh. "This explains so much."

"It does?" Bud turned to her. "How so?"

"Why your aura is so bright. Why you can work the glamour without my aid. Why my wings went so willingly onto your shoulders."

"Why I've always wanted to fly," Bud murmured. "Why there is a glamour book on my father's bookshelves." Except for his father's early death, there was longevity in his family's past. "My family has lived in Oaktree Falls for centuries. I can probably trace my roots back to Rosebud's time. This is unbelievable!"

Yet, somehow, he knew it was the truth. He did not question the revelation, for deep inside he felt the rightness of the King's statement.

"If it helps you to believe," Glory rested her head on his shoulder. "I will assist you in your search for your heritage."

"Mayhap, your friends here," Queen Celandine indicated Murphy and Jack, "will be of assistance in that regard."

"To be sure," Murphy lilted. He elbowed a still silent Jack. "It will be our greatest pleasure."

Jack slanted a distrustful look at Triumphant. He spoke with reluctance. "I will help where I can."

"I'm to remind you," the King added, "lest you forget, that there is still the small matter of your third wish."

"That's right!" Glory lifted her head from his shoulder. There was an excitement building in her that was catching.

"I need time," Bud stammered. "To think. Do I have to make this wish now?"

The King waved his hands in front of his chest. "A wish is not to be taken lightly. What say we leave you alone in the throne room, for a time or two?"

How could Bud tell everyone that he had tried for days to find an answer to the curse and had come up with nothing? They all looked to him with such expectation in their eyes? Even with learning the truth of his heritage, why should now be any different?

"I have to release you" Bud reminded King Aloysius. "As you have touched me."

A new warmth shone in the King's eyes. "I am grateful for your consideration."

Bud immediately incanted the glamour he now knew so well to free King Aloysius.

Bud then said, "Allow Glory to remain with me while I make my decision?"

A royal nod appeared to be enough to satisfy the King and with the Family Most Royal leading the way, everyone filed from the throne room, leaving Bud and Glory alone.

Time to think.

Time to absorb this new knowledge.

Time to wrap their arms about each other.

Fingering the flowers resting on Glory's brow, Bud studied her perky nose, her heart shaped face and moistened cherry red lips. "What shall I wish for my love? Tell me what you want."

"I cannot," came her pained reply. "'Tis not permitted for me to influence your wish in any way."

"I can hardly believe it." Bud kissed her rosy lips. "I have faerie blood running through my veins."

"'Tis a miracle," Glory kissed him back, wrapping her arms about his neck and threading her fingers through his soft, thick hair.

"Love is the key." His strong hands cupped her face. "I love you, you love me."

"'Truly."

Frustration lit Bud's eyes to a stormy gray. "But it's not enough."

"So it seems."

"Do you know anything that will help me decide?" Bud questioned. "Anything at all?"

"I know nothing and can offer no help. 'Tis up to you."

"There are so many ways to phrase a sentence. One word misplaced and the entire meaning can be changed."

She sought to encourage him, unknowingly echoing her mother's words earlier to Father. "You will know when the time comes."

"But the time is now. Your father is right. I feel it as surely as I can feel you in my arms."

"Mayhap it's for the best I leave you alone while you make your decision. My presence will only serve to distract you."

He shook his head. "You always distract me. When you're not in the same room as me, you're in my mind." He pressed a hand to his chest. "You're in my heart."

He turned one of her small palms over and placed his lips to the soft skin, then rested his cheek there. "Distract me with your lips and hands. Hold me and tell me how much you love me."

So, Glory did exactly that. And when she emerged from the throne room some twenty-five minutes later, the bloom on her cheeks, her lopsided wings and disheveled hair left no one in the ante-chamber, human or faerie alike, in doubt of what had just occurred in the most royal of rooms.

The King coughed and blushed.

The Queen smiled knowingly.

Triumphant chanced a look out of the corner of her eye at Jack only to find him staring at her. She looked away as though pretending not to notice.

Herald, grinned widely. He was yet to experience physical love but he could imagine well enough.

Then the waiting began.

≈ CHAPTER 20 ≈

Pacing the long length of the damp throne room didn't help. Neither did pacing the width or walking in circles clockwise and anti-clockwise.

Peering out the irregular shaped knotholes of Tree Most Royal, Bud absently noted he was in the uppermost region of the trunk, a very long way from the ground. He looked down at his wet palms and over at the moisture glistening on the interior bark, knowing the dampness to be a result of Glory's tears.

If he couldn't restore the balance of the forest, the Kingdom of Faerie would be at risk. There was more at stake than his love for this most incredible woman who had stolen his heart and taught him how to love.

Arguing incessantly with himself, he asked why? Why him? Such an important decision to be made and one that could alter so many lives.

Responsibility weighed heavily on his shoulders. In the short time since he'd learned the truth he felt as if he'd aged a thousand years. Pushing back his glasses, he rubbed his blurry eyes. He didn't want to make this decision, but knew he must. It was too easy to make careless wishes. He must use this last one and use it well.

The chair the King had requested for him had long since disappeared and the only remaining seat in the room was the Royal Throne. It was an incredible piece of architecture. Built from both solid and super fine branches, it had been polished to a high sheen and decorated with hand carvings of the forest in the back and sides. Bud recognized the images of birds and insects along with fauna of the region. The seat itself was luxuriously padded with a mixture of silky oak and maple leaves.

Bud sat down on the throne, placed his elbows upon his knees and buried his head in his hands. Royal Throne was sentient, and as time slipped by, a peace he had not felt in ages began to descend over Bud. Leaning backwards, he rested his head against soft leaves and smoothed his hands repeatedly over the length of the armrests, enjoying the lustrous texture.

Slowly his mind stilled, his worry lessened. His breathing grew more regular. In, out. In, out. Closing his eyes, the tension in his neck and shoulders eased and he relaxed enough to appreciate the sensation of calm enveloping him.

During the quiet stillness an idea, a possible answer to his incessant questions shot through to the inner recesses of his muddled mind with the startling clarity of a lightning bolt. A sense of rightness settled on his shoulders, sending him surging from the throne and running across the room. Throwing open the doors to the antechamber he stood in the frame of the doorway and as the startled assembled crowd stared back he thought it a wonder no one could see the answer blazing in neon above his head.

"Your aura," Queen Celandine stuttered with a mixture of astonishment and awe. "'Tis radiant."

"Indeed," agreed the King, the back of his hand covering his eyes as if blinded. "'Tis a day for revelations." He spoke eagerly. "You have received a Knowing. 'Tis plain for all to see."

Only a few weeks ago Bud believed faeries didn't exist. Now he found himself not only believing but also wondering if he looked anything at all like his ancestor Silversleeves?

Aloysius was staring at him. "There is some similarity."

Bud was certain he hadn't spoken aloud. "There is? You can read my thoughts?"

"Nay. Silversleeves was a friend. A good one until the madness took him from us. There is much of him in you." Aloysius peered over Bud's shoulder. A frown of irritation creased his smooth brow. "You have been sitting on Royal Throne?"

"I needed somewhere to think."

"No one sits upon Throne except me."

"It calmed and soothed me. Cleared my mind."

"Truly," the King responded. He was clearly surprised at this news. "Throne did not throw you off?"

"No. Should it have?"

"Aye. A loyal throne would." Aloysius glared accusingly at Throne as if it were a traitor. "No one but the King sits upon it. Truly, 'tis another miracle on this very strange day."

Bud was beginning to tire of all this 'tis and truly stuff. "I know what to ask for."

Without waiting, he walked back into the throne room, giving him a few moments to work out how to phrase what he knew would upset Glory. A muscle at the corner of his eye twitched. He knew she wouldn't agree with what he was about to do.

He turned as she caught up with him. He took both her hands in his. "Do you trust me?"

There was no hesitation on her part. "I do."

He admired her ability to trust so easily. "My wish may not be the one you are hoping for."

Glory's smile slipped a fraction. "What do you mean? Surely you will wish for my hand?"

Seeing her sudden pallor, he gripped her hands tight in his. "There's nothing I want more, believe me. I hope my wish will enable us to be together, but I fear there is a greater purpose for which it must be used. It breaks my heart not to request your hand, but even if I did there would still be the constant danger of

Silversleeves' curse to contend with. The inability for you to live in my world and me in yours still exists. I have family who would be devastated if I left them permanently. As your family would be if you left them. A burden has been placed on my shoulders. On all of our shoulders. I must try to right that wrong."

Bud's resolve wavered. He wanted to throw his cares to the wind, whip Glory up in his arms, carry her away and comfort her, as only he knew how. "Trust me," he urged, gazing into eyes that held a mixture of innocence, hope, love and fear. "Trust me."

She trembled but spoke without hesitation yet once again. "Without reserve."

"Good girl." He tugged her into his arms kissed her soundly, mindless of everyone watching. United, they then stood before the King and Queen. "Can you confirm what you said earlier that a wish once made must be granted, no matter what?"

The King nodded his head. "We do."

Bud steeled himself, took a deep breath to bolster his courage and said, "Then I'm ready to make my final wish."

There was apprehension in the King's eyes as he turned and walked to his throne and stepped up to the dais. He raised his hands to silence the chatter.

Signaling to Bud, he said, "Step up beside me ancestor of Silversleeves, and let us all be witness to this historic event. Daughter," he gestured to Glory. "Come stand beside us also."

Glory took her place at Bud's side, tears glistening like polished dewdrops in her eyes. She smiled a tremulous smile and spoke clearly for all to hear. "Whatever you wish for, my love, I will willingly grant."

In that moment, Bud loved her more than he ever thought possible. What a strong, courageous woman his Glory was. Her faith in him held no boundaries. No matter how this all turned out, he was a richer man for his having known her.

Surveying the room, Bud noted the raised expectant faces, some showing fear, others hope, and one or two outright objection. He knew what he was about to wish for could change all their lives. He only hoped it was for the better. He had the opportunity to rectify the mistakes of the past. To redress the lines of communication between his world and theirs. To right a great wrong.

Bud prayed to God he was right. If not, Glory and he were doomed to lives of abject unhappiness. Apart.

Closing his eyes, he uttered another silent prayer to God to bolster his flagging courage. He inhaled a deep breath, opened his eyes and spoke before that courage deserted him.

"I, Bud Chandler, descendent of Rosebud the human and Silversleeves the Ancient One, do make my third and final wish as granted by Gloriane. This wonderful faerie, my lover and the woman I want to spend my life with, has shown me what love is. She has broadened my horizons, and opened my heart. I am a better man for knowing her. My wish is for both human and faerie alike to be free of the curse created by my great ancestor. For it to be gone, dispelled into the ether until it exists no more so that we may all live side by side in peace and harmony forevermore."

The room was hushed. Would Bud's wish work? Was the answer something so simple? Was his love strong enough to break a glamour created by one of the greatest Ancients to have ever lived?

A buzzing, similar to the sound of high-tension wires surged through Bud, sending uncomfortable niggles of electricity up his spine. A loud hum began to vibrate throughout the room and the tree in which they all stood began to shake.

It came from within, it came from without and it seemed to go on forever.

Fear clutched at the core of everyone's heart and they clung wildly to each other as their world swayed about them. Bud would have laughed at seeing the strange sight of Jack holding on to

Murphy who was, in turn, repeatedly crossing himself, except the rumbling and shaking increased to a deafening roar. A thunderous explosion ripped through the air and it was as if the very roots of Tree Most Royal were being ripped loose from the sodden earth.

Lightening flashed, followed by a clap of thunder of such magnitude that many cried out in fear and crouched against the walls of Tree, hiding their heads under their arms, thinking the world was at an end.

It went on and on and didn't stop until every last leaf had been shaken free from Tree Most Royal. The rumbling and swaying subsided and in its wake came an unnatural, prolonged silence.

Glory lifted her head and plucked a petal from Bud's hair. "'Tis encouraging to find we are still alive."

"Did it work? Are we free of the curse? Do you feel any different?" He stood and held out his hand and tugged her into his arms, her feet lifting off the floor.

"The world shook but I do not know if the curse has gone? I feel no different."

"I believe something happened."

"The understatement of the year," Jack interrupted, pushing himself as far away from Murphy as possible.

"'Tis hopeful you were successful, me dear fellow." Murphy brushed leaves from his arms. "This old Irishman does not care to be repeatin' such an event again in this lifetime."

"Aye," Queen Celandine agreed, hugging Triumphant to her with one arm and clinging to her husband with the other.

"Tree Most Royal is strong," the King smiled gravely at his wife. "And courageous too. He still stands and we are alive."

Already, Tree Most Royal had begun to sprout new leaves and the stripped vines showed signs of recovery. That was good news. Wan't it?

"How do we know if the wish has worked?" Bud voiced what he

was certain everyone was wondering.

Breaking free of Bud's arms, Glory flew the short distance to a nearby knothole and peered out. "'Tis but a simple matter. I will remove myself from your presence."

"No!" Bud surged towards her. "I will not put you in danger or pain."

"There will be no pain if it has worked," she replied logically.

Bud wasn't ready for logic. "What if it hasn't?"

Gripping the edge of the uneven opening, Glory leaned out. "'Tis not something I care to contemplate. It has worked. I'm confident of it."

"Glory!" Queen Celandine rushed over to her daughter and gripped an arm. "Let us experiment in a controlled fashion."

But before her mother or anyone else could stop her, Glory shrugged off her mother's hold, and flew out the knothole, away from Bud, and away from the safety of his presence.

"Guards! Quickly!" The King ran to the knothole and peered over his Queen and Bud's heads. "Follow her. If the curse is not broken she will die!"

≈ CHAPTER 21 ≈

In the ensuing panic every single faerie, except for King Aloysius simply vanished or flew out every available knothole. "Release me Bud, if you will? I cannot leave to search for my daughter." Bud immediately recited the words, and before he could ask the King to take them all with him, he flew out the window!

Standing alone with his two friends Bud was once again rendered helpless.

Peering down from his vantage point, Bud could see nothing but a carpet of foliage and flowers blanketing the ground below. All the plants and trees had been stripped bare, although new buds were already forming and growing at a rate that only magic could have had a hand in.

It appeared Newberry Forest was enchanted. He didn't want to think that his wish might have had anything to do with it. By sunset the forest would once again be verdant, as if nothing momentous had happened.

"Hell's bells!" Jack leaned over Bud's shoulder. "Stuck up a tree and no wings in sight. We're as useless as fleas without a cat."

Murphy patted Jack on the back. "No need to be afraid. Bud will know what to do."

The hairs on Jack's neck fairly bristled with irritation. "Who said I was afraid?"

"No one did," Bud snapped. "But I am. If my wish hasn't worked, I'll never see Glory again. She will die and it will be my fault."

"You have faerie in you." Murphy seemed to be the only one who had remained calm. "Can you not zap on some wings and fly after her? Or perhaps cast a glamour to get us out of here?"

The idea held merit. Could he do it? Damn it all! He had to do something. Anything was better than standing around helpless up inside a tree. "I'm damn well going to give it a try."

He didn't question how or even if he could but he immediately recited, with a few modifications, the glamour Glory had taught him a week ago.

"Wings be light, wings be airy
Place a set on this beginner faerie"

A millisecond later Bud possessed a set of wings and they were firmly attached to his shoulders. Another millisecond later he was zooming through the air with only a smidgen of control. The wings whirred, stirring up leaves and blossoms in his wake as his speed increased.

"Hell's bells," Jack spluttered, looking as if he was ready to expire of an apoplexy.

"That's it, boyo," Murphy cheered Bud on. "Be off out that knothole over yonder. Don't worry about us. Go find that wee girlie 'afore the archangel comes alookin' for her."

"Wings," Bud shouted. "Take me out the window." And as he flew towards the knothole inspiration struck him. "Tree Most Royal, please show my friends the way out."

He didn't know if Tree heard him and he didn't wait to find out. Glory's life was in jeopardy and there was no time to waste.

Not knowing which way to go, Bud felt the tug of Glory's presence and knew she was still alive. She was crying. He could feel her tears welling up within him. Listening to those tears, he tamped down his panic. He would be useless to anyone if he cracked now.

Find Glory first. Crack later.

Bud followed the lure of Glory's tears. Allowing them to be his guide he flew first one way, then the next, testing his gut instinct, the knowingness in his heart. Certainty drove him toward the center of the forest, flying deeper and deeper into its unknown depths.

He flew fast, his flying a death-defying act, but all the trees in the forest were watching out for him. Whenever he thought he was about to collide with a branch or trunk, they somehow moved to accommodate him. The wind also seemed to be pushing him onward, informing him in its own way he was heading in the right direction.

"Glory?" he called aloud, over and over again until his throat was raw and his voice a mere croaky whisper. "Where are you?"

He gave up calling for her and allowed the wind to take him where he needed to go. On and on he flew, until Bud couldn't begin to imagine Glory having flown this far.

Ahead in the distance, he could see the largest, tallest most impressive tree he had ever seen. It towered above all the rest, its branches reaching out as if to encompass the entire forest. Not one single leaf had been lost in the great shake. All around, as if surrounded by a ring of protection, was a stand of a hundred or so smaller ancient oaks, with a clearing between them and the large tree. Surely, this was the Tree of All Knowingness.

The discordant notes of wailing rose up through the branches and his heart squeezed and he dropped several feet as his wings stopped moving. No! Do not give up. She lives. I know she does.

From his vantage point high among the branches encircling the Great Tree was a multitude of faerie kneeling on the forest floor. Fresh cries drifted up to clutch and squeeze the life out of his soul. His heart plummeted, and so did he when his wings stopped beating again.

His damned wish hadn't worked. Thunder hammered in his ears, rendering him deaf. Tears welled in his eyes, leaving him blind. His throat closed, rendering him breathless. He had killed her. The one true beauty to have touched his life was gone. His glasses slipped from his face. Past caring, he let them fall. He didn't need them to see the truth. It was all revealed below him.

Bud made what could only be described as a semi-controlled crash landing and he heard himself cry out a broken, "No!" He forgot about not touching the faerie. He forgot about the implications of such an act. All he could think of was that his darling, innocent Glory with a heart of gold, was gone and it was his fault.

With no mind for their safety, he shoved his way through the thick throng. "Let me through," he pleaded, his throat hoarse with pain. "Let me through."

Desperation spurred him forward.

Wretchedness tore his heart to shreds.

"Out of my way," he bellowed, and this time the sea of faerie separated, allowing him a path through to where Glory lay.

Her immediate family was hunched in a small protective circle around her. The King straightened and turned to Bud, revealing moisture glistening in his eyes.

Queen Celandine took an unsteady step towards him, held out her trembling hands and spoke with such passion that his knees nearly buckled. "My son."

What did she mean my son? He had killed her daughter and she spoke as if she loved him.

"My son." The King held out his hands also.

"My brother," Triumphant and Herald cried one after the other, an indefinable emotion etched in every feature of their ageless faces.

In unison and to Bud's utmost bewilderment they bowed their heads and stepped aside finally allowing him to fall on his knees before the prostrate form of Glory on the forest floor. Her cheeks were flushed red and she was gasping for air. Emerald tears sparkled in her long thick eyelashes.

"Dear God in Heaven! You're alive!"

Glory held her arms out to him and mouthed his name, the word a mere whisper. "Bud."

Leaning over her, he scooped an arm beneath Glory's shoulders and crushed her to his chest, burying his face deep within the mass of her wonderfully wild hair. His control barely in check, he pulled her onto his knees, and cradled her gently, afraid he would hurt her more than she already was.

He kissed her repeatedly. "I'm sorry. I'm so sorry. It didn't work and now we're all doomed."

Oblivious to the crowd surrounding him, all he could think about was how he had hurt the most precious woman in the world. Glory. His wonderful Glory.

He shrugged off the Queen's hand when she tried to talk to him. The King tried as well, but he was blind to their solicitation.

"Why?" he shouted, rocking his head back and staring up to the heavens as if he would find an answer there. "I give you my life in exchange for hers," he sobbed. "Take me. Take me instead."

Glory reached up and caressed his cheek. "Do not cry for me."

"I'll never leave you my love. I'll stay here with you in your world. The curse will not beat us. I *will* find a way."

"Nay. You don't understand." A new flood of tears spilled down her cheeks. She cupped his cheek. "There's no need."

"There's every need," Bud reiterated. "I'll never leave your side again."

"Listen to me Bud. There's no pain. Truly if you choose to stay, well and good, though you need not feel compelled to do so. Listen and understand. The curse is broken. My tears are not of pain or sadness. They are joyous ones."

His stricken eyes stared blindly into hers and it took several long agonizing minutes for the truth to seep into his battered brain. The tears on her cheeks were not from pain or sadness? They were from happiness? "Don't tease me Glory."

"The curse is lifted. I am well." Bud really looked this time, realizing the rosy cheeks were those of one who was healthy and not dying.

He finally took notice of her parents as they crouched down beside them. "Aye," King Aloysius said gruffly, a huge warm grin belying the tears on his bright countenance. He slapped Bud heartily on the back. An action intended to allay his apprehension. "Like a charm. We cry with gladness. Joy is uppermost in our hearts. 'Tis time for celebration."

Bud studied the faces of those crowding around them. He had been so frantic, so blind with worry he had misinterpreted the signs.

He brushed Glory's teardrops away with his fingers and palms. "I thought I had lost you. You've no idea what I went through when you flew out that window. Don't ever do anything so dangerous again! You hear me!"

"I hear you." Glory touched her lips to his chest, over the area where his heart still beat too loud and too fast.

"Promise me."

"I make no promises. Promises can be difficult to keep."

"You'll promise me this."

She rested her forehead against his. "If you tell me how you got those wings on your back then I will?"

"It was nothing," Bud laughed and colored. "I just said the words and they appeared. I was meant to find you. The forest showed me the way."

"Nay," Triumphant didn't believe him.

"It did," Bud insisted. Nevertheless, he saw doubt in everyone's eyes.

He would have spent time convincing them, but the King interrupted. "Mayhap you will tell us about it sometime. But for now, let us head back to Tree Most Royal. Your friends will be needing our assistance."

"Not yet," Bud insisted. "There is something I would ask of your daughter?"

"You've already had your three wishes," said Aloysius.

"This is not a wish. It's a request."

"A request," Aloysius echoed. He looked to his wife and winked. "A few minutes then."

Bud took Glory's face in his palms and stared into her eyes, stopping every second or so to plant a kiss on a new area of her face. "It's not a difficult request. All I ask is that you promise to love me for the rest of our lives together."

"I don't need to promise what already exists between us. My birth was ordained and so was yours. Our union is written in the stars. I love you Bud, with my heart, my soul and I will worship you with my body each and every chance I get."

"With the curse broken we can be together forever. In this world and in mine as well."

"Together," Glory murmured, nuzzling her face into the crook of his neck, safe in the knowledge she was free to touch him as much as she wanted. Whenever she wanted. "Forevermore." She let out a whoop of laughter. "Forevermore!"

Elation lit her eyes. Joy danced a wild jig in her heart. Jumping to her feet, she dragged Bud up to stand before the only remaining obstacle preventing a formal union between them.

"Father? Mother? With the curse broken, do I have your permission to Cleave with Bud within the Knowing Circle?"

Queen Celandine dabbed the last trace of moisture from the corners of her husband's eyes who appeared to be quite overcome with emotion. She spoke for him. "Aye, daughter. We anticipated such a request and spoke earlier with Albertus in case such a momentous event occurred. After much discussion, we reached an agreement. If Silversleeves' curse could be broken, and if Bud is agreeable, then aye, a Cleaving would be permitted. The Ancients will not repeat their mistake a second time."

Glory turned back to the most important man in her life. Bud Chandler. "Will you Cleave with me as my parents once did, here within the Knowing Circle?"

"Is that the same thing as an engagement or marriage because that is what my next question was going to be?"

Glory beamed and she seemed to shine and sparkle all over. "Truly? Then I say yes. But to have official Faerie Sanction we must promise ourselves to each other within the Knowing Circle." Doubt clouded her eyes and her sparkle dimmed. "You do wish to Cleave with me, do you not?"

Wrapping his arms about her, he lifted her up and twirled them around and around.

The wings on his back stretched and opened and began to whoosh backwards and forward and they rose above the ground so that everyone could see them. "I do," he shouted in a clear voice. "I do."

Then he whispered for Glory's ears only. "Again and again and again."

And on such a promise, as the two lovers sealed their love with a kiss, the clouds dispersed and a beam of light from the sun above chose to shine down upon them in a radiant and benevolent blessing of its own.

≈ EPILOGUE ≈

Deep in the darkest corner of Newberry Forest, tucked away in a cave made invisible by an undetectable glamour, Silversleeves raised his eyes to the roof of the cavern as the world shook. A curious lightness stole like a thief into his stone-cold heart. Unafraid, he stood, his feet planted firmly on the cave floor.

Raising his arms to the unseen sky, he cried out. "Rosebud! At last! A love to equal our own has come to pass."

Every single day for over five hundred years, he had tried and failed to break the accursed curse he'd so foolishly created.

The centuries had proven to be interminably long and painful and had taken their toll. He was old. Ancient in title as well as years. How tired and feeble he felt but when the curse lifted he experienced a bliss he had never felt except in Rosebud's arms. The tight band of his own making, the ever-present reminder of his folly evaporated, leaving him strangely lightheaded. He looked downwards and a dry, husky chuckle rattled past his lips. His spirit was so light his feet no longer touched the ground below.

"Now I am free."

Donning his best robe, he released the glamour shrouding the dark cave and as night descended, he lay down upon his straw bed and drifted off into a peaceful slumber.

Rosebud stood at the opening of the cave, the night sky glowing behind her with a million twinkling stars. She was as beautiful as he remembered and she was holding out her hands, entreating him in that soft loving way he remembered so well.

"Come my love," she whispered hauntingly. "Come. It is time. I have waited for you for far too long."

With the release of the curse, Silversleeves was finally free to follow his heart. In death, he would be with his love. "I never stopped loving you," he spoke brokenly, a single tear running unchecked down his cheek as his spirit began to lift away from his frail body lying prone on the straw bed.

"Nor I you," she smiled. "Come to me now, my love. Our blood lives on in a child from our love. The balance has been restored. Come to me. Let me dry your tears and banish your loneliness for all time."

"At last." Without fear, Silversleeves reached out his hands and relinquished the last silken strands of his earthly life.

He didn't look back. A glow of light surrounded Rosebud and as his hands grasped hers, the glow spread out encompassing them both until they were but one band of golden light.

Together they flew like a shooting star across the night sky in a brilliant arc of light towards the heavens.

Towards home.

The End

THE GREENWOOD WITCHES TRILOGY

Book 1: The Silver Rose out 14 April 2015

When the Bells of Marylebone toll for the mortal witch, Rosa Greenwood, she is forced to make a choice that will change her life and, that of her sisters, forever. She must bind her life to another within thirty days to balance her unstable magic, or sacrifice it for the remainder of her life. If she fails to do either, she will be hunted down by Marylebone's Dragons and killed before she can turn rogue.

What game is Marylebone playing by sending Immortal Warlock Aden Dragunis to Raven's Creek and into Rosa's life when he has vowed never to love again? But Rosa possesses the silver rose he crafted centuries ago for his deceased Beloved. Is he prepared to break his vow of service to Marylebone and sacrifice everything to ensure Rosa lives.

The Jade Dragon

Book 2: Out June 2015

The Spell Weaver

Book 3: Out August 2015

A Note From Rowena

I often dreamed of becoming a writer. Before that, I dreamed of becoming an actress, a ballerina, a singer, a hairdresser, an adventurer, a magician, you get the picture. Reading while walking was another passion until I fell down a manhole while reading Joan of Arc. She was about to be burnt at the stake. My only thought was, "Save the book!" So that's me. A book worm at heart!

If you would like to know more about new releases you can subscribe to my newsletter at www.rowenamayosullivan.com.

Lastly, a very big **THANK YOU** for taking time to read Footloose & Faerie Free. If you enjoyed it, please consider telling your friends or posting a short review. Word of mouth is an author's best friend and much appreciated.